T0119829

Changes and Chances

CHANGES
AND CHANCES

STANLEY MIDDLETON

NEW AMSTERDAM
New York

Copyright © Stanley Middleton 1990

First published in the United States of America in 1992 by
NEW AMSTERDAM BOOKS
New York, NY

Published by arrangement with Century Hutchinson Ltd., London.

Library of Congress Cataloging-in-Publication Data

Middleton, Stanley, 1919–
Changes and Chances / Stanley Middleton.
p. cm.
ISBN 1-56131-004-2 (cloth, acid-free paper)
I. Title
PR6063.I25C4   1992
823'.914—dc20
90-40015
CIP

First printing.

Manufactured in the United States of America.
10 9 8 7 6 5 4 3 2 1

This book is printed on acid-free paper.

To Anthony Whittome, with thanks

'All the changes and chances of this mortal life.'

(*Prayer Book*)

'I am ruminating,' said Mr Pickwick, 'on the strange mutability of human affairs.'
'Ah, I see – in at the Palace door one day, out at the window the next. Philosopher, sir?'
'An observer of human nature, sir,' said Mr Pickwick.

(Charles Dickens: *Pickwick Papers*)

'. . . and life time's fool.'

(Shakespeare: *King Henry IV Part I*)

The boy on a bicycle swerved with a flourish into the shadowy drive. Tall, wrought-iron gates were fastened back, and through shrubs and leaning trees he could distantly see the light over the front door. Touching his brakes and obedient to his mother's instructions he ignored the turn to the right and rode, cautiously now, into darkness at the back of the house. He dismounted, searched with the aid of a flash-lamp for a bell, found none and hammered smartly on the right-hand upper panel of the door. As there was no immediate answer, he knocked again and began to untie the box from the carrier of his bicycle, propped now under an unlighted window.

There was a drawing of bolts and the door was opened a few inches.

'Well, what d'you want?' A female voice.

'I've brought some things.'

'Who for?'

'Mr Hillier. From Top Fare. He's expecting me.'

A chain rattled loose; the door and yard were suddenly lit.

'You'd better come in then.' The boy stepped inside into a dark room; he was perhaps thirteen. 'Give your feet a good wipe. There. On that door-mat.' He could make out the rectangle by the outside light and vigorously cleaned his bootsoles. 'One more for luck,' she said. 'That's it.'

She banged the door behind him, bolting it, and switched off all light. Next she felt for and opened a second door, pointed him into a poorly lit but spacious corridor, led him along coir matting and finally through into a brilliantly illuminated, warm, deliciously-smelling kitchen.

'What's your name?' she asked. A grey-haired, not unfriendly woman in a white apron. He still clutched the box in front of him.

'Peter Fowler.'

'You Mr Fowler's son, then?'

'Yes.'

She lifted a white telephone, announced the arrival and listened to instructions. On large mesh trays rock cakes, macaroons, cornflake and chocolate twists and cheese straws stood in rows, fresh from the oven.

'I can see to that,' she answered. Further murmured instruction. 'Oh, all right then.' She replaced the phone. 'I'm to take you up to him. You're honoured. Come on, then.' She spoke brusquely, as if put out.

They left the redolent kitchen by another door, and walked into the foyer.

'Upstairs,' the woman ordered, then more kindly, 'Can you manage the box?'

'Yes, thank you.' It weighed heavily on his arms, but he did not complain.

On their way upwards they met two men edging down. The woman and boy stepped aside as the men, making no acknowledgement, continued with their conversation. Their voices, the boy noted, brayed, as if they were confidently addressing a public meeting.

'It is not so much a matter of compliance . . .'

'But you remember . . .?'

'I remember perfectly well what was said at the time, though as you are aware I had no confidence whatsoever in . . .'

'Gerard, Gerard,' the second man laughed throatily, 'if the Archangel Gabriel . . .'

'I cannot imagine he would have made an appearance in such . . .'

The boy and his mentor were on their way again. The men had disappeared, still talking at the tops of their voices. The woman tapped on a glassily polished door and was bidden to enter. She ushered Peter in first and stood with a hand on his shoulder, protecting him.

'And what have we here?'

The woman relieved the boy of the box, placed it on the desk at which the man was sitting, removed the cover and began to empty it. Four bottles of whisky, intact and wrapped in tissue paper, a tin box of Oxo, a bottle of assorted spices, a slab of cooking chocolate.

2

'Yes, Mrs Mead,' the man said. 'The feast can begin.' He looked at the boy. 'They must have been heavy. I thought your father would bring them himself; he was insistent that there was no need for me to come down.'

'I came on my bike, sir,' the boy said.

The man beamed as if that settled all argument.

'Is there a bill?'

'In the box, sir.'

Mrs Mead scrabbled, produced the slip of paper, handed it over. The man donned half-glasses, reached for a large cheque-book and humming to himself filled it in, thoughtfully, as if date, name, amount, signature needed concentration. Before he had finished he looked at Mrs Mead, asked uneasily, 'Have we all arrived?'

'Except the Stokeses.'

He blew out his lips and turned to Peter, gently stroking his fair greying hair with his left hand. One would guess his scalp was tender. Pen in hand, he spoke to the boy.

'What sort of party are we having then?'

'Hallowe'en.'

'That's tomorrow, isn't it? No.'

'Bonfire Night?'

'Nothing so spectacular.' He smiled, completed his writing, tore out the cheque, delved into trousers pocket, found a fifty-pence piece. 'Thank you very much.'

'Thank you, sir.'

'Thank your father.'

'It's his pleasure, sir.' Again a pained smile twisted the thin face.

'It usually is. Mrs Mead will spare you a bun, I'm sure.'

The man seemed loth to release them, but as he said no more, Mrs Mead opened the door. Boy and man wished each other a solemn good night. The box remained where it was.

At least a dozen or fifteen people crowded the hall, many talking, most eyeing the descent, demonstrating interest, surprise, indifference. Once in the kitchen Mrs Mead waved two full plates in front of the boy. He chose a jam tart.

'Sit down, and eat it.'

The kitchen gleamed, was hot, and quiet compared with the hall outside. That had been lit by a high chandelier and crystal

3

clusters of wall lamps, but gloomy overall with oak panels and broad balustrade, chill above the grey, patterned mosaic floor. Here bar-lights and heat dominated. The boy mounted the stool and bit, careful to avoid spattering crumbs.

'What school are you at, Peter?' He told her. 'The grammar school, are you? You must be clever?' Mouth full, he did not reply. 'Have another.'

'Thank you.' He held the new tart flat on his left hand as if to try a conjuring trick. 'Was that Mr Hillier?'

'Who else do you think it was?'

'I liked him.'

'Did you now? I suppose he has good points.'

'I see.'

'You see what?' Her voice snapped. 'Come on. Eat your tart. I've plenty to do.'

'I'm sorry,' Peter Fowler said.

'For what?'

'I've annoyed you.'

Mrs Mead wiped her hands on her apron. She had a high colour.

'You're an odd young man.' She shook her head. 'No, you've not annoyed me. Why should you? Do you like the tart?'

'It's delicious.'

'But not so good as your mother's?'

'The pastry is different.' Then reluctantly, 'But better.'

'Don't tell her so.'

'I shan't.'

They grinned conspiratorially as the kitchen door opened.

A young woman in a grey dress which shone dazzlingly stood in front of them. She touched her blonde hair, assumed a clownish expression and asked Peter, 'Is it good?'

'Perfect.'

'There's a diplomat for you,' the lady said. She was beautiful, slender with long hands. 'Could we have the coffee at nine-fifteen, please? That will be half-time.' She used the word to please the boy, he thought.

'Have they started?' Mrs Mead.

'They're just going in . . . or were.'

'Is Mr Hillier down?'

'Yes.'

4

'Hasn't he changed, then?'

'I think so. He looked quite smart.'

The telephone interrupted them, shrilly. Mrs Mead started, staggered but recovered to answer: 'The Firs.'

They could hear a female voice, then Mrs Mead's reassuring reply.

'Yes. He's safely here. He's eating a jam tart, and as soon as he's finished that I'll set him on his way. No trouble. Not at all.' She replaced the instrument. 'Your Mum, wondering if you'd arrived all in one piece.'

'She worries.'

'All mothers do. I would.'

'Right,' the young lady said. 'Nine-fifteen.' She disappeared at speed.

'Is that Mr Hillier's daughter?' Peter inquired.

'It is not.' Mrs Mead's voice sprang quick and hurtful as a trap. It seemed not difficult to incur her anger. 'You'd better be off now. Don't want to upset your mother more than's necessary, do we?'

They crossed the kitchen, corridor matting, the dark room. Lights leapt outside; bolts, chain and key rattled. The boy found his bike.

'Good night, and thank you very much.'

The door banged shut and before he reached the front of the house, the yard lights were doused.

Four days later when Peter Fowler came in from school his mother greeted him with, 'Mrs Mead from The Firs rang up this afternoon.'

'What did she want?'

'You made a good impression on her, apparently.' Since Peter made no comment his mother continued, 'Would you like a job up there on Saturdays for a few hours? In the morning?'

'Doing what?'

'Helping her out.' His frown demanded expansion. 'Presumably with the cleaning.'

He put down his case. 'I don't know.'

'Both she and Mr Hillier liked the look and sound of you. It'll earn you some extra pocket-money. You needn't make up your mind just now – well, not this very minute – but I said I'd ring her tomorrow, and then we'd go up together to see her if you're interested.'

'What's my Dad say?'

'I've not told him yet.'

On Saturday morning mother and son set out by car. Mrs Fowler had dressed herself most carefully as if for a parents' evening or concert at the school. They parked in the avenue outside and walked to the back door.

'It's a huge house,' Peter said. 'It looks bigger by daylight.'

'And when you're not on your bike.'

Mrs Mead answered the bell, which existed but not where one expected it. Courtesies were exchanged.

'You should have come to the front,' the housekeeper said. The room behind the back door was large, lit by two sash windows and a light above the door, and was quite bare. The quarry-tiled floor, blue-grey and red squares, lacked all covering; neither table nor chair could be seen; two highish shelves, eighteen inches apart, ran round three walls but were empty. The place did not seem dusty, merely unused; paint on windows and doors looked recent. The visitors were hurried into the kitchen where clearly no great culinary process was in motion.

Mrs Mead, after a question, made instant coffee, sat the two down and outlined the nature of the duties: polishing silver, oak panels and staircase, some furniture, door-knobs; running errands.

'He's good at washing-up,' Mrs Fowler offered, socially.

Mrs Mead pointed behind her. 'We have a machine.'

She suggested three or four hours according to the length of the tasks, to be paid at one-fifty an hour, beginning at nine or ten. All was businesslike but friendly, put swiftly without delay. All knew where they stood.

'What do you say, Peter?' Mrs Fowler kept her tone neutral.

'I'd like to try, please.'

Mrs Mead lifted the phone from the wall and outlined the prospective agreement to her employer. She replaced the instrument, sat down with them, said, 'He'd like to see you before you go. Both of you. No rush. Before you go. When

6

you've finished your coffee.' She pressed them to another home-made Shrewsbury biscuit. 'There's no hurry.'

The trio made their way upstairs. The foyer below was lighted by a wide front door in stained glass and the aura was solemn. A piano tinkled as Mrs Mead rapped at the study door and without waiting for an answer immediately showed them in. Three walls were book-lined, and under the window Mr Hillier's desk, large, oak, solid with a cushioned chair, gleamed in subdued light under its pile of papers. Two rows of shelves continued above another door; this now opened and Mr Hillier came out, tugging at the sleeves of his cardigan.

'Mendelssohn,' he muttered.

'Mrs Fowler and Peter,' Mrs Mead announced.

'Sit down, please.'

Mrs Fowler took one of the two hard-backed chairs placed side by side, while Peter motioned to Mrs Mead to make use of the other. When to his surprise she obeyed, the boy assumed a position at attention behind his mother. They might have been preparing for an old-fashioned formal photograph. Mr Hillier's right hand doodled on the dark green leather of his desk-top as if still performing Mendelssohn. He looked out of the window at his front garden; from where he stood, Peter could see three silver birches against the cloudy light.

'It's all arranged, then?' Hillier asked nervously, still averting his head.

Mrs Mead again repeated the agreement, rather disagreeably, as if to call her employer to sense.

'Yes.' He swung round. 'Is that in order?' he asked Mrs Fowler.

'Thank you.'

'Good, good. We shall enjoy having Peter here. Are you strong?' he demanded suddenly.

'Not bad, sir.'

Hillier dropped his head, grimaced into a small smile, and lifted his face again. The eyes, wide open now, were bright blue, staring at the mother.

'We know each other, don't we?' he burst out, though the voice was barely above a whisper.

'Yes.'

Peter saw his mother's neck flush.

7

'Adrian Hillier.' The man spoke, clearing ambiguities, but still with hesitation. He seemed slow this morning, slothful. 'You were Alice . . . Alice . . .' Mrs Fowler did not help him out. 'It does not seem very long . . .' He broke off again, gathered his wits. 'That's very satisfactory, then, Mrs . . . Mrs Fowler. Yes. Thank you very much.' He looked at the boy. 'You'll start next week,' he said in a normal voice. 'Good then. Thank you. Thank you.'

He resumed his Song-without-Words on the desk-top and Mrs Mead had the Fowlers on their feet and quickly out of the room. She seemed perturbed by the recognition of Mrs Fowler, perhaps suspecting chicanery on the part of the employer, Peter guessed, but politely let them out of the great front door, warning them to be careful on the five steps.

'I wonder who does the garden,' Mrs Fowler said, quite recovered.

'Me. From now on.'

'Some hopes.'

They laughed together, like equals.

Peter Fowler found Mrs Mead rigorous in the direction of his work.

He enjoyed his Saturday mornings at The Firs, but earned his money. The housekeeper knew exactly what she wanted, and how long each task should take; if it was improperly carried out, then the boy had to repeat it. However, he relished their conversations, the home-made cakes and steaming coffee in the break. Mrs Mead quizzed him about his school work, the history, algebra, French and Latin, while her constantly reiterated refrain, 'That must be difficult for you,' puzzled him. When he shook his head, she smiled her relief.

Mr Hillier made no appearance. He was up and about in so far that Mrs Mead carried his coffee to the study at eleven, but there was no sound of piano or footsteps. The telephone was answered by the housekeeper. Saturday morning was occupied by furniture polish, elbow grease and silence above.

Peter had already questioned his mother about her acquaintance with Hillier. Mrs Fowler did not seem very forthcoming.

'He was a student at the university.'

'He didn't live here? His parents didn't?'

'No. London, I think. I'm not very sure.'

'Where did you meet him?'

'At a disco. The college where I did my secretarial training used to invite some male students from the university.'

'Was he rich, then?'

'He hadn't got a car.'

His mother allowed him half a dozen questions and then would break off the conversation, not as though she had anything to hide but as if the subject did not arouse much interest in her. It had happened twenty-two or -three years ago. Mr Hillier looked greyer now but he hadn't changed all that much. Peter's questions elicited the fact that they had acted in a play together, but she couldn't remember the name. It was a light comedy, and she had been the young sister of the heroine. Mr Hillier had played a man-about-town, something of the kind, a friend of the family.

'Was it a success?'

'We enjoyed it.'

'Was Mr Hillier a good actor?'

'I can't remember. He spoke rather well. Or so I thought.'

'And were you?'

'I just acted myself. Anyhow, I didn't have much to do. I can remember one line: "At eleven o'clock somebody was pacing the terrace." It created a sensation on the stage, or was supposed to. The audience laughed on the last two nights.'

His mother shook her head as if at the extreme foolishness of the world, or young people, or her waste of time and opportunity.

'Did you know my Dad then?'

'No. I'd be seventeen, and I didn't meet your Dad until I was twenty-three at least.'

'You were twenty-six when you married him.'

'That's right.'

Peter enjoyed these exchanges with his mother, who constantly varied her approach. Sometimes she was brusque, too busy for confidences, while on other occasions she would let out what he would have kept secret.

'When I first met your father, I thought what funny legs he had.'

'Why?'

'It was the way he stood, I suppose. Or the trousers he wore.' Alice Fowler laughed, a seventeen-year-old again.

One Saturday morning during the coffee-break Mrs Mead asked, 'You're finding your way round now?'

'Yes, thank you.'

'Mr Hillier is pleased with you.' That meant she was. 'There'll be an extra day or two's work for you in the Christmas holidays if you want it. Clearing up.'

'Thank you.'

'Mr Hillier told me to ask you and your mother if you would like to come to dinner next Thursday. Is that possible?'

'Well, yes. I'll see. We're not usually out. Thank you. I know what my Mum'll say.' He sniggered.

'What's that?'

' "I've got nothing to wear." '

Mrs Mead laughed, rocking on her stool.

'You're so sharp, young man, that one of these days you'll cut yourself. You just tell your mother that there'll be no need for dressing up. It'll be early, seven o'clock, so we don't keep you awake all night, and it will be very small: Mr Hillier, me, your Mum and you. Small and informal. You can help me. He's pleased with you, and this is his way of showing it. I told him, straight out, that boys didn't want dinner-parties, but he insisted in that quiet way of his. "Just you go and inquire, Elsie," he said. "You might be surprised." He acts eccentrically, if you know what I mean. I can't ever quite make him out.'

'I've never been to a dinner-party before.'

'Well, here's your chance to begin.'

Alice Fowler fluttered, hesitated, but after a prolonged telephone conversation with Mrs Mead accepted the invitation and stayed late in town after work one evening to buy a new dress about which she became immediately uncertain. Peter was invited up to inspect. It seemed quite startlingly beautiful, plain but shining, with a skirt that billowed.

'Turn round,' he ordered. 'And again. Magnificent,' he pronounced.

His mother blushed, and touched her hair.

'Is it?'

'What's my Dad say?'

'It's no use asking him anything. He wouldn't notice if I dressed up in a paper bag.'

Her husband, in fact, had grumbled in a half-comical way about their outing, saying he was left to fend for himself, that while they feasted on the fat of the land he'd be left to the mercy of the chippy or the Chinese take-away.

'That'll make a change for you.'

Mr Fowler stroked his moustache and screwed up his eyes.

'You see how she treats me,' he groaned to his son. 'I'm wasting away.' He patted his rotundities, winking.

They arrived exactly on time, six-fifty, after a rush. Mrs

11

Fowler had been delayed at the office of the insurance company where she worked, exactly as she feared, and so was left with less than an hour to bathe and dress. Peter, completing his homework, provided her with a cup of tea and zipped her dress. She smelt delicious, exotic; her hair shone; she wore silver earrings he had never seen before, but a small frown played on her forehead.

'Let me have a look at you,' she ordered. He wore, following instructions, his best school blazer, flannels, black shoes and a new white shirt, an early Christmas present. She tugged and jerked and straightened. 'You'll do.' She turned to concentrate on the dressing-table mirror.

Mrs Fowler parked in the street and led her son round to the back although the lights shone above the front door. Mrs Mead whirled them straight through to the hall where they hung their coats in the cloak-room. She eyed them with approval. Mr Hillier made a silent approach from upstairs, shook hands with the mother, nodded affably to the son. The house felt comfortably warm.

In the small sitting room Mrs Fowler refused sherry, saying she was in charge of a car. Hillier stoppered the decanter, denying himself.

'What about wine with dinner?' Mrs Mead asked.

Again Mrs Fowler refused.

'We won't bother,' Hillier said.

'Don't do without on my account,' Alice said, embarrassed, reddening.

'My drink is water bright.' Mrs Mead laughed and carried off Peter to give a hand loading the service trolley.

The dining room blazed; they ate at one end of a polished table which could accommodate ten. Hillier occupied the head with Mrs Fowler on his right, Mrs Mead and the boy on his left, nearest the door, where they could slip out.

The meal was simple, but each ample plateful satisfied. Cod goujons, potatoes in jackets with cold beef and salad, a trifle with cherries on thick cream, cheese and coffee. Hillier ate sparingly; Mrs Mead seemed quite at home at her master's table, delivering information about the sauces to Peter, tempting him.

Conversation did not flourish at first; the food demanded

full attention. Meat melted in the mouth; the salad was full of extraordinary surprises; the trifle involved a hundred variants of sweetness.

The boy had expected to hear his mother and Mr Hillier talk about their appearance in the play or their dancing together, but the subjects were not raised. Peter's success at the house, his education so far and the options open to him were discussed at length, mostly by the women. Mr Hillier asked in the course of this if Peter could see any sense in learning Latin, and admitted he could barely translate half a dozen words on a gravestone these days. Mrs Mead expounded then, learnedly, the theory of the transfer of the effects of training; it sounded impressive. She had read all about this at her training college. She had been a teacher, it appeared, but had given it up to take this position at The Firs.

'No,' she answered Mrs Fowler, 'I don't regret it. I'm very comfortable as I am. And education is never wasted. One thing they taught me at college was to read. If I worked in a school, I guess I'd be so busy with their concerns I'd have less time for adult books.'

'Who's your favourite?' Peter interjected.

'I'm reading Arnold Bennett now.'

'He's a very uneven writer,' Mr Hillier murmured.

'Anybody who is any good is that,' Mrs Mead snapped. This was her first display of sharpness this evening. 'He writes a great deal, and some of his books are better than others. Just like Shakespeare. It's to be expected.'

Mr Hillier bowed his head, smiling at the rebuke.

The housekeeper seemed most at ease, expansive, encouraging them to try this delicacy or that, or to expand on some short comment. She was mistress of the feast. The topic which – oddly, in Peter's eyes – interested Mr Hillier most was the management of Top Fare, the problems of staff training, stock replenishment, store theft, commercial success. In his soft voice he plied Mrs Fowler with question after probing question. She, who sometimes helped her husband with his accounts, his VAT, his orders, was able to answer satisfactorily, to anticipate the next question and suggest both questions and solutions which he had not raised. Their exchanges were lively; both valued opposition. Mrs Mead and

Peter sat silent, fascinated, amused. Alice kept up her end; Mr Hillier's politeness did not hide his acuity. The two interested each other.

They retired for coffee to the small sitting room.

The move silenced Hillier, who sat with legs out straight smiling to himself, hands restless in pockets. Peter knew this room well, with its tall glass-fronted bookcases, its dull water-colours, its leather armchairs and smell of furniture polish. He tried to read the titles of books, but could not. Mrs Mead's arrival with the coffee brightened the air.

'You're all very quiet,' she admonished.

'Silence is golden.' Mr Hillier.

'We went off that standard years ago.'

The housekeeper asked the guests how they intended to celebrate Christmas. Mrs Fowler said she grew to dislike it year by year. She and her husband were busier and there were presents to buy, and meals to cook, and no time for anything.

'Do you have visitors?'

'No, but on Boxing Day morning we shall walk round to my sister-in-law's. I suppose she's pleased to see us; I hope she is. Peter enjoys it.'

'And my Dad. He and Uncle Gordon have a glass of whisky in the morning.'

'Are there no children?'

'No. Neither my sister nor my sister-in-law has a family. Peter's the only one.'

'You're unique,' Mrs Mead concluded.

'We're not very fertile.' Peter was surprised at his mother. 'But it's an unpleasant world to bring children into.'

'Do you think so?' Mrs Mead to the boy.

'I've not much choice.'

They all laughed. Delicious chocolates were issued, though Mr Hillier refused them. Peter sat smoothing his gold wrapping-paper. The coffee had a richness about it that distinguished it from the morning offerings, welcome as they were. They talked about keeping pets; Mrs Mead said she was trying to persuade Mr Hillier to adopt a cat.

'He looks a cat man, don't you think?' She spoke over her employer's head.

'I'm sure a cat would sit on his knees and purr.'

'What do you think, Peter?' Hillier asked patiently. 'You hear how these ladies are bullying me. Should I give in?'

The man spoke breathlessly, almost as if translating from another language.

'If I lived here,' the boy answered, 'I'd have a cat and a dog.'

'And a horse,' said his mother.

'Or an elephant,' he replied, with sociable cheek.

The two women recalled pets of their youth. Mr Hillier accepted a second cup of coffee. Silences between anecdotes grew longer until Mrs Fowler found her voice to say they'd have to go. No attempt was made to detain them; coats were found, thanks pronounced and the visitors left by the front door. Mr Hillier seemed more wraith-like, standing back, nervously touching his hair, slipping away.

Mrs Mead accompanied them outside, down the broad steps, and stood coatless in the wind on the gravel drive.

'Thank you very much again,' Alice Fowler said. 'We've really enjoyed ourselves.'

'It's good for Mr Hillier. He knows and meets a good many people, but he's no friends to speak of. He's a shy man.'

'We were glad to come. And the meal was lovely, out of this world. Peter won't taste anything like that again for a long time.'

'Oh, nonsense.'

'Thank you. It was a treat. Don't catch cold out here.'

Mrs Mead ascended the steps, crabwise.

When they were seated in the car, Peter's mother said, 'I knew Mrs Mead.'

'When?' His mother had said nothing on their first visit.

'She was the head girl at school when I was in the second form.'

'Why didn't you say something?'

'It doesn't do to talk about women's ages, and that would certainly have come up, expecially in front of men. Her name was Elsie Hooper. She seemed a grown-up woman to me; I was only twelve.'

'Was she nice?'

'Stately. She's a bit like that now.'

'Do you think she's in love with Mr Hillier?'

His mother turned, laughing, towards him. 'Now what on

15

earth makes you come out with such a thing? You read too many books, our Peter. What do you know about love?' Mrs Fowler was interested, tapping the steering-wheel with the butt of her right hand. 'Does she live in?'

'She's always there.'

'There must be plenty of spare rooms in a place that size. You wouldn't think an educated woman would want to be a housekeeper. That's not much more than a servant, is it? And not well paid, either. And the Hoopers thought they were a cut above most of us. I think he was a bank manager.'

'And who was Mr Mead?'

'You have me there. Mead? Mead? No.'

On their steady way home Peter asked, as dark lime trees flashed past, 'Was Mr Hillier as quiet when you knew him?'

'No. Not really.'

'He never comes out of his room while I'm there.'

'I wonder why he asked us?'

'Perhaps Mrs Mead made him,' Peter answered. 'Do you think she recognised you?'

'I'm sure she didn't. I was only a little girl.'

'Shall I tell her?'

'You can please your dead aunt.'

He considered that his mother did not sound altogether content.

3

With a touch on a button Adrian Hillier cut off his record-player.

He stared at Mrs Mead and held his chin in his left hand. The first movement of the Brahms Clarinet Quintet had been concluded. In a slow voice, as if talking to himself, he lectured his housekeeper. She stood easily, hand on a chairback, listening; she was used to it, enjoyed it, profited.

'That is romantic and contrapuntal, high art combined with a complicated view of life, deep feeling expressed through a learned form. And yet,' he leaned back, approaching some climax, 'to me . . . to me the effect is that of a cup of cold, clear water. Why this is so I can't determine.' Frowning, he searched his mind.

Mrs Mead, without moving her place, shifted from foot to foot.

Her employer often addressed her in this academic, subdued way as if to convince her by his intensity rather than his eloquence. More than two years ago, soon after she had begun here, he had lectured her thus as he removed her clothes.

His movements had been gentle, delicate, and the voice had caressed her with a skill equivalent to that of his hands. He had spoken, as he undid buttons and zips, of historical inevitability. She had been terrified, shocked that this quiet man should so dominate her, so overwhelm her with passion and kindness. Once her initial protests, even tears, were quieted, this copulation seemed inevitable. That word stuck; she could remember none of the arguments, nor the interwoven compliments and endearments, only 'historical inevitability' and the thin, electric body of her employer as he laid her naked and compliant now to the floor of his study.

She could not, on recollection, be altogether surprised. Their bodies, hands, shoulders had touched, perhaps by chance at first, during the six weeks she had worked here. He attracted her and he knew. This quiet man who had confessed to a nervous breakdown, with his books and music and plays, was a sexual expert who had roused her as her husbands had not. And yet, once their sexual bouts were over, they resumed their rôles as employer and employed. She had not once expected more. Thoughts of marriage had never entered into the relationship. He was deeply considerate, but so he had seemed in the weeks before his first sexual advance was made. Each learned the other's needs, the intimacies of bodies, but without verbal familiarity. Even at the height of sexual ecstasy, Elsie Mead had never yet used his first name. They could dress together and resume discussion of meals and routine cleaning or hospitality without trouble. The housekeeper longed for the moments when he would rise and kiss her lips, or ease her on to his knee, or calmly, insolently fondle her breasts or genitals.

She had not expected this, would have refused the job had she foreseen this consequence, but now found a deep satisfaction. Her middle age dropped from her; her body became desirable in her own eyes. In principle she could not approve of her own attitude; in practice she was fulfilled. She enjoyed her work, the comfortable flat at the top of the house; her own home was profitably let. She had never been so well-off, so well regarded.

On that first morning, once the shock and terror had been soothed away, she remembered that her feeling was one of thankfulness that she had taken a bath, that her underclothes were clean. That was trivial; she wondered if she had not prepared herself every morning, unconsciously, for her employer's assault. It had shaken her; she had tried to repel him, but her resistance was in no way as strenuous as it ought to have been. She had welcomed him in, or so it now seemed. Even at the first attempt he had revealed to her pleasures she had never learnt with her husbands whom she had genuinely loved. Perhaps, she wryly considered, she needed the thrill of illegality, of risk, to rouse her.

It became clear that she had satisfied some need in him. Once as they lay naked together he had said, 'I was without hope, but it's not so now.' She had leant to kiss his shoulder, saying nothing, rewarded.

This morning he would make no sexual overture. He sat, hands clasped between his knees, pursuing his thoughts. 'The music is artificial, an artifice, and in my mind unconnected with life. Thus its clarity, its refreshment for me. But for Brahms it must have described, as music can, his deepest emotions, his longing, his discontents.' His hands wrestled together and were lifted to his chin. 'My life is a failure, is incomplete by its own low standards. It has skidded past. Who is to say that Brahms did not view his own achievements as equally unsatisfactory? We do not know. Certainly he approached the writing of a symphony with great diffidence. And women. He never married.'

Hillier smiled at his housekeeper, hopelessly lost.

'Have you anything interesting to report?'

'Peter said yesterday that his mother had been at school with me.'

'At Queen Elizabeth's?'

'Yes. She's five or six years or so younger than I am.'

'She never mentioned it?'

'No. She told the boy.'

'So you won't remember her?'

'No. Her name was Alice Hogg. Peter is going to bring some photographs of her as a girl to see if they ring any bells. They won't; I mean, why should they?'

'I remembered her quite well,' Hillier said. 'She seems staid now, bland.'

'And she wasn't when you knew her?'

'On the contrary. Have you met her husband?'

'I've seen him. And I've spoken to him on the 'phone. He's making a big success as manager of Top Fare. Very obliging.'

'Is it well paid?' he asked.

'These jobs aren't, are they? I don't know.'

'Are there not bonuses for increased business?'

'I've no idea; I expect so.'

The silence possessed them totally, each occupied with self.

'Would she make you a good friend, do you think?' Hillier began. Mrs Mead grimaced, unanswering. 'I often wonder about you in that flat of yours. This is a dull house.'

'I've never been so happy.'

'Good God!'

19

'I have more time to myself than ever before in my life. I'm comfortable. I live within my means. I enjoy myself.'

'Doing what?'

'Talking like this to you.' Was that a euphemism? She did not know. 'Listening to your friends, and their music, and their drama. I'd hate to be chained night after night to the television. I have books. I can borrow yours. I visit the library every week. I belong to a film club. I'm in good health. There's much to be thankful for.'

'Yes.' He nodded, as if he were dropping asleep.

Adrian's father, John Vernon Hillier, had come out of the Army at the end of the war, had joined his own father who ran three profitable electrical shops and had then expanded the business beyond all expectation. He organized a television hire service and was a millionaire inside ten years. His boldness had terrified his own father, whom he soon bought out as his empire continued to spread. Eight years ago, when John Vernon was sixty-two, he had suddenly sold off his many concerns on advantageous terms and settled with Megan his wife, a woman who had encouraged his schemes but now seemed ready to garden in the country, to travel abroad, to decorate her homes and her person. Their only child, Adrian, had disappointed them.

Megan had insisted that the boy went to university, where he'd worked hard and taken a good degree. After National Service, mainly in Germany, he had worked for one of his father's concerns, occupying a junior managerial position, but had shown none of the old man's entrepreneurial flair. He gave satisfaction but lacked ambition, seemed prepared to occupy his present post, or some equivalent, until he reached sixty or sixty-five, and to shade in the rest of his life in concert halls or theatres or with books. Marriage had made no difference. His wife, Suzanne – of French extraction, educated in Paris – was as little concerned as he, or so it appeared, with promotion to the high echelons of commerce. There had been no children and after nearly ten years she had left him for a dull representative of a continental electronics consortium to whom she was now married, with a home in Switzerland.

His parents blamed him for that fiasco. They were not keen on Suzanne during the years of the marriage, seeing her as dull, housebound, supine, her only advantages a slight prettiness, good dress sense, a faintly foreign accent and an excellent table. Megan, on whom the social duties of the older Hilliers descended as John Vernon worked himself into the ground, did her best with Suzanne, but confessed defeat.

'Why,' she ground out at her son, 'of all the women in the world do you have to pick out that puppet?'

Adrian Hillier could not answer. He loved women, attracted them, but had chosen his wife as a kind of sacrifice to his parents' expectations. Here is the answer to my dullness, a foreign lady who speaks French as fluently as English, who can discuss wines and appear exotically on social occasions. It had been a sad mistake which he should not have made. They had no children, not for want of trying, and he quieted his conscience by claiming to himself that his own behaviour would have been better had there been a family at home to catch and hold his interest. Instead he had womanized without great enthusiasm, had neglected his wife, so that when she announced her departure with Pierre Lemercier his first reaction had been relief.

His mother had shrugged off their separation, as though she had expected it. She showed little sympathy, asked acidly if Suzanne was a Catholic, or this Lemercier, though she knew that Adrian's wedding, against her wishes, had been a quiet affair at a register office. Megan's mind was engaged elsewhere encouraging her husband to retire, but without much success so far. A slight heart attack and a set of favourable offers from contesting multinationals a year later added conclusive weight. Her son wondered about his mother's influence on her husband. She had spoken plainly to the invalid: 'What use is it to you that nobody in North London can buy a washing machine without your being involved?' John Vernon gasped back: 'Quite apart from the fact that washing machines are useful, you lead a pretty comfortable life on that account.'

He had retired, sure that his financial position, like that of his wife and son, was rock solid. The older Hilliers had taken a world cruise, bought a house, a château rather, in France, and lived quietly rusticating. John Vernon did not wither; he rode a horse and dressing like a farmer swung his bucolic walking

21

stick; at night he played himself at billiards. Every two months they pulled up roots for a further excursion into unknown regions. When Adrian visited his parents, a rare occasion, the old man seemed different as if he had acquired a new personality. His father had died unexpectedly from a massive heart attack three years ago, aged sixty-seven.

By this time Adrian was in trouble.

At his parents' instigation he had retired from his job. Megan said they had seen to it that his income, unless he went raving mad, was sufficient to allow him to lead a life of cultured leisure. He had done enough humdrum work; now he could please himself. The son found himself baffled; he had often expressed dissatisfaction with the tiresome hours in his office, but at the age of forty he found he could not occupy himself without them. He had tried to write first a book of aphorisms, then a novel, and had failed to complete either. Reading, concerts, theatres occupied him to some advantage, but could not settle his conscience. He needed thirty or so hours a week of acknowledged, gainful boredom to satisfy him as to his place in the world. His father's energy had descended to him in this oblique, useless guise.

He became more melancholy, was treated with drugs and, against his conscious wishes, for depression. The woman with whom he was living, a spirited Manchester girl who was beginning to make a name as a director of television drama, could stand no more of it and walked out on him. Then his father, that immortal, had died, leaving him a substantial fortune and a sense of gaping loss that seemed quite unrelated to reality.

His mother, Megan, had little time for moping and said so. She, on her husband's death, had sold the château and the place in Kent and bought a more convenient house in the Cévennes from where she conducted raids on interesting places and people around the globe. Younger in appearance, more relaxed after John Vernon's demise, she determined to please herself and made no difficulties about it.

'I'm not giving myself time for dejection,' she announced. 'There are too many things to be seen and done. Mumps and dumps are in my view the fruits of idleness. I supported and stabilized your father, though he wouldn't have admitted it, through his years of work and his retirement, and now he's gone I don't intend to spend the rest of my days in useless sorrow.'

Megan, a schoolmistress from Aberdyfi, had met her husband at a Royal Artillery dance in Tywyn, and had spent the rest of the war teaching at a grammar school and bringing up her son in her parents' home. When John Vernon was demobilized, she joined him in London, lost her Welsh accent, found herself much at ease and encouraged her man, not that he needed it, on his swift upward climb through the commercial world. She believed in education, status, and after that money. She provided the first, to her husband's amusement. There was soon enough of the third to necessitate, at least in Megan's mind, a series of changes to larger, more commodious houses, and fees for expensive preparatory and public schools for Adrian. The boy had been at the time neither happy nor grateful, but had struggled his way through and had chosen, a preliminary intimation of awkwardness, to study economics at Beechnall University rather than follow some more cultural, civilized courses at Oxford, Cambridge or (Megan had taught French) at the Sorbonne. From the mansion in St John's Wood she watched her only child choose to disregard every opportunity she had provided.

The boy was popular in an unspectacular way, worked hard during university terms, travelled dutifully with Megan in the summer vacs and baffled his craggy Welsh grandparents who could not but admire their daughter's dizzy rise into the plutocracy. Adrian's quiet arguments with them about politics, religion or music impressed, reminding them, they claimed, of Mrs Hillier's uncle Gareth who had died at the age of twenty-two having just achieved his MA in Mediaeval Welsh with distinction. Adrian's attitude to his father, whom he saw only occasionally in school or university holidays, seemed too guarded for safety, unappreciative of advantages presented. The young man was, in their old canny eyes, too unworldly even for a hard pew in chapel.

The widowed Megan advised her son to pull up his roots and start elsewhere. 'You've plenty of money. You'll have even more when I die. Look round for somewhere interesting and start again.' He followed her counsel, but kack-handedly. His down-market decision to buy The Firs in the city where he had been at the university seemed typical of him, dully wrong. He might just as well have moved from his present house to one exactly similar in the next street for all the good it would do. 'If you'd gone into a hut in Northern Norway or the South Seas, that would have been sensible, because you very soon would have come running out. The idea is to change your mode of existence, not to settle down like some old man in a huge place with trees all round it. You'll moulder away.'

Adrian smiled at her. He was beginning to recover, could shrug off criticism.

'Whatever will you do there?' she persisted.

'Chop branches off the trees.'

'I think you will.'

'We haven't, all of us, your talent for living in far-flung places. I'll survive.'

His mother loved him then, for his bland awkwardness. He'd never occupy a large place in the world as his father had, but his own niche was not unattractive to her. If only he could keep his head.

Now, this morning, under the cold sky blue with thin washes of cloud, he clasped his hands and stroked his chin, lifting his head from time to time to speak to his housekeeper. He tapped with a fastidiously clean finger-nail a single letter lying on the vast top of his desk.

'I'm troubled, Elsie,' he said.

Mrs Mead assumed interest.

'This missive,' it was like him to use an outlandish word, 'is from my ex-wife. Her name is now Lemercier and she lives in Geneva. In it she informs me,' he spoke at snail's pace, 'that she will be in London and that she wishes to visit me.' He scraped at the stubble under his lower lip with his teeth. 'Why would she want that, do you think?'

Mrs Mead wisely made no answer.

'She is a very conventional woman. She has no financial claims on me. If she had, she would make them through her solicitors. But all that has been cleared up for long enough. Her husband is quite capable of keeping her in the manner to . . .' he allowed his voice to trail off, unwilling to parody himself.

'Has she any children?'

'No. Neither by me nor by her present husband.' He lifted the letter by one corner, dangling it. 'Nor do I imagine that she looks back on our marriage with any affection.'

'She was in love with you at one time, I expect?'

Hillier frowned at the housekeeper's sentence. 'She left me.' He stroked the letter. 'Not without cause.' He sniffed, shook his head. 'Can we put her up without undue difficulty?'

'Easily.'

'I'll think about it.'

'When will it be?'

'The New Year. January the . . . I've forgotten.' He did not re-open the letter. 'I'll think about it.'

4

Peter Fowler was burnishing the woodwork in the hall of The Firs when the young lady he had met on his first visit rang the bell. He opened the door on the chain; he had exact instructions.

'Hello,' she said. 'Valerie Fitzjames.' She obviously expected to be invited in. 'I've come to see if I can give a hand.'

Peter asked her to step inside, and sought out Mrs Mead.

'I don't want her,' she said, angry at once.

'Shall I tell her so?'

'Yes. No. You hold on there.'

The housekeeper wiped her hands and instructed the boy to stay in the kitchen. After a very short interval he heard the front door close, and Mrs Mead returned.

'That's got rid of her,' she said with satisfaction. 'There's a dinner-party tonight. Theatrical friends; she's one of them. Wanted to know if she could help me at all.' She grimaced, sourly. 'What she wanted was to see Mr Hillier.'

'Why?'

Mrs Mead considered him, or his question, at length.

'If you want my opinion she's setting her cap at Mr Hillier.' Peter knew the phrase. 'I told her he was out. He is, but she didn't believe me. Not that I care much what she thinks.'

'You should have given her some work to do.'

'And have it to do all over again myself?'

'Isn't she a bit young for Mr Hillier?' he asked.

'You get back to your panels,' Mrs Mead instructed him, grimly. As he opened the door she said, 'Men. They've no idea.' Peter waited, but nothing more was forthcoming.

At coffee-time Mrs Mead raised the subject as soon as she sat down. 'What did that girl say when you opened the door?'

'"Hello. Valerie Fitzjames. I've come to see if I can give a hand."'

Mrs Mead stirred her coffee with violence.

'That's a daft name, Fitzjames,' she began. Peter waited. 'Don't you think it is?'

'No.' Hesitating. 'Not really.'

Mrs Mead burst out laughing.

'You're right. It's because I don't like her. She can't help her name. Unless she's made it up to look better in theatre programmes.'

'I'm a bird-catcher.'

'What does that make me? Fermented honey. Or a field.' She drew his attention to the roses on her apron. 'O'er the flowery mead.'

'I like talking to you. You teach me things,' Peter said, flattering.

'But I don't like her. I shouldn't tell you that, should I?'

'What about Mr Hillier, though?'

'What about him?'

'Is he in love with her?' Peter giggled at his boldness.

'What do you know about love? Have you found a girl-friend?' He shook his head. 'It won't be long. No, Mr Hillier's at a difficult time of life, and he'd been quite seriously ill before he came up here. He doesn't need young fly-by-nights bothering him.'

'Do you think she would?'

'I'm sure of it. Now, you drink your coffee.'

Before they had finished Mr Hillier tapped at the kitchen door and came in. He was wearing his outdoor clothes.

'I thought I could smell coffee. Any chance of a cup? No, I'll have it down here, because I have to go out again.' He drew up a stool as the housekeeper poured. 'I've been in your supermarket, ordering my Christmas spirits.' They dutifully laughed. 'Anything exciting or untoward here?'

'Miss Fitzjames came. Did you ask her to call?' Accusatory.

'No, not that I remember. Did she want anything important?'

'She wanted to help.'

Hillier consulted the oracle in his coffee cup.

'Odd,' he said. 'She'll be here tonight. Mrs Mead is not keen on her,' he said to Peter. 'She thinks she's pushy – always where she shouldn't be.'

'Certainly I don't like her strolling in and out of my kitchen.'

27

'She means well. What do you think, Peter?'

'She's pretty.'

'Typical man. Already.'

'And lively?'

This talk sparked dangerously and the boy held his peace.

'It takes all sorts to make a world,' Mrs Mead said, pacifically, to appease them or herself.

Hillier drained his coffee, drifted out. Peter was dismissed brusquely to his next chore.

In the weeks before Christmas the housekeeper and Alice Fowler became very friendly, exchanging telephone calls and short visits. The friendship excited Mrs Fowler, while her husband at first affected a rough amusement.

'What do you two women find to talk about?' he asked.

'The shortcomings of men.'

Mr Fowler was pleased then that his wife had found a companion. He spent increasingly long hours in the supermarket, felt guilty about it and took comfort from Alice's easy acquaintance with so sensible a woman. Peter enjoyed seeing Mrs Mead in the context of his home; there she was less stiff, less striking, better dressed, more even-tempered. The two women giggled together over their teachers at the grammar school, the sports day, the prize distribution. Neither had kept in touch with the Old Girls' Association, nor attended reunions, but those memories seemed important to them. The boy wondered if his schooldays would loom large in his future. When he broached the topic to his father, Mr Fowler answered, 'I quite enjoyed grammar school, but they wanted it all doing their way. That was the snag. They didn't prepare you for life. They didn't seem to connect what was going on in school with what was happening outside. The old saying, "A man among boys and a boy among men," certainly applied to some of the masters. I don't suppose I should be telling you this, but it never does anybody any harm to keep his eyes peeled.' Mr Fowler stroked his bristly moustache and hurried off to his next worry.

The two women discussed Valerie Fitzjames in the boy's hearing. Miss Fitzjames, who worked at a hospital as a minor administrator, had been appearing too regularly at The Firs for Mrs Mead's liking.

'They're discussing a festival, or so they say, and it's often one o'clock in the morning before she drives off. God knows what time she has to be at work.'

'It sounds as if the festival's started.'

'It can't do Mr Hillier any good. He's been very seriously ill with nervous trouble. He needs quiet and regular hours, not young women leading him a dance.'

'Does she know his history?'

'I doubt it. He plays his cards very close to his chest, doesn't like to give too much away about himself. For instance, I guess he's very much richer than he lets on.'

'What makes you say that?'

'The stubs of the cheques he's sending off to charity. That's good, mark you, but they're not amounts from a man of moderate means.'

'The upkeep of that house,' agreed Mrs Fowler, 'must be tremendous.'

'Oh, he'd run six like that and not feel it.'

'And does this Fitzjames woman know?'

'How can she? She sees that he's not short. And God knows what he lets out. Sometimes he's like a child . . . I don't know.'

'He's very attractive still.'

'You can say that again.'

'What about his former wife? Does he have to support her?'

'She's coming to see him in the New Year.'

'Why?'

'Why, indeed? It can only mean trouble.'

'Is that what he thinks?'

'That's the drawback with him, Alice: he does not think. For a man of his education and experience (I believe he was manager of some very large electrical concern in London) he doesn't seem to consider consequences.'

'What does he do all day?'

'That's another thing. He's on with this dramatic club in the city, the Phoenix, but most of the people are out at work in the daytime; they're amateurs. He reads and listens to music. He does some electrical work for the plays, or pays for it to be done, and paints scenery and sells tickets. Sweeps the floor, for all I know.'

'Miss Fitzjames isn't there in the day with him?'

'No. Not as far . . . No.'

'And he's a good employer?'

'Perfect. Considerate and polite. He likes things done properly, but who's to blame him?'

The other subject they discussed was Peter's future. At some time during the next academic year, the boy had to make up his mind about the subjects he'd take at GCSE. His reports were fetched out and considered.

'He's interested in languages rather than science,' Mrs Fowler said.

'He'll have to make the choice in the end, so he might as well pick something he's already good at.'

'What do you think about computers, computer studies?'

'It sounds very up-to-date, and everybody should know something about them these days, but my step-nephew, who works for ICI, says the market's getting crowded, especially at the top end. Why don't you ask Mr Hillier? He went to university, and he was in business. And he's fond of the boy. Do you want me to approach him for you?'

'If you please.' Courtesy matched formality.

'I will then. It's my opinion that Mr Hillier's better employed dealing with sensible problems and not this everlasting theatre. He'll consider it carefully, and make inquiries for you. He's a clever man, but he's wasting himself.'

'Why is that?'

'I can't say. Perhaps things have been too easy for him. I don't know.'

They had returned, without qualm, to Topic Number One.

On the next Saturday Adrian Hillier made an appearance, questioned Peter about his progress at school and invited the boy and his mother to discuss the matter with him. Mrs Fowler was to telephone.

The meeting proved business-like and short. Hillier questioned Peter again, coached the mother in the questions she was to put to the staff. The boy had no idea of the career he wanted, and Hillier said that that was not unusual. He himself had not known, even at university, even with his parents 'baying at my heels', what he had wanted to do. Yes, it seemed sensible, and he stroked his chin, for Peter to add German to his French and Latin. 'Might even be better to do Japanese or

30

Russian, only they don't teach them, do they?' He laughed his sly laugh.

He dismissed them politely but at speed.

When the meeting was reported to Mr Fowler, the father seemed unexpectedly angry.

'What the hell's it got to do with him?'

'We asked him . . . through Mrs Mead. He's interested in the boy.'

'The proper persons to ask are his teachers. They know what's what. Hillier was born with a silver spoon in his mouth. He never had to fight for a place as our Pete will.'

'It's sensible to look out all the information that we can.'

'You wouldn't ask the postman or the milkman. It's years since he was anywhere near a university. There's constant change and you must take account of it.'

'Gerry,' Mrs Fowler spoke in a low, dangerous voice, 'what have you got against Mr Hillier?'

'Against? A-bloody-gainst? Nothing. He, or that Mrs Mead of his, is a good customer. I just don't like my business being bruited all over Beechnall.' The verb surprised his wife.

Two days later Fowler, hurrying in from work, rushed into the kitchen. 'I'll tell you something about that Mr Hillier,' he gabbled, teeth white under the moustache.

'Well?'

'He owns a very large block of shares in Top Fare. I don't know whether it's the majority, but a considerable interest.'

'Where did you learn this?'

'From a man in head office who was down today. He was talking about some alterations and he let on that a big shareholder, a member of the Board, actually lived in this town. Adrian Hillier. No other.'

'What did you say?'

'I said, "He's a customer." '

'And?'

'And nothing.' Fowler dashed his hand down.

'So that makes it all right for me to ask him about Peter's education?'

'What the bloody hell's that got to do with anything?'

She could see he was pleased.

Gerald Fowler had owned a large grocery shop, which had

31

been demolished in a council reorganization scheme five years before. He had worked hard, had done quite well for himself, but had not been finally displeased especially as Top Fare had immediately appointed him manager of a small supermarket, and then two years later promoted him to a larger emporium in a good shopping area. He had not expected this; the managing director usually drafted in some graduate from London for these superior positions, some young man on the way up.

His promotion had been a constant topic between him and his wife.

'I don't know whether it's a change of policy on the part of the board to use local men. They're the sort of organization that goes in for whizz-kids, I'd have said.'

'You're the exception proving the rule.'

'They probably pay me less than one of their London wonder-boys.'

'Look, you've done them well. Somebody's noticed it.'

'I've never known them promote a local man to one of the really big places.'

'Because they haven't found anybody up to your standard.'

Mrs Fowler's praise was by no means hypocritical. If the city council had not decided to pull down his old premises he would still be a self-employed grocer. He had not done badly; he knew his customers, he was obliging, he worked long hours, but the work was physically arduous and would prove more taxing as he got older. Moreover, there was no scope for expansion, and this riled him. He'd work on for the next twenty years, not making much progress, turning an honest penny, keeping his head above water, his detached house painted and heated, in debt to nobody. He had deserved more, she thought.

When the plans for the rebuilding of the streets in the district round his shop were first published, Fowler was thrown into alternate anger and despair. He'd fight, he shouted to his family, stand for his rights. He badgered councillors, his MP, the local papers; he attended, inaugurated protest meetings. His name became known. There was talk of his being invited to stand for the council, but in all this activity, and he organized his time well, conviction grew in his mind that nobody would ever employ him again at his age, that he would be unlikely to rebuild his business in the reorganized district, the nature of which would be radically changed. Without hope, he applied therefore to Top Fare, his application supported by two Conservative councillors, one an ex-Lord Mayor, and his bank manager. The firm had interviewed him at length three times, and had appointed him temporarily for six months to the Carlton, their most elderly supermarket. At the end of the sixth month, they had extended his period of probation, though with an increase in salary, and had confirmed him in his position at the close of the year and fifteen months later promoted him, after an impressive interview in London, to his present job.

'The best thing that ever happened to you was when the council closed you down,' his wife argued.

'You could say so. It didn't feel like it at the time.'

'Is this the end of the road with you this time?'

'Probably. They might move me to some larger place they're opening somewhere else. Or at least they might inquire.'

'Would you go?'

'Depends where it is. I couldn't afford to buy a house in London, however much they paid me. And what about your job? Or Peter's education?'

Fowler was doing well, knew it, but could hardly believe his luck.

Adrian Hillier summoned Mrs Fowler for a conference on Peter's future. As Mrs Mead was out at a concert, he prepared the coffee himself. He had made inquiries amongst business acquaintances here and in London, and it did not seem to matter, he thought, what subject you studied at university. Provided you had done well, showed you weren't afraid of work there, looked personable and could speak up for yourself, they'd consider you for management training. Of course some graduates qualified later in law or as accountants, and that carried extra weight, but Peter could make up his mind about it in the sixth form when he was deciding what course to follow at university.

Hillier spoke softly, but energetically.

In his study the air was pleasantly warm and lights glowed on the multi-coloured dust covers on his books. He had seated his guest at his desk while he occupied one of the smaller upright chairs by a book-laden table. He perched straight, with knees

33

together, and reminded Alice of the headmaster of her son's grammar school; both had seemed young, grey-haired men, enthusiastic but not prepared to overstate a case. His voice was low and the delivery quick; he did not hesitate. He thought for a moment before answering a question, but once he began to speak he did so without hiatus, hands clasped in his lap. Once his information had been given and discussed, he had little small talk. He asked after Mr Fowler's health, but made no comment when she praised her husband's assiduity at work. No mention was made of Mr Hillier's connection with Top Fare. He poured her a second cup of coffee, rather strong, and in his gentlemanly way seemed relieved when she said she must leave. He accompanied her outside, shook hands by her car, commented on the weather, saying that only puritanical compunction or prejudice prevented him from spending January and February in Tenerife or Mauritius, but he nevertheless stood coatless in the misty cold.

When, on their next meeting, Alice reported the conversation to Mrs Mead, the housekeeper seemed affronted.

'He never said a word to me. And he'd washed up your coffee things and put them away.'

'Is that unusual?'

'Well, yes, it is.'

'Perhaps he didn't consider my visit of any importance. Or perhaps he forgot.'

'That's not likely.'

Mrs Mead made a thorough investigation of their exchanges, pulled a sour face when she learnt that Alice had been allotted the swivel chair, paid more attention to her employer's behaviour than the sense of his advice.

'He was thoroughly polite,' said Mrs Fowler, puzzled.

'I'm glad to hear it.'

'Why do you say that? I've never found him anything else.'

The housekeeper pondered. 'Mr Hillier's a very nice man, an excellent employer, straightforward and decent as the day's long.' She sounded as if she dictated a reference. 'But . . . and I don't want to exaggerate this, or start ideas in your head, or appear to be issuing warnings. But . . . I will put it no more strongly than this: he is something of a lady's man.' Mrs Mead had lost her sangfroid, was blushing, rolling her shoulders, trying to look Alice in the eye.

'You mean,' Mrs Fowler tried to speak calmly, 'that he's not to be trusted sexually?'

'That is what I do mean.'

'But, Elsie, you live in the house with him. You see him every day.'

'I should know then.' She recovered equilibrium.

'You don't mean to say that he has . . . ?'

Mrs Mead raised a cautionary hand.

'I don't mean to say anything . . . except this: be careful, on the watch. You knew him when he was a young man. I don't know what he was like then, but I know what he is now, and that's why I'm warning you.'

'There was nothing of that kind when I saw him.'

'I'm glad.'

'He was, well, exactly as I'd expected him to be. Very helpful . . . most courteous.'

Now both blushed again, Mrs Mead who thought she had given away too much about herself, and Mrs Fowler who remembered the shy, overpowering student who had seduced her. They dropped the subject, in suspicion, self-doubting.

On Boxing Day the Fowler family was invited to The Firs in the afternoon for a drink. The party was small and Mr Hillier lethargic. Peter had received a fountain-pen from his employer, and an illustrated copy of *Pickwick Papers* from Mrs Mead. As the four sat in the smaller drawing room they were joined by a foreign lady, ushered in by the housekeeper. Introductions were made: Mme Lemercier. She took an armchair. Mrs Mead was instructed to find herself a seat. Mr Hillier rose with a subdued joviality to fill or refill glasses.

Conversation was low-key, hard work, until Mme Lemercier learnt the nature of Gerald Fowler's work, when she began to question him about the running of a supermarket. She spoke knowledgeably, compared the policies of her local store in Geneva with those in Paris, in Lyons, in Toulouse and in Zürich. She seemed especially interested in attempts to catch the customer's interest, in the use of displays, the constant changing of the placement of stock.

'That annoys me,' she said. 'If I want to buy, let's say,

breakfast cereal, then I don't want to enter into a voyage of discovery. I want to walk straight to the shelf where it was kept yesterday.'

'You, madame, know your mind.'

'Don't most of your customers?'

Fowler gave her a lecture on the psychology of salesmanship. He spoke fluently, with conviction, from experience, not as if he'd committed a few pages of a hand-book to memory. When he outlined the difficulties of ordering for the neighbourhood where his shop stood, serving two council estates, a large middle-class area and a substantial group of houses where the really affluent lived, he waved towards Hillier, he became eloquent.

'Do such people patronize your place?' Mme Lemercier queried. 'Don't they shop in the centre of the city, or by telephone?'

'They shop,' Fowler pronounced, 'where they have a wide variety of choice, a high quality of product, reasonable prices and easy parking facilities.'

'In that order?' Hillier asked.

Fowler rubbed his chin. 'I often think price is the main consideration.'

'With rich people?' Mrs Fowler, interrupting.

'Yes. In this part of the world, at least.'

Mme Lemercier now opened an investigation into Fowler's views on shoplifting. Again Fowler was clear, incisive, with statistics to hand. His security men had apprehended five in this last week. All would be prosecuted. These were clear-cut cases.

Adrian Hillier wondered if robbery of this kind was caused not so much by unemployment and shortage of ready money, as by a need for excitement. Fowler refused final judgement, except to guess that lack of cash was almost always an ingredient.

'We have to be careful with the girls on the tills. It's very easy for an intelligent person to make a dishonest profit for herself.' He explained how this was achieved.

'You won't be able to employ any of us now,' Mr Hillier said. 'Not that I'm thinking of applying. It must be boring.'

'Do you,' Mme Lemercier inquired, 'appoint clever people or dull to these posts? It must be a difficult decision for you.'

'I prefer the intelligent, but I look into background, upbringing, need for income. I look for those with children, with a mortgage, for whom the loss of a job would create real problems. Of course there are other things: appearance, speech, temperament.'

'Does the firm employ a psychologist?' Madame.

'The firm issues us with instructions about the taking on of staff, as about a hundred and one other things. But in my opinion common sense and local knowledge are paramount. Presumably these guides were drawn up in the first place by professional people; I don't know. They are useful, but lack detail because they cover a hundred and one environments. What is suitable in the West End of London will not do for, let's say, Skegness or South Shields.'

Gerald Fowler set out his stall to impress Mme Lemercier. When she began to talk about the advantages and drawbacks of travel by car on the continent, he plied her with questions. Madame grew animated comparing French or Swiss motorists with those of England or America.

'Do you prefer living on the continent to England?' he asked.

Mme Lemercier smiled at Hillier. 'It is the people who contribute most to the quality of life. Fine scenery, proximity to recitals or theatres, a pleasant house, money are all important, but it is neighbours, friends, loved ones who determine the richness of my existence.'

'In that order?' Adrian Hillier again, not serious.

'Have you a family?' Mrs Fowler asked to avoid embarrassment.

'Only my husband. We have, unfortunately, no children.'

This initiated a discussion about married couples who decided against children, and about those who confined themselves to an only child.

'Would you have liked brothers and sisters?' Hillier asked Peter. The boy had barely spoken, had listened intently, interested in the voices.

'I don't know. I expect we would have quarrelled. I was going to have a sister, but she died.'

'Oh, I am so sorry,' Mme Lemercier said to Mrs Fowler.

'I was alone,' Hillier announced. 'Unique.'

'Has it done you harm?' Mrs Mead, challenging.

'Probably.' Hillier picked up his glass, held it to the light.

Mme Lemercier expatiated on French and Swiss education, on nurture and nature. Now she threw in sentences in French as she described known Parisian or Genevan mothers about their business of rearing children. The voice rippled vivid, rapid and direct, but her hands stayed unmoving and her face lacked all animation. An attractive woman, Mr Fowler decided, but without expression, not making the best of herself. She knew her subject, but clarity not charm was her aim.

The Fowlers left soon after four, accompanied to the front door by the other three. In the hall, they stood back to admire the lights on the tall Christmas tree.

'I can smell the forest,' Mme Lemercier said.

'Do you have Christmas trees in Switzerland?' Peter asked.

'Oh, I do. But then I am English.' She did not sound it, as she laid a hand on Peter's shoulder. In this multi-coloured half-light she excelled, seemed beautiful. 'I think the custom is pretty well universal these days. In Europe, at least. Isn't that so, Adrian?'

Hillier murmured something inconclusive, mentioning Prince Albert and German precedents.

'I hate Christmas cards,' Mrs Mead offered. 'Always have done.'

'Do you sell them, Mr Fowler?' Madame.

'Yes. And next week they'll be out again at reduced prices, ready for next Christmas.'

'Will people buy them then?'

'Oh, yes; we'll clear the lot.'

'I'll have to call in,' Mrs Mead said huffily, condemning herself.

'They're a bargain,' Fowler told her.

'Is that quite the idea?' Hillier asked.

'If you are talking about idealism, then money shouldn't come into it. If I had to defend my action, I'd say I was giving the not-so-well-off the chance to send good-class cards.'

'A year late,' his wife chaffed.

'It's the thought that counts,' Mrs Mead said. 'Or so they say . . . whoever they are.'

After hand-shaking the Fowlers congregated at the bottom of the steps, staring at the lights through the closed front door. As they stepped towards the car the outside lamps snapped on, illuminating their path.

'A pleasant little function,' Mr Fowler asserted, opening up, fumbling with keys.

'I'll drive,' Alice told him. 'You've had one or two too many.'

'A good idea.' Fowler crossed to the other door. While they were fastening their seat-belts he began, 'I'll say this for Hillier. He doesn't throw his weight about.'

'There was no call for it.'

'People with money like to let you know that they occupy a privileged position.'

'And so they do.'

'I agree. All I'm saying is that Mr Hillier didn't make a song-and-dance about it.'

'Perhaps he doesn't feel the need for it, especially with us.'

'Unnh? Who's this Mme Lemercier, if that's her name?'

Mrs Fowler giggled, changing gear, making him wait. 'That's his former wife.'

'How do you know that?'

'Mrs Mead. She keeps me up to date.'

'And is she staying there?'

'No idea.'

Fowler considered this. Since they had left the house he appeared less steady, his speech more slurred, his head looser on the trunk.

'They must have parted on amicable terms?' No answer to that. 'Does she often visit him?'

'I don't know. Mrs Mead told me she was coming but I thought it was later, in the New Year.'

'Has she brought her husband over?'

'Look, you know as much as I do now.'

They were passing Top Fare, the windows plastered garishly with Christmas offers. The interior was faintly lit.

'The source of our wealth,' said Peter from the back seat. His parents laughed, then fell silent until they reached home.

39

As they stood on the street Gerald Fowler said, fiercely, as if the words were forced out of him, 'If I divorced you, I wouldn't want you dropping in on me.'

'That would depend on the circumstances.' Mrs Fowler checked the car doors.

'There'd be hurt, and damage, and soreness. Certain to be.' Gerald's fists were clenched; he looked ready to fight.

'Not of necessity.' Mrs Fowler spoke pacifically, guiding Peter through the gate.

'Yes. There would. Couldn't be otherwise.'

The mother opened the front door. Peter entered.

'Put the lights on, sweet,' she ordered. Her husband stood in the street still. 'These are morbid thoughts for Boxing Day.'

'For any bloody day.'

— 5 —

'They had sexual intercourse together.'

Mrs Mead, visiting Mrs Fowler a week after Christmas, spoke with vehemence.

'How can you be sure?'

'I took him a morning pot of tea, and there they were in bed, mother-naked.' She scowled. 'Oh, I didn't actually catch him in the act, but no one is going to tell me that they lie in bed with their clothes off and go no further.'

'Were they embarrassed? When you walked in?'

'No. I'd knocked, of course, and waited for an invitation to enter, but, no, I can't say they were.'

'Mr Hillier seems so shy. I'd have thought . . .'

'No. "Put it down there, Elsie, thank you very much." As he would on any morning. "Could you bring a cup for Suzanne?"'

'Perhaps the fact that they had been married . . .? Or that she is a French lady?'

Mrs Mead hacked a scornful laugh, short as a cough.

'And that's another thing. "Elsie," he said to me, "what do you think of Suzanne's way of talking?" That's what he calls her. "She speaks beautiful English for a foreigner," I said. "When we were married," he said, "she spoke English with the same sort of accent as mine." I didn't know what to say to that.'

'It sounds like criticism, don't you think?'

'Perhaps. He has a sly way of putting things.'

'And how did you find her?'

'Oh, I've no complaints. She was affable, amenable to my suggestions, not awkward. Very friendly, indeed. But I never found out why she'd come.'

'Perhaps she was just curious to see how her former husband was living. They may have parted without too many tears, and . . . You'd know better than me. Does Mr Hillier confide in you about such things?'

41

'Yes and no. Sometimes he'll tell me something that quite plainly he'd do better to keep his mouth shut about, and then he can be just as secretive. In some ways he's uncertain of himself. "I'm just off to London," he'll say, "for a round of giddy pleasure." And then he won't go. "I've changed what passes for my mind again." I don't know.'

'When he was married to Mme Lemercier, he wasn't nearly as rich as he is now.'

'And you mean she's come over for a further cut of the spoils? It was certainly never mentioned, not hinted at, in my hearing. But they had ample time to themselves.'

'How long did she stay?'

'She came on Christmas Eve and left the day after Boxing Day. Went on to some relative in Weston-super-Mare.'

'I wouldn't like to be away from home over Christmas,' Mrs Fowler said.

'There are no children. That makes a difference.'

'I'd think people cling to each other all the more in that case.'

'In my view, people who can have children, but don't, are generally selfish.'

They argued that over satisfactorily, pleased with each other.

When Mrs Mead made as if to leave she blurted out, 'Mr Hillier was impressed by your husband.'

'In what way?'

'He just said that Mr Fowler seemed much in command of his work and was very articulate about it.'

'I'll pass that on. Gerald'll be pleased. Mr Hillier will understand these business matters.'

'I don't know whether he does or he doesn't.'

'Doesn't he keep up his business connections, then?'

'He attends meetings from time to time in London; they're all marked up on his calendar. And he gets sheaves of paper about them. But how important they are, or how much notice he takes of them, I don't know. Occasionally gentlemen drop in on him to discuss his money, or his concerns. He's not put out by it; at least as far as I can tell. But he doesn't talk to me about such matters. He's very good at figures, that I can tell you.'

Talk rambled; the women laughed over the vagaries of men, well settled into their chairs.

'I don't understand my husband sometimes,' Alice Fowler confessed.

'Why is that?'

'One minute he's so ambitious he's going to turn the world upside down, and the next day nothing will ever be right again.'

They fell silent.

Mrs Mead heaved herself about on her seat, sighing heavily as though she were physically pained.

'My second husband committed suicide.'

The words fell heavily clear. Mrs Mead had never spoken to Alice about her life before she lived at The Firs. Now the drawn features, the pallor, the rapid breathing suggested that she must come out with it.

'I'm sorry.' Mrs Fowler's voice whispered.

'I've been unlucky in marriage. My first was a disaster. I met that husband soon after I left college and I was in my first job, but it was over and done with inside a year. It set me back, I can tell you. And it was nine years later, I was thirty, when I married my second. I didn't know if I was doing the right thing. He was my headmaster, and twenty-eight years older than I was. A childless widower, very good at his work, extremely kind to me. I liked him, I can tell you; I admired him. He seemed young for his age, lively. I was taken aback when he invited me to dinner out of the blue. I wasn't sure what I wanted when he asked me to marry him; I hummed and haa-ed. But in the end I agreed. We were happy, I'd have said.'

'Did you go on teaching?'

'Yes, it seemed sensible. There weren't any children.' She laughed roughly. 'There was sex. Frank Mead was a vigorous man for all his age. But when it came to retirement at sixty-five, we'd been married seven-eight years then, he didn't want to leave. "I'm better," he used to say, "than I was twenty-five years ago. I know my way around now as I didn't then." I thought he'd find plenty to do, voluntary work, teaching illiterates or Indians, Oxfam, the WEA, Men of the Trees, the hospice, the Lions, all of which he'd had connections with while he was at work, but no. He hung about the house. Oh, he was jolly about it at first. "I'm going to remedy the defects of my education," he'd say. "Now for the first time in forty-odd years, I've the time to sit down and read seriously." '

'And did he?'

'I doubt it. He never went out. He'd potter in the garden or do little jobs about the house, but for instance I'd have to come home at night and prepare the evening meal.'

'Didn't he do the shopping?'

'Not really. We had a freezer. But he wouldn't have peeled the potatoes or shelled the peas.'

'Didn't you say anything about that?'

'You know me, Alice. But he answered, very reasonably, that he was no sort of chef, that I'd spoilt him and so on. It's true I'd always been keen on cooking, and didn't allow him to interfere, that is while we were both out teaching. I'd made a rod for my own back.'

'Did he do any housework?'

'Well, yes, after a fashion, when I got on to him. To tell you the truth, I don't know how he occupied himself. Sitting about. Brooding. I told him to get out to the law courts or the library or the cricket matches, but he never did.'

'Was he religious?'

'Not in the sense that he attended a church or chapel. I mean he'd be reading prayers in the school assembly fine as the next man, and I daresay he'd claim to believe in God, but it didn't make an atom of difference to him. I believe in Greenland, that it's there, but I can't say it affects me in any shape or form.'

Mrs Mead spoke with a cheerful resolution as if she could manage her life, smiling albeit grimly, gesturing, straight-backed in her chair. Then her face twisted into gravity, as if she had suddenly tasted something bitter.

'I don't know why I'm telling you all this rigmarole, Alice. I've never spoken about it to anybody before.'

'Not Mr Hillier?'

'He doesn't encourage confidences of that sort, though he likes talk. You don't mind, do you?' They exchanged murmurs of support. 'Now, where was I?' She waved her hands as if this were a street chat in which she had slightly lost her way. 'He grew very depressed. I made him go to the doctor's, but he wasn't willing. He had tablets, but he wouldn't take them regularly. It surprised me, because he lectured the children at school about obedience and using common sense, but it didn't apply to him. I made him go away with me on holiday; I needed it anyway. He used to be super on foreign vacations when he was at work, full of gusto, the life and soul of any party he was with. Like a young man. But not now. He moped about, wouldn't walk or talk or do anything; it was hell. He acted like a fractious, sulky child.'

'What did you do?' Alice broached her question tentatively, breaking an awkward silence.

'What could I? I called the doctor again for him. The man did his best for us, but he couldn't be with us all day and every day. I could not believe the change in Frank. He had been a vigorous, well-directed, energetic man, a leader of men, and now he drooped about the house, put on weight, wasted his talents. It was awful.'

'And all this was due to retirement?'

'So it seemed. I did suspect some physical cause, but the doctors didn't think so. He was just into his seventies now. And then one day I came home and found him. It's what I'd been dreading. And yet he'd seemed better for a week or two. I thought I'd detected signs of . . . On that day we were having trout. A young man on the staff used to go fishing and we . . . Frank loved them, with almonds. He'd perked up, had been quite himself for a day or two, and I thought this was just what he'd enjoy, do him good. I felt cheerful.'

Mrs Mead paused, staring glassily at the wall.

'Shall I fetch us a cup of tea?' Alice Fowler in fear.

'No, hear me out.' The drawn face struggled to recompose itself. 'I found him in the garage. There was nobody about the house. That was unusual. I went to look for him in the garden. He was in the car in the garage, door not locked, with a piece of hose on the exhaust. He'd tied it so it wouldn't slip off. I hadn't gone in the car that day because a colleague at school who lived in the next street was learning to drive and I sat with her, there and back; she had to have a qualified . . . His poor face . . . And he'd propped a note up over the dashboard, in his big writing. Sealed in an envelope with my name, Mrs E. A. Mead, fancy putting that on it, apologizing for what he was about to do. The best thing. I would be happier. Seventy, only seventy.

45

No age these days. He wore his best suit, with a tie. You wouldn't think they'd bother about such things.'

Her face had cleared. She shook herself straight.

'I don't know why I'm telling you this, Alice, except to show how little we understand each other. You're not forty yet . . .'

'Next year.'

'I'm forty-five. I don't fathom myself. Marriage has been a tragedy for me, and twice. Perhaps I deserve it. What do you say?'

'How can you be . . .?'

'I'm no angel. I've not always done as I should. I knew my mind too well for my first husband. And I . . . No, why should I load you with my . . .? It's happened, and nothing I can say or do will change it.'

'I'm sorry. I'd no idea.'

'I don't go blazoning it round the world.'

'How do you manage? Sometimes when something unpleasant has happened to me, I can barely lift my head.'

'Alice, if I spoke the truth I'm the same, but I'm as happy now as I have ever been. Except perhaps when I was in the sixth form or when I was first married to Frank. I went on teaching after the death, but I had no heart for it. And then when Mr Hillier moved up here, I took the position with him. I'm not earning as much, but on the other hand I'm not spending as much. And it's interesting. I owed it to myself to hide out of the way somewhere.'

'Will you go back to teaching?'

'It depends. I'm not sure that there will be jobs going. And classrooms aren't what they were. This post has proved exactly right for me. So far. I say that because when you've had the sort of experience I've had, you're always looking over your shoulder for the next blow.' She sat poised now, on top, in control of herself. 'Mr Hillier had already sacked one housekeeper after a month's trial.'

'That doesn't seem like him.'

'What do you mean?'

'He seems so quiet. Won't say boo to a goose.'

'Don't you believe it. He can be as ruthless as the next; you should see him sometimes. But I've been up there for eighteen months now, and nothing's gone awry. We've had words, but we get on. We're almost of an age, you know. I'm older than he is, but we were born in the same year. And I'm out of the road, and saving money, and finding my way back.'

'You always seem,' Alice Fowler answered, hesitantly, 'so sure of yourself. And you've been so kind to Peter.'

'I like that boy. I did the first time I saw him. Sharp, but polite with it. And I'd had dealings with his father. I knew something of his background. And Mr Hillier took to him.'

'Yes. He really likes to go up there.'

'I say to myself,' Mrs Mead continued, as if she had not heard the last sentence, '"Elsie," I say, "you're in domestic service now." And that puts me in my place. "You're down a few notches," I tell myself. My great-grandmother was a skivvy. "Clogs to clogs in three generations."'

'You don't regret it, do you?'

'I regret nearly all my life, Alice. It seems hardly the thing to say at the age of forty-five, but there it is. I've touched nothing that's turned out as it should.'

Again Mrs Mead pulled herself together. Alice Fowler, reduced by these revelations, sat with knees together to contain her trembling. Her sitting room seemed icy, and yet Mrs Mead, after the bout of confession, sat upright and easy.

'You won't mention this to anyone, I hope, not even your husband?'

'I wouldn't think . . .'

'You'd be surprised what people spill.' Again she smiled, without mirth. 'Now I really shall have to be going. I appreciate the chance to come here. And talk . . . and talk.' The echo sounded an appeal.

6

'I haven't seen anything of Mrs Fowler recently,' Hillier said to his housekeeper as they sat in her kitchen.

'I'm not surprised, with this weather. And she holds down a full-time job.'

'Have you come across her?'

'Once, since Christmas. We ate a mince-pie at her house one Saturday afternoon.'

'Is she friendly?' he wanted to know.

'Very. Why do you ask?'

'She's stiff with me, on her best behaviour.'

'Perhaps that's as well.'

Hillier stroked his chin, stirred his coffee, examined his pockets. 'What's her husband like? How does she make out with him?'

'You've met him.'

'There's a reason behind these questions.' Hillier's voice had become vague, a whisper. 'Top Fare are considering Fowler for promotion.'

'How do you know that?'

Hillier laughed silently, teeth strong.

'I'm a shareholder. The managing director's personal assistant asked me if I knew him. If they promote him he'll have to go away. Will that upset their apple-cart?'

'It depends where they send him. Presumably she needs the money; that's why she works. But if she could find a reasonable position and a good school for Peter, she'd like to see her husband get on, I'm sure.'

'They don't seem much alike.'

'What do you mean by that?'

'I've only met him once, socially, and she seemed very much more reserved than he was. Downcast eyes. The "low voice of your English dames". Does she have to do as she's told?'

'I doubt it. Not these days. But you knew her years ago, didn't you? I take it she was quiet then.'

'I was in no position to judge, Elsie. We used to dance together. She was rather diffident, yes. But not a nonentity. Lively in a way. There was something behind her, inside there, even then. Wouldn't you say that was the case now?'

'I don't go in much for amateur psychology,' she rebuked him. 'I like her. She's a bit like her son, but that's not surprising, is it? Are you particularly interested in her?'

'No, I don't think so. Should I be?' He laughed again, challenging her to make something of it.

The same afternoon he announced that he 'expected' a visitor.

'Why didn't you tell me this morning? Surely you didn't forget?'

'No. I've only just found out. On the telephone.'

'Which bedroom?'

'The usual. Front.'

'Oh, she's important, is she?'

Hillier wrinkled his mouth at her impertinence.

'She's a he,' he answered. 'And he's elderly. He hates the winter. He must feel very down to have let me persuade him to leave home.'

'Where does he live?'

'Yorkshire. He's quite a famous man. He's a poet.'

'What's his name?'

'Stephen Youlgrave.'

'No,' Mrs Mead answered, unwilling to admit ignorance, 'I don't think I've heard of him.'

At the evening meal Hillier brought down two thin hardback volumes by the poet, *A Hard Winter* and *Between the Cherubim*.

'I thought you'd perhaps like to look at these.'

'When shall I have time?' Ungratefully.

'Make it.' His eyes were bleak. She thanked him.

In bed that night Mrs Mead opened the books; both were inscribed: 'To Adrian Hillier, with good wishes' on the title page. Mr Youlgrave's writing was small, extremely neat, rather like printed Greek. She concentrated on the earlier volume, then the title poem, 'A Hard Winter', which did not stand first.

49

She read with determination: frost-bound runnels, dirt-ingrained hands, fir trees beautified, the low sun, all hardness, redness, ice; the words were striking, clinging, not exactly unusual, but carefully chosen, like carvings, lapidary; a college lecturer had used that sarcastically to her once; she would remember parts, she thought. Somewhere in the middle of the second four-line stanza she dodged and stumbled, lost, astray, groping for meaning. Annoyed with herself she began again; again she found herself baffled. This time she tried grammatically, to parse, to find subject, predicate. Ambiguity spread. Her eyes were heavy and she closed the book.

'Did you look at friend Youlgrave?' Adrian Hillier asked, sliding past next morning.

'I did. Can you understand it?'

' "It"?' he said foxily. ' "It"?' He put a finger on his lips, perhaps enjoining her to silence. 'Not in the same sense as one understands an article in *The Times*.' He was through the door.

Youlgrave arrived in the early evening. Hillier drove to the station to pick him up. The poet was tall, with whitish untidy hair, a red face not well shaved and a breathy voice. He shook hands with Mrs Mead, weakly, his fingers like ice. Hillier lugged two suitcases upstairs.

At dinner, and Hillier instructed his housekeeper to dine with them, Mr Youlgrave was affable in a guarded way. He had what she described to herself as an 'educated' accent, but he spoke mumblingly, without force. Twice he stopped eating to battle with coughing fits, covering his face with a large ironed handkerchief. He congratulated her on the cooking, saying he had not eaten so heartily for long enough, and gave them a schoolmasterly discourse on aristology, the art of dining. He said it came from the word for breakfast, and that led to a mazy, inconclusive questioning as to whether the Greeks considered the early meals, breakfast or lunch, the best. Mr Youlgrave mentioned some other word for dinner. The two of them enjoyed themselves in this slow display of learning between mouthfuls. By instruction no wine was served, only glasses of iced water. All three smiled at intervals, thinly, cunningly, with sincerity.

Next morning Mrs Mead served the poet with breakfast in bed. His pyjamas were spotless, the hair on his chest frizzily grey, that of his head whiter and sticking out in spikes. He coughed, thanking her and inquiring about the bleak weather. At half-past ten he returned his tray to the kitchen, stayed for a mug of coffee and stood with hands in pockets at the window watching the sparrows, blue tits, greenfinches hanging upside-down and pecking at the reticules of nuts. He spoke slowly, but told her in a friendly way about his garden and his difficulties with it.

'Though I can afford to have a man in to keep it neat, he doesn't do it to my liking, and this irks me. Do you understand that? Of course, I am lucky in that old age hasn't incapacitated me altogether, so that I can continue to live in my own place. I look forward with dread to the day when they'll carry me off to a home for the elderly.'

Mrs Mead apologized that she had not fetched down his breakfast pots, because she had not wanted to interrupt his writing.

'You have more faith in me than I have myself,' he said, slowly.

'You are not working then?'

'No. I'm having what the glossy advertisements call a "winter break". The trouble is it lasts most of the year.'

He shook his head, in no hurry to leave the warm kitchen.

Later Mr Hillier inquired how she was getting on with the guest.

'The word I'd choose,' she answered, 'for him is "gentle-manly".'

'I'd be glad if you'd talk to him when you can find the time. He'll enjoy that. He likes female company, but is unused to it now.'

'Hasn't he been married?'

'Twice. The first wife died, the second was a catastrophe; he's divorced. He has a son, but rarely sees him; he's independent.'

Over dinner Hillier put a question to his housekeeper, though she could not be sure how serious he was.

'What would be a good night out for Stephen and me?'

'The film of *Little Dorrit*?'

'I've considered that. It's a full day's work. Six hours' sitting. We'd need to go out twice. Anything else?'

'Why not go to the pantomime?'

'What is it?'

'*Cinderella* I think. There's plenty in panto today for adults. Too much in my view. And besides you can always watch the children enjoying themselves, shouting out and going on stage.'

'Would it suit a couple of old pessimists like us? What do you say, Stephen?'

Youlgrave slowly cleared his mouth of trifle before he answered.

'I last went to a pantomime in the late twenties or early thirties, when I was a boy. *Aladdin*. I don't recall much about it. The Widow was a man who brought the house down baring his bottom to the audience. And the main song was "Ramona".' He looked in interrogation from one to the other. 'Is that right?' His head began to nod to a rhythm, and then diffidently he sang. 'Ramona, I hear the mission bells above. Ramona, they're playing out their song of love. I bless you, caress you . . .' He shook his head. 'No, that's wrong. It was Charmaine. "I wonder why you keep me waiting".' He smiled at Mrs Mead. 'Memory.'

'You could take Peter Fowler with you,' she said.

'Good idea. And the boy's mother. And you. Make a party. We'll see,' Hillier enthused.

Now Youlgrave spoke about theatre-going, and instantly Hillier was alight again. Soon they were immersed in the difficulties of reducing *Hamlet* to two hours, and the impossibility of casting it amongst amateurs. Mrs Mead left them to it.

She had been impressed by some lines she had read in *A Hard Winter* describing the blue and silver change of a room when the electric bulb had been suddenly switched off on a moonlit night. The new luminosity flooded, but not quickly, the objects in the place, but only when the eye became accustomed. It had seemed perfect to her, so much so that she had put on her dressing-gown, pulled back the curtains, turned off her reading-lamp. This had not been successful because the street lamp, high on curved concrete, took over, not the moon. There had been a moment of delay, a growing accustoming to the new source of illumination, but it had none of the magic of Youlgrave's verse. That had seemed set apart, lifted up; reality for all its strangeness could not match it. The rest of the poem had been beyond her, and though she blamed herself for the incomprehension, this score of words caught, snagged, tugged at her imagination.

In conversation Youlgrave was invariably lucid. He spoke slowly, and his grammar and enunciation were old-fashioned, accurate, leaving nothing to chance or the listener's imagination. That lecturer at college used to quote Eliot about an old man in a dry season; that was the prosaic Youlgrave.

'I am a dodderer,' he said, 'a ditherer.'

Mr Hillier had not been able to obtain five tickets for the pantomime until the Monday of next week and at first Youlgrave had not wanted to stay so long, but was now, not altogether reluctantly, persuaded.

'Aren't you comfortable here?' Mrs Mead asked him, the battle over.

'Yes.' And the long pause for thought. 'But at my time of life I enjoy making a martyr of myself. I'm better off here than I am at home. My bungalow up there will look after itself; my neighbour will feed the cat. There will be no letters of importance to read, nowhere to go, nothing much to do. But in my crabbed age I feel I ought to live uncomfortably, fight the winter for myself, struggle out to the shops, groan over aching joints and meals to be prepared. Whereas here you pamper me, tempt me into idleness and hedonism.'

'You could write us a few poems in return.'

'Ah, that's another matter.' He left the room.

Mr Hillier took down his *Who's Who* to enlighten the questioning Mrs Mead. 'Well, yes. Let's see. He's just seventy-five, born Manchester, youngest son of William and Grace. His father was a clerk. Twice married: (1) Anne Harcourt-Jones; one son. (2) Emily Kemp. dissolved. Educated Manchester Grammar School, St John's College, Oxford. M.A., D.Phil. University of Göttingen. Lecturer in English Language and Literature at St Andrews, Reading; professor at Durham and Birmingham. Armed Forces 1939–45, Royal Engineers, Intelligence Corps. Eight named volumes of poetry. Queen's Medal. Litt.D. twice. Hobbies: reading, ailourophilia – that's cat-loving – gardening. There you are.'

'Why doesn't he call himself professor?'

'I suppose he does in academic circles. Professor emeritus.'

'Have you known him for a long time?'

'No. I met him on a cruise. He invited me to visit him. I did.'

'Is he well-off?'

'Comfortably. Not rich.'

Strictly at eleven each morning Stephen Youlgrave entered the kitchen for coffee. He sat on a stool, knees drawn up, warmed his hands round the mug and slowly, breaking them first into inch-long fragments, ate two home-baked biscuits. Though he used a plate he left a scatter of crumbs when he retired to his room, exactly at eleven-thirty. Hillier never attended these sessions.

On Saturday the professor announced to Mrs Mead, 'I've begun a poem.'

'Is it good?'

'It's only at the stage of the first draft of the beginning.'

'How many lines?'

Elsie Mead had been out shopping and dashed sweetly about the kitchen and larder, storing her purchases, pleased with herself.

'Twenty, perhaps . . . thereabouts.' He crumbled a shard of biscuit. 'That's a not inconsiderable length for one sitting. I have the drift, the schema now, and these lines actually written.'

'Would you recite one for me?'

'No. They're sketches as yet. Hints. Outlines. Very un-satisfactory. And in any case I do not like to talk about work I'm engaged on.'

'Oh, I'm sorry.'

'There is no need to apologize, Mrs Mead. Not in the least. This is a taste for secrecy which I have acquired from long habit or, worse, from superstition. You are not to know my unreasonable ways.'

'You don't talk about your poems, then?'

'Not until they're complete. And then not if I can help it. They should speak for themselves.'

'Are you pleased with them? Sometimes? Or with some more than others?'

'Relief is what I feel. It is out of the system. No, Mrs Mead,' he held up a veined hand, 'that is ungrateful. Sometimes I have the notion, I put it no more strongly, that I have approached my topic, suggested something worth reading or pondering over. I am trying to express this feeling in as quiet, as understated a way as I can.'

Elsie Mead shook her head, smiling.

'You don't understand me,' he said, 'and I don't blame you. You won't have read any of my verse.' He did not stop to check the accuracy of his assertion. 'I am now in my seventy-sixth year and have been retired from university work for ten of those years. I was, like you, a teacher.' Hillier had been purveying information, she concluded. 'I taught Anglo-Saxon and Middle English and pre-Shakespearian literature. Not a very useful profession, you may think, either vocationally or from the point of view of leisure, pleasure.' The rhymes seemed dragged across his lips. 'But it occupied my time. I was, I may claim, a successful practitioner in a shrinking field. I wrote one decent textbook, superseded now, that held the market for twenty-five years, and brought out half a dozen useful editions. I did not let my pupils down, either the gifted or the mediocre; I catered for them all. The most highly regarded Chaucerian scholar of today, he's in America, of course, was a student of mine.' He sipped his coffee meditatively, mug between hands. 'I expect you find all this autobiographical material rather dull. I never approach a subject head-on these days. The meandering and indirect suit my style of life.'

Mrs Mead concluded he had made a small critical jibe against himself.

'Do you follow me?' he demanded.

'I think so. I enjoy listening. You talk about things that haven't impinged much on my life.' He reminded her of the man who lectured at her training college on the philosophy of education, who spattered around important words like 'pragmatist' or 'heuristic' or 'existentialist', or once, she put it in her note-book, 'banausic', who seemed to be sketching a significant foundation on which everyday, humdrum classes on reading or composition or arithmetic, even science, were raised. Some of the students complained that this was useless rubbish, but she valued it. Others wanted tips on how to keep

55

order among rowdy fourteen-year-olds, or the titles of books suitable for bright teenage girls. She wished to be educated herself, directed outside the school-room round, to be learned above average, to count the stars.

'Who is your favourite poet, Mrs Mead?'

'Keats.'

'You read him at school?'

'And at college.'

He placed cup and saucer on plate by the sink, and walked out.

On Sunday morning she asked if he had made progress with his poem. He had, but rubbed his chin, not adding to his monosyllabic reply. The housekeeper, in no hurry because they lunched late on Sunday, sat waiting.

'I have been trying to sort out,' he began, 'what I have attempted in verse. That's a vague echo of Milton. There must be a certain amount of literary inspiration, if not direct plagiarism, in my work. Not that I think that matters. My earliest volume leaned somewhat towards my Anglo-Saxon studies.'

'Did you do some translations, then?'

'No, not in that volume. I did a version of the "Seafarer", like others, and "The Dream of the Rood", and "The Battle of Maldon", and though they were published in specialist journals they were never collected. No, it was the comparison I put to myself, the attempt to find common ground, similar virtues in modern men. Saxon times would have seemed hard to us. I would have hated life then. The cold, the discomfort, the brute advantages of strength or birth. No.'

'Weren't they civilized?'

'In many ways, yes. Highly so. Beautiful jewellery, poetry, religion. But they lacked hot water in large quantities for all, central heating, dry, unmuddy roads. Think of tooth decay or earache.'

'People who have harsh winters, like Russians and Finns, appreciate the Spring the more,' she answered. 'And Canada.'

'That's right.'

On Monday morning he offered further comment without prompting.

'I look back over my life and am amazed what bits remain in

the memory. I can see the reason for some; those were occasions when I was unusually elated or downcast. But other significant incidents are there, very clearly, as if to challenge me to win, form something out of them.'

'Mr Hillier thinks he has never made a success of anything in his whole life.'

That remark was followed by a long silence, as if Youlgrave were drumming up courage to answer. In the end he spoke very slowly, his voice like gravel.

'I suppose that if one had a tremendous victory, in a field where strictly measurable standards are possible, such as, let us say, the Olympic Games . . .' Again the drawn-out pause, more painful since he made no attempt to ape struggling thought, but sat perfectly still as if expecting a message, a visitation, a blow, an unwelcome stimulus. 'If one won a gold medal against the strongest possible opposition, and in so doing broke the world record by a wide margin, then one could consider that one had done well, that the training, the sacrifice, the physical distress, even former failures had been amply recompensed by the achievement. But according to temperament there might well come a time when that winner would hold the triumph as worthless, would feel that he could have spent his youth and strength in a more worthy pursuit. Or another would look back to the great day and find the rest of life anti-climax.'

'We take some satisfying,' she said.

'You agree with Mr Hillier, then?'

'On the whole. But then I've done nothing outstanding.'

'Would you consider I had?' Youlgrave asked.

'Certainly. You were a professor. You are a poet.'

He sighed, dramatically now, stood up to leave but noticed that his cup was half full. He drained it, thanked Mrs Mead politely and limped for the door, brow crumpled as suit.

'He's an odd man, but I like him,' she told Adrian Hillier.

'Odd? In what way?'

'Well, he's always about to tell me what his life or his poetry are about, but he never gets round to it. He brings up some interesting point, and that occupies him until he leaves.'

'Is that deliberate, would you think?'

'No idea.'

57

'What I'm suggesting is that he's preparing you for the confession when it arrives so that you can make head or tail of it. Is that right?'

She shrugged. 'I just don't understand his poetry.'

'Go on.'

'I make headway with a line or two, grasp it, and then off he goes somewhere else unconnected and I'm lost.'

'There's no continuous thread of narrative or argument?' Hillier queried.

'There certainly isn't. It's as if something beautiful and interesting and memorable is going on, but in three or four foreign languages. Except, of course, it is all in English . . . of a sort. Now, when he speaks to me I can understand him perfectly. He may touch on subjects beyond me, but I feel that if I'd read a bit more or been better educated I would be able to keep up with him. With his poetry I think he could easily puzzle someone as learned as he is. Can you understand him, for instance?'

'I'm not as erudite as he is.'

'Never mind that.'

'No. Honestly. No.' Long pauses spread between the words. 'I can't. But it may be prejudice on our part, you know. We're demanding this continuity, whereas he is loading his lines with doubletons and ambiguities, small piles of meanings, which we should stay and sort out, or let them sort us out emotionally, before we move on to the next line or two prepared for what's coming.'

'That's daft. You can't just have heaps of words and nowhere to go with them.'

'My dear Elsie!' Hillier laughed. 'You give me a good line or two of poetry. Something good, mark you.'

'You're making fun of me.'

'No, I'm not.'

Hillier waited, finger-tips together, altogether sweet.

'Oh, all right. "The sedge is withered from the lake/ And no birds sing".'

'Why is that so good?'

'It's so bleak. It gives an immediate picture, both to sight and sound, that sets the mood of the poem. The Knight is ailing; he's loitering; he's pale and then this wintry scene. We feel something dreadful is happening or has happened.' She delivered with conviction.

'Or will happen.'

'Oh, you.'

'But it has this effect because you are trained in . . . have a wide experience of . . . the kind of language Keats is employing. You accept it and so you are moved by it. Now, poor old Stephen adopts a different tack. He dispenses with a widely accepted code. The result is that you, with your Keats-expectations, or Milton, or Pope or Shakespeare or whoever, fall back baffled.'

'Can he understand what he's written?' she pursued.

'By that you mean "Can he give a prose paraphrase of his verses?"' He rubbed his chin. 'I doubt it, in the sense you want, I very much doubt it. But then I don't think he'd want to.'

She shook her head.

Hillier, who had been impressed by the housekeeper's intelligent fluency, felt bound to continue.

'Shall I put another of your objections for you?' he asked. 'Less tactfully than you would.'

She nodded her agreement.

'I guess you wonder if he wants to be understood, if the real trouble with Stephen is that, in spite of his skill with words, his learning, he is afraid that he has nothing important to say and so covers it with this riddling verse. Is that about it?'

Mrs Mead did not answer.

'Of course,' Hillier spoke slowly, but without hesitation, 'that is a charge which can be brought against any modernist. That's why it is so difficult to distinguish between the bogus, the meretricious and real poetry.'

'I don't think Mr Youlgrave is bogus.'

'You're probably right. But the temptation is there. And he is, in many ways, uncertain of himself.'

'He's certainly never come round yet to saying what his poetry is about.'

'Keep at him.'

'He'll be back home before I can pin him down.'

Hillier eyed her, not without respect. 'You're something of a hard case, Elsie. I shall have to watch you. Tell you what. Cheer me up, will you, with a piece of poetry?'

'You'll only laugh.'

'Not I. Something inspiring.'

Without delay, but not looking at him, she began. Her voice was quiet but had about it a hushed tone – suitable for high moments, he guessed, in the schoolroom.

> The rain had fallen, the Poet arose,
>   He passed by the town and out of the street,
> A light wind blew from the gates of the sun,
>   And waves of shadow went over the wheat,
> And he sat him down in a lonely place,
>   And chanted a melody loud and sweet,
> That made the wild swan pause in her cloud
>   And the lark drop down at his feet.

'Good God,' he said, 'Who wrote that?'

'Tennyson.'

'Yes, a lot of "ands" about.'

'I learnt it at school. I have never forgotten it.' She defied him. 'It ends:

> For he sings of what the world will be
> When the years have died away.'

Her hands were clenched; her mouth a strong line.

'Very good,' he said. 'Very good.' He seemed moved, pensive, caught up or out by her recitation, or the speed of her response, her sincerity. He nodded to himself, humming.

'He's started a poem here,' she blurted out, 'but he won't repeat any of it.'

Hillier looked at her with solemn respect.

7

The women and Peter enjoyed the pantomime; the two men sat silent, very wary. The boy occupied the plush seat between the housekeeper and his mother; Mr Hillier was next to Mrs Fowler and Youlgrave sprawled by the gangway so that he could 'stretch his legs'. They all enlivened the interval with deliciously sweet ice-cream with nuts, with sugary wafers shaped like scallop-shells.

'The trouble with us, Adrian,' said Youlgrave, 'is that we don't understand the code.'

'We're just ignorant, that's the top and bottom.'

'Don't say that.' Mrs Fowler simpering.

'These speciality acts are new to us because we don't watch television much.'

'They're funny in themselves,' Mrs Mead objected.

'Not very. We've no experience. Any catch-phrases are lost on us. We are hearing them for the first time. The rest of the audience are expecting them, so that they feel personally served when they roll out.'

'And any mention of pop groups or footballers is wasted on us,' Youlgrave told them. 'We represent the innocent ear.'

'I'd never believe it,' Mrs Mead averred, 'if somebody told me that educated people had to have pantomime explained to them.'

'The fractured nature of modern society,' said Hillier cheerfully.

'Was it different in your day?' Mrs Fowler asked. Hillier bowed to the older Youlgrave.

'I don't suppose so,' the poet answered, 'but the story was paramount. No, that's not true. The laundry, the bread-making scenes, the songs had more relevance to the narrative, had less initial value, had to work harder for their applause. But you must remember the wireless, the radio, arrived with my boyhood and the rot had set in.'

'How are you enjoying it, Peter?' Hillier asked.

'It's great. Very exciting.'

Adrian Hillier delivered the Fowlers home first. He, Elsie Mead and Youlgrave drank a nightcap together in the study.

'A successful evening?' Hillier asked the housekeeper, shifting coffee and whisky nervously around.

'Very. Peter was absorbed.'

'I didn't laugh as much as I expected.' Youlgrave spoke without disappointment, directing criticism towards himself.

'Mrs Fowler was highly amused. And you, Elsie.'

'I tell you,' Mrs Mead's straight face was rosy, 'the first thing I did when I came home was to change myself. I'd wet my knickers laughing at those ugly sisters.'

'I'm glad,' the poet said, gravely.

The next morning, the day of his departure, Youlgrave appeared at his usual time in the kitchen. He was dressed in an admirable three-piece suit of greenish tweed, a clean shirt with a silk tie, polished brown thick-soled shoes.

'Are you ready?' she asked. Mr Hillier was to drive his guest over to Grantham after lunch to catch an East Coast express.

'Of course.' He had shaved closely, fixed his hair, discreetly used after-shave lotion.

'Are you looking forward to it?'

'Strangely enough, no. Any more than I had looked forward to coming here. It's rather foolish for old men to gad about in Winter. Life's too dependent on home-comforts. But . . .' He blubbered his lips, rubbed dry hands together. 'This has been good. Adrian and I hit it off. And I have enjoyed our little exchanges here in the morning. Perhaps I'm a social being after all.'

'And you've begun a poem. Have you done any more to it?'

'A few lines, and many alterations.' He cleared his throat. 'But that is something.'

Mrs Mead drew up her stool.

'Mr Youlgrave, there is something I'd like to ask you.' She waited.

He cocked his head. 'Go on.'

'Is there any special way I should read your poetry?'

'I don't exactly understand you.' He spoke as hesitantly as she.

62

'I'm often puzzled. When I read a new poem, new to me, that is, by a poet I know such as Keats or Tennyson or Rudyard Kipling, I often can't make it out first time, but after three or four readings I think I've mastered it.'

'But with me you're still baffled?'

'Yes, and that makes me think I'm doing something wrong, that I'm approaching it in the wrong way. Am I?'

'A poem, Mrs Mead, has existence, as words on paper, words as sounds. You can read it, can approach it in any way you like. I mean, you could learn it off by heart.'

'Would that help?'

'I don't know. A poem is what I wrote down plus what you make of it. If you don't see it as anything but meaningless babble, then . . .' He threw his arms wide.

'That may be my fault.'

'Very likely. But it doesn't alter the failure as far as you're concerned. But whether you should read my poems as you read Keats, I don't know. In some ways, yes, but . . . You should read them with the same expectation you bring to Keats.' He coughed, deep in his hollow chest. 'But I expect you will want to reply that Keats has earned your expectation as I have not. And I'd agree with you.'

Her face expressed disappointment.

'I tell you what,' he continued. He shook a finger at her as though to compel her attention. 'When I get home, I'll look out and send you a little book I published a few years ago called *Burrs*, you know, those prickly seed-heads that stick to your clothes. It's not long, about thirty-five poems, all unconnected, all dealing with memories. Thus the title, the bits and pieces which have stuck in my mind. Two, at least, are about lilac; one about a boy in my class killed over Hamburg; one about my father at the seaside; one about aeroplanes at night at the beginning of the war. But you'll see. At least you'll know what I'm about, dredging up little anecdotes and brooding on them.'

'Thank you.'

He detained her with a wrinkled hand on her arm.

'Thank you. I have not enjoyed a holiday so much for long enough.' His eyes were rheumy.

They shook hands again after a very early lunch. He left in

silence. He had made an impression on her, so that she began to miss the quiet, phlegmy voice.

'Did Professor Youlgrave make his way home safely?' she asked Hillier.

'I guess so. I'd have heard otherwise.'

'Hasn't he 'phoned?'

'No. He'll be keeping his head down.'

His booklet, *Burrs*, arrived inscribed 'With best wishes, Stephen Youlgrave' but without mention of her name. She showed it to Hillier.

'Any letter with it?' he asked.

'No. He sent these because he thought I would understand them better.'

'And can you?'

'No. Not really.'

'It's a hard world.' Hillier looked mischievous. 'I had a card from Valerie Fitzjames.' Mrs Mead knew this already; she collected and kept an eye on the post. 'She's in Tunisia; she wanted me to go with her.'

'Why didn't you?'

'I'm like Youlgrave, a bit of an Anglo-Saxon, staying here to face the Winter out. Besides . . .'

'Besides what?'

'Oh, nothing.' He had decided, she concluded, against an unfavourable comment on Miss Fitzjames.

The next day when she took up another bright card with his breakfast he asked her to ring Fowler at Top Fare and arrange for him to call in at The Firs.

'Morning, noon or night?' she asked.

'That's up to him. As it's a business matter, there's no good reason against coming up in working hours. Whenever it's convenient; you know my commitments.'

She arranged the assignation.

The interview was short, a mere half-hour immediately after Top Fare had closed, but thereafter it was discussed at every meal in the Fowler household.

Mr Hillier, Gerald Fowler had reported, had been very polite, but was no more than a messenger for the board of directors.

'How do you know that?' his wife pressed.

64

'Because he said so.' Father tickled his moustache. 'The MD had asked him to make inquiries. They were pleased with my work here on Mansfield Road.' He waited.

'So they should be.'

'But they wanted to know if I wished to go further. And so this was a first, informal interview, saving time and trouble and money later on. Mr Hillier stressed that we might probably have to move, with consequent disadvantage if we went south.'

'Wouldn't the firm help?'

'With moving expenses, that's all. Not with a mortgage.'

'How do they expect to get anyone? Anyone from up here at any rate?'

'There are plenty of applicants. They can pick and choose.'

'Would they hold it against you if you decided to stay?' Alice asked.

'I put that to him. He said he was speaking without his book, but he didn't think so. That was his line the whole time, that he wasn't doing this officially, that he was sounding me out. And I'll tell you another thing he said.' Fingers again consulted moustache. 'Top Fare is doing well, and that means they'll be getting offers from bigger concerns to buy them out.'

'And would they sell?'

'He thought so. And that would mean a change of board, of policy, of organization, of personnel. One couldn't promise a steady course.'

'So what was his advice?'

'I'd have to make my own mind up. "Go home and consult your wife," he said. "And Peter. It concerns them as much as you. It's a risk, but it might pay off. Or it might not." He was like that all the time, was Hillier. You know, he speaks in that quiet voice, very friendly, but never quite looking at you.'

'Do you think he was warning you against a move?'

'No, I don't. Isn't he always like that? Shy? Not laying the law down? You know him better than I do and it's so, isn't it?'

'Yes, it is. And what do you think about the risk?'

'I look at it like this.' Fowler looked at wife and child. 'I derive a good deal of satisfaction from my present job. I wouldn't be in it if the council hadn't pulled my shop down and put me on the street; I should still be a self-employed grocer. Financially, there's not a great deal in it, but I'm not so

65

physically pressed. Though that might be a disadvantage. Bus conductors are less likely than their drivers to have heart attacks, because they move about. But this job is more interesting; it has wider implications.'

Peter listened to his father, who seemed to enjoy the sound of his own sentences.

At every spare moment the move was discussed, the same points reiterated, the same emotions aroused. Mrs Fowler threatened to consult Adrian Hillier, but her husband disparaged the idea. 'You won't find out any more from him than I did.' Both adults were easily angered; the boy kept out of their way.

On Saturday morning everything at The Firs was as usual. Hillier was not to be seen. Mrs Mead had forgotten that Gerald Fowler had visited the house. Jobs were to be done, panels needed burnishing, brass polishing.

'Did anybody say anything?' his mother inquired on Peter's return.

'What about?' He'd make her come into the open.

'Oh, our Peter! Your Dad's job.'

'No, I didn't see him. And Mrs Mead didn't know he'd even been. She knew he wanted to see my Dad. She didn't seem very interested.'

'There's no reason why she should be, is there?'

'She likes to keep an eye on Mr Hillier.'

His mother laughed, harshly.

Gerald Fowler puffed out his chest, but his face was haggard, his eyes unbright. After sleepless nights he allowed his name to go forward. Mr Hillier said he would pass the message on. 'Then it's out of my hands.' Fowler thanked him, and watched out for the postman.

At the end of January Stephen Youlgrave unexpectedly invited Hillier and Mrs Mead to visit him.

'Can he put us up?' she asked.

'It's a three-bedroom bungalow.'

'Is he capable of looking after us?' She clapped a hand to her mouth. 'That's why he's invited me, so I can cook for you.'

'I'm not so sure. Do you want to go?'

'Do you?'

'Yes. Yes and no. I'd do him a good turn if I could.'

66

They arranged for Mrs Fowler to look in at The Firs every day while they were absent. An electrician installed time switches so that the house would be lighted between the end of daylight and eleven o'clock. On the Saturday morning Peter was to appear and use the duster and vacuum cleaner. His mother drove him up there and they spent a quarter of an hour looking over the whole house. They could not get into Mrs Mead's top-floor flat, which was double-locked. They admired Mr Hillier's squadron of suits in the wardrobe and his wealth of shirts, ties, shoes.

'He never looks particularly well dressed,' Peter commented.

'Always neat, isn't he?'

They fingered the excellent cloth, commended to each other the variety of subdued colours in his ties, the bright newness of his footwear.

'If I were rich, I don't think I'd waste my money on clothes,' Peter said.

'Why not? You wouldn't miss it if you were well-to-do.'

'He doesn't go out a great deal. A concert now and then. And down to his theatre.'

'How are you so knowledgeable?' his mother asked. 'You're only here once a week.'

'Mrs Mead tells me. She thinks his theatre's a waste of his time.' They closed the wardrobe door and looked out of the tall windows. The trunks and branches of the trees in the garden below shone black against the winter sky. Huge houses in their own grounds stood opulently haphazard below on the slope. Forest-sized trees towered, limes, oaks from an earlier period when these hills stretched wild, wooded and untamed, hunting country.

'It's high here.' Peter.

'Yes. You can look over your neighbour's grounds. It will be beautiful in the summer, though; you won't be able to see a single house for the leaves. I wonder if he realizes how lucky he is to live in a place like this?

'It's a bit like a fort,' Mrs Fowler said. The great wrought-iron gates had been locked.

'Would you like a lot of money?' Peter inquired.

'I'd like more than I have now, that's for certain. I'm not sure whether I'd want as much as Mr Hillier has.'

'Why not?'

'When you've been brought up as I have, you believe you ought to go to work every day. You need training to spend your time without a job and yet think, know you're not wasting your life. That's half the trouble with Mr Hillier; he's never sure that he's occupying himself properly.' She sounded confident. Her son smiled to himself.

They walked swiftly about the house, admiring carpets, straightening pictures, mother and boy pleased to talk to each other, conscious of the superiority of this house and its furnishing, willing to examine, describe and share the effect of such size and beauty.

'You needn't go out at all,' Peter said. 'You could just walk round all the rooms and corridors in the Winter.'

'I don't know whether that's good for you,' his mother answered. 'That's another advantage of going to work: you meet people. As you do at school.'

'They've gone to meet people in York.'

'Well, I hope so.' She breathed deeply. 'Mrs Mead will tell me.'

Elsie Mead returned impressed and almost voluble.

'It's one of the best holidays I ever had. The weather wasn't too nasty; it didn't stop us from going out. We went to the Minster and to a performance of *An Enemy of the People* and to *The Mikado*.'

'Mr Hillier would like that.'

'I'm not so sure. They don't do it right.'

'Did you visit that Viking Jorvik affair?' Peter wanted to know.

'No. I'm not sure it was open, though Professor Youlgrave had something to do with it in the first place, I think. Nor did we visit the Railway Museum; Mr Hillier has an interest in that. Well, vaguely. He mentioned it, anyhow.' Mrs Mead bent forward. 'The best thing was the conversation.'

'Mr Hillier's not much of a talker, is he?'

'Neither of them. But Professor Youlgrave came out with

68

some fascinating things. Do you know, I wrote them in a big diary? I scribbled it all down before I could forget.'

'What did he talk about?'

'Literature. His bungalow was a beautiful place, and crowded with books. In every room there were shelves, all packed solid. Wall-high sometimes.'

'Old, were they?'

'No, not all. Some of them were, of course. Valuable, I should think. But some looked brand new.' She squared her shoulders. 'One day, I was cooking a light lunch. I insisted on it when we were in, and Stephen, he made me call him that, started talking about poems and novels and so on, and I asked him if any good books were being written nowadays and he said, yes, there were. Are you interested in all this?'

'Oh, yes.'

'He said the young men had lost all shackles, that they wrote with a lacerating power about terrible extremes of behaviour. It was almost as if they were being driven mad by what they observed.'

'And he didn't like this?' Mrs Fowler was wide-eyed.

'Oh, yes. They had to do it. And often they did it well, with marvellous use of what he called "trope", metaphors and so on. They were not afraid to squeal and bawl, to wound themselves. "They're like the prophets of Baal slashing themselves with knives and lancets." And when I said, "That didn't do *them* much good," he laughed and poked his finger. "Does literature have much effect?" He gave me some stories to read by a man called Martin Amis.'

'What were they like?'

'Horrible. But Stephen told me that Amis had given up logic. He's like an evangelist, a tub-thumper, except that he's talented. He thinks, Stephen said, that the results of a nuclear war are dreadful beyond imagination, but that people just won't see it, grasp it. "I believe that," I told him. "Amis is working for an emotional upheaval inside his reader which in its small way mirrors the terror of surviving the bomb. And also to show what extremes of behaviour human beings are capable of, so that we can't comfort ourselves by saying that nobody would ever be mad enough, or angry enough to press the button." '

'Did he approve? Professor Youlgrave, I mean?'

'Yes, he did. Amis smashes you with hammer-blows because he does not think reason has much validity these days. Reason cannot or will not comprehend such terror. I said to him, "Hasn't anything like this ever happened before?" And he said that we'd never been in the position of being able to destroy the whole world. On the other hand, if I meant had people never written with such ferocity before, well they had, but language grows duller in time, we lose the key to the code, blunt the edge so that Pope's savagery looks mere formality to us now. That's what he said. We did some Pope at college. If Amis survives, he told me, it would be on account of his literary talent, or because his message seemed still to have relevance.'

'It all sounds very highbrow,' Mrs Fowler said.

'I enjoyed every minute. You couldn't just sit there and nod off. Stephen seemed very serious about it all, but he never raised his voice. Just spoke on and on. That's another thing he said. That to these young men his work seemed flat, without passion and, if not boring, irrelevant. I said, "Do you mind that?" He said he didn't. He wrote his poems in the way his temperament and experience allowed.'

'My, you've got a wonderful memory, Elsie.'

'No, I haven't. I scribbled it down every day. But it was such a change. We mumble to each other about our colds or the cost of living, but he seemed to let himself go from time to time. This wasn't all in one session. I wouldn't say he wanted to convert me, it was just that he couldn't help himself.'

'Do you think he'd been affected? That he thinks now that all he's done or taught and written was wrong or wasted?'

'Perhaps. He never said as much.'

'Could you understand these stories better than Mr Youlgrave's poems?'

'Oh, yes. Sometimes you had to read very carefully, and sometimes I wished I couldn't understand what I was reading. They terrified me. When Stephen asked me what I thought about them I said, "There are some things you shouldn't write about, they're too private, or too horrible." '

'And what did he say?'

' "I know what you mean, Elsie, but circumstances alter cases." Then he rubbed his temples in that way he has. Both he and Mr Hillier touch their faces when they're thinking. "The freedom of our times and the temperament of these young men make it possible for them to write as they do. We don't like it, Elsie. It disturbs us. But I'm glad they are able to set it down." And he put his arm round my shoulders and gave me a squeeze. He's a lovely man, he really is."

'Ay, ay.'

'Oh, no. Don't get me wrong. There was nothing untoward.'

'I didn't suppose there was,' Alice Fowler smiled broadly, 'but I can see you enjoyed yourself.'

'It was marvellous because I was learning all the time. If you didn't know something, and Professor Youlgrave didn't either, he'd have a book on it. He was looking things up day and night. And Mr Hillier. They had their heads in books all the time. It was very good for him. It was like being at a university.'

'Is he a fit man?' Mrs Fowler asked, keeping her friend cheerful.

'For his age. He had serious internal operations some year or two ago, but he's fine now. He complains about his slowness, and I guess he's in pain sometimes . . . with his joints. But he's strong, I think, has a sound constitution.'

'That's good.'

'Those two men, quiet as they are, have livened me up. I thought my life was over when Frank died.'

'But it isn't?'

'By no means. But I'm boring you to death with all this rubbish.'

'No. I'd like to see your notebook.'

'Um. I'm glad I took it with me. It gave me the opportunity to write things down and not forget. You'd not make much of it. Nor anybody else.' She offered no hint of allowing her friend to read it but smiled to herself, pleased with her secrets.

— 8 —

On the last day but one of January it snowed.

'I hate this weather,' Mrs Mead hissed to Peter as he polished the panels of the hall. 'You like it, don't you?' The boy nodded. 'It makes these hilly roads impassable. The corporation won't do anything about them until too late. We're right out of their way up here. And then they'll pile it in the gutter and the pavements will freeze. It's like a bumpy ice-rink.'

Peter Fowler realized that something more than snow was preying on Mrs Mead's mind. He held his peace, waiting. Sooner or later she'd come out with it.

Over coffee she began. 'You've not come up on your bicycle, have you?'

'No, I walked. I started early.'

'It's not fit.' Then violently, 'Mr Hillier has not slept for the last two nights.' She stalked to the kitchen's one window which overlooked a wide patch of lawn, a shrubbery and a row of lime trees in front of a brick wall. Ground and branches were thickly covered. 'Snowing again. It's too bad.'

Peter hid his grin. Did Mrs Mead blame the snowfall on Mr Hillier's insomnia? Her face was fearsomely grim.

'He's quarrelled with that theatre of his.'

The boy shook his head.

'The Phoenix Company, or whatever they call themselves. He's worked like a dog for them; he's paid bills, put down money all over the place for them, and now look. But he's resigned.'

'Were they cheating him?' Peter.

'They took some decision he didn't approve of, I don't know what it was exactly. He's too upset to say much to me about it. That Valerie Fitzjames was concerned in it.'

'She'd be on Mr Hillier's side, though, wouldn't she?'

'Well, no, not so far as I could make out. She wasn't. But they're no better than a pack of children squabbling in the schoolyard.' She eyed the boy. 'I'm sure you're not like that.' The thought cheered her momentarily, as she clasped her warming coffee mug.

Mr Hillier made no appearance, nursing his grievances in silence up above. The telephone was dumb. Just before Peter left, Mrs Mead led him to the study to 'see the snow'.

'It's beautiful,' she averred. Snow lay inch-thick on each branch; surfaces, paths and roofs shone smooth in the grey light. 'It looks even better from my rooms upstairs,' she said, but did not take him there. Clambering down in his wellingtons, he asked, 'Is Mr Hillier out in it?'

'No, he's in bed. He's not slept. He's really unwell.'

The boy reported this to his mother, who telephoned on Sunday morning for some news. Fowler had trudged in the snow to his shop, where he'd spent an hour or two in contemplation. 'Seven days a week,' she had mocked him, but he'd taken it in good part: 'The weather's not fit for anything else. I have my best ideas walking round an empty place. It's as different, I tell you, from a working day as it would be if I was strolling through the park or sitting at the riverside fishing.' She laughed, for he was no angler, but she admired him. He was out of her way; Peter was upstairs doing homework; she had vacuumed dining and sitting rooms; the dinner was prepared, meat already in the oven. In spite of snow, she felt on terms with the world.

'Mr Hillier's not very well, Peter tells me.'

'No. I don't know what to do with him.'

'Have you had the doctor?'

'No, he won't hear of it, but I shall call him here if there's no improvement.'

Mrs Mead invited her friend up for an hour that afternoon. She'd be pleased with company, saying she couldn't desert her employer for any length of time. With some difficulty Alice Fowler did the short journey by car.

The Firs seemed dark, if warm. Elsie led her friend to her flat on the top floor, a first visit. They admired the snow-capped landscape, still fresh as an Impressionist painting. Wind gently shifted branches without moving snow.

Mrs Mead poured tea from a large china pot which would have satisfied a family thirst. They approached Hillier's health obliquely by way of weather, Peter's Latin, Fowler's assiduity, the stupidity and indolence of the young typists in Alice's office. It was as though they deliberately postponed the main item on the agenda. At last, conversational apprenticeship served, Mrs Fowler put the questions and received short, gloomy, non-committal answers before both settled with second cups.

'I tell you, Alice, he's like a zombie. He lies in bed, unshaven and grey as a corpse. His eyebrows stick out, the only live part of him. He doesn't clean his teeth, he hardly eats. When he has to get out of bed for the lavatory, it's as though he's nearing exhaustion; he staggers and holds on to the wall, and groans. And he doesn't cover himself, if you know what I mean. His pyjamas gape open and I can see everything he's got. And that's not like him. He's so neat and polite, and precise in every way. If you saw him you wouldn't believe the change . . . inside these two or three days. It's as if he's another man.'

Mrs Fowler lifted cup and saucer, waiting.

'It started a week last Monday. Apparently, at this time of year they have a committee meeting to prepare a schedule for next year. They've done half this year's programme, and now they start to make their suggestions. There are all sorts of readings and social gatherings and talks, but the main idea is to decide on the half-dozen principal productions for next year. These are discussed by a new committee called "the play group". I ask you. Typical daft title. Usually there's not much change, but this year there was a big upheaval. I don't know why; I don't know if he knows. There was, anyway. Mr Hillier rather welcomed this. "We need new blood," he kept saying when they were elected in November. I bet he doesn't think so now. He was on it. Not chairman, or anything. Just an ordinary member. Even though he puts so much time and money into it.'

The ladies sipped tea, staring out over snow, trees, roofs, mist.

'Well, they had this meeting and there was an argument. There always is with them. They're like squabbling children. He told me about it when he came back. His view was that an amateur company such as theirs should put on performances that the commercial theatre cannot afford to mount. The

74

classical repertory. The Greeks, he said, Shakespeare and Jonson, Restoration and Eighteenth Century, then Shaw, and Arden and O'Neill and Miller and Pinter. He's not against the moderns, horrible as some of them are, and he's not averse to a crowd-puller or a Christmas show, but this lot want a whole series of musicals and entertainments. "It's better to do *The Boy Friend* to a full house than *Timon of Athens* to thirteen relatives and the caretaker's cat," one of them said. They argued and he lost, but asked them to convene another meeting. They agreed, but named last weekend as the time when they'd make final decisions. In the meantime they'd seek suggestions. You know, consult the members and all that. Or so they said. Mr Hillier said they intended nothing of the sort. You can't do a proper survey of anything in three or four days, but he was overruled again.'

'He was upset by this?'

'To tell you the truth, he wasn't. "There's always been this song-and-dance set," he told me. "There always will be. And they've some sense on their side." But this time they'd won a large majority on the committee, and were prepared to throw their weight about.'

'How come?' Mrs Fowler kept up the pressure.

'Not by cheating. Or so he said. They'd spent a lot of time chivvying members and had whipped up considerable support. "This will increase the paying customers. We need a more active membership and much larger." And this must have gone down well, because they managed a considerable majority on the play committee. There were only two or three of Mr Hillier's mind. Anyhow, they had their meeting last weekend and pushed their programme through. Now, he did seem very down that Sunday lunch-time when he came back: "I don't spend my time at that place to have them put on things they can see done twice as well in the London theatres." I said, "A lot of them perhaps can't get to London, or can't afford to." His face really fell, then, and his eyes filled with tears. "Christ, Elsie," he said, and he never swears, except as a joke, "don't tell me you've joined them?" If I'd hit him over the head he couldn't have looked worse. I wondered what I'd done. But after they'd voted their new schedule through, he resigned.'

'What did they say?'

'Begged him not to. Thanked him for all the valuable work he'd put in. Said he was indispensable, added weighty judgement, hoped he'd change his mind.'

'But he didn't?'

'No. He made this speech. Very short, he said, very quiet, wishing them every success because the Phoenix would always hold a warm place in his heart. But they had set off on a course so radically opposed to all his principles that he had no option but to resign. There and then. The chairman, the biggest hypocrite of the lot, implored him to sleep on it and he said he would. He never said another word at the meeting, didn't stay behind for a drink as he usually does, came straight home. He wrote his resignation on Sunday afternoon and delivered it by hand to the chairman's pigeon-hole straight away. That's after he'd spoken to me.'

'And that's that?'

'They've tried to ring him. He's spoken to several notables on the phone. And Valerie Fitzjames came round herself on Tuesday; she absolutely insisted on seeing him. She was dressed to kill, more like what Frank used to call a Piccadilly whore than a decent girl, and reeking of scent. She was up there for an hour or more and when she came down I could see she'd been crying. Her eyes were all smudged.'

'Did she say anything to you?'

'She thanked me, and sniffed, and dabbed at her face with a tissue.'

'And Mr Hillier?'

'I never saw him that night. And it was next day, Wednesday, he took to his bed.'

'Were they shouting at each other? He and this Valerie?'

'No, it was as quiet as the grave. These doors are pretty solid, though. He could have murdered her and I'd have heard nothing. He said a funny thing on that Sunday when he told me all about it. "You think it's all a storm in a tea-cup, don't you, Elsie?" '

'And did you?'

'Well, yes. And he'd said as much himself: "Nobody'll die, Elsie. Nobody'll have his living taken away." '

'And yet?'

'Exactly. He came down that Wednesday morning and he

looked ashen; he hardly spoke, but when I carried his coffee up I thought he was better. He sat there in his chair, with nothing open on his desk; he'd done no reading or writing. But he took this sensible line with me again. Wasn't it foolish that an unimportant matter like this should make him feel so ill? I just said it was a pity, and that they ought to show more appreciation of all he'd done, but I thought to myself, "If he can express it as clearly as that, then he's on the way up." He pecked at his lunch, and went straight to bed, and there he's been ever since.'

'It must be very important to him?'

'I think it is. He said something to me, Alice, that impressed me: "I'm not a religious man," he said, "in any shape or form. There's no after-life; we're here only the once, and we have to get our little act together because there's only this one chance. And mine is to let the people see the great dramatic classics performed, outstandingly well if it's possible. If the likes of the Phoenix don't do them, nobody else will these mercenary days." '

'Did he act himself?'

'Not really. He did the prologue or whatever you call it in Anouilh's *Antigone*. I went to see it. He recited it in his ordinary voice, dressed in an ordinary suit, and I thought how good it was. I said as much to him. There was no ranting and raving, because there was no need. It contrasted with these Greeks in their tunics. Mark you, they looked lovely, especially the girls, but his quiet voice explaining, putting it in front of us, saying some striking things but without acting it stunned me; I couldn't forget it for long enough.' They both suddenly listened, heard nothing. 'I'll just nip down and see if he wants anything. I'll tell him you're here. It might help him if he knows the world's going on much as it was before. Pour yourself more tea.'

Mrs Mead slipped away leaving Alice Fowler to stare about her. The room was plainly furnished with a table, four dining-chairs, two russet armchairs, a settee and a glass-fronted bookcase. A flowered screen stood in front of the fireplace; the radiators needed no assistance. Three gold-framed pictures – oil-paintings, stormy, dull landscapes with trees – were hung on the gold-striped wallpaper. Paintwork glistened white; the heavy velvet curtains shone sunny yellow; a gilt chandelier hung from the middle of a chalk-pale ceiling; the wall-to-wall carpet was a warm, autumnal chestnut; the fender glistened. The furniture gleamed new, hardly tarnished. The ceiling was flat; this was no converted attic. Alice walked to the window enjoying the lacework of branches, the stretches of snow, the broken patterns of roof and wall, of brightness, dark and dazzle.

No sounds came from below. The door remained firmly shut. Alice moved towards the bookcase. Dickens in fading blue occupied almost all of the top shelf; the rest were miscellaneous, fiction and poetry, Lawrence, Conrad, Woolf, a beautiful edition of *Vanity Fair*, three Jane Austen, four Brontës, *The Vicar of Wakefield*, *Tom Jones* in two volumes. It was not unlike Alice's own bookcase at home: prizes, the classics of the language, gathered over two generations.

Silence below. Radiators stirred and ticked.

The door flashed open; Mrs Mead had mounted the stairs without a creak. She shrugged vigorously in answer to Alice's inquiring glance.

'I'm just looking at your books.'

'Yes.' Mrs Mead, surprised. 'Yes. They're for show really; I never take them out. Sometimes I think I ought to. It's the paper-backs in my bedroom I really read. Some I buy, and Mr Hillier hands me over anything he thinks I might find interesting. And my *Golden Treasury*.'

'How is he?'

Elsie shook her head, bemused, uncoordinated.

'Just the same. Lying there, slumped. Won't talk. Barely says "yes" or "no". Groans. It's awful. I asked him if he'd like to see you, but he just turned away, and that's not like him. If he didn't want to do anything, he'd always give you his reasons. But he just screwed his head away. I asked him if he wanted anything and he didn't bother to answer.'

'I'm sorry.'

'If he's not any better in the next day or two, I shall send for the doctor whatever he wants. "They've a whole armoury of drugs," I told him. "You might just as well make use of them," but no, there was nothing to suit him. "I know what's wrong with me, as you do, Elsie," he said, "and I don't see drugs changing that." I said to him that if they wouldn't alter circumstances, at least they'd make him more able to cope, but he wasn't having it.'

'It's sad.'

'It's daft, Alice, if you ask me. It's as if he wants to be as he is, chooses it deliberately.'

'Is that possible?'

Mrs Mead shrugged, lifted the teapot in query, returned it to the stand. 'I'm at my wits' end,' she reported glumly. 'When I went in now, he'd been crying. His eyes were full and there were drops running down his cheeks.' She stopped, angrily, clenching her fists, face red. 'I don't like to see a man cry. It's not right, somehow.'

'It might help clear it out of his system.'

'If,' Mrs Mead spoke sternly, 'he'd lost his wife or was ruined or had committed a bad crime, there'd be some excuse. But this, this!' She slapped her thighs in exasperation. 'He just can't get his own way about acting silly plays.'

'Perhaps he doesn't see it as we do.'

'I'm sure he doesn't. But what difference does that make? When Frank died I felt as if the world had come to a sudden end. There was a man who'd given his life to advancing the prospects of his pupils, had been compulsorily retired and could bear it no longer. He didn't know how not to be a hundred-per-cent full-time schoolmaster. And I couldn't understand that. I still can't. There's some weakness there. But he was older than Mr Hillier, and had been made to stop doing what he did exceptionally well. I blamed myself then. I ought to have done more for him. I ought. God knows what, but I ought. But I thought he'd manage. I admired him. He'd always been on top of his world. I knew he was depressed; he was sometimes while he was still at work, but I was sure he'd recover. He didn't. He killed himself. We always think it's somebody else it happens to, suicides and murder and so forth, but it was me this time. I was worried about him, but I didn't in any shape or form expect that. He'd been cheerful, well, more so, when I left that morning.' She pulled herself upright, a gesture of stupid bravado, one minute in the chair, the next with ramrod back as if she'd lash out with her hands. Now she walked towards a single, small photograph which stood on the mantelpiece.

'That's Frank,' she announced at length. Alice stood and joined her. The photograph showed a balding, moustachioed man wearing spectacles, with a sugary expression. 'He used to say he looked like Rudyard Kipling in that picture.' She held the portrait at arm's length before handing it to Alice. 'He was outstanding at his job, if old-fashioned. He'd have hated schools today. He'd sufficient energy to do what he was trained for, but not enough to find another line, start at the bottom and climb up. He felt society had no need for him, no place.'

'He had you, Elsie.'

Mrs Mead laughed, a dry bark. 'A fat lot of good that counted.' Ruefully she received back the photograph and restored it to the mantelshelf. 'And now there's another.'

'He's not as bad, though, is he?'

'Bad? Who knows what they feel? I don't. Frank never allowed me to see him in the state Mr Hillier's in. He never showed it. The morning of his death, he'd shaved and parted his hair and wore a collar and tie as he did every day of his life. His shoes were polished, his waistcoat buttoned properly. But what was going on inside that head . . .?' She stared at the photograph. The pair stood dumb and gloomy.

'I shall have to be off,' Alice said finally, barely able to breathe.

Mrs Mead snapped a glance towards the television set. A digital clock greenly marked 15.38. She did not argue. The two women tiptoed down the stairs together, beaten.

'Let me know if there's anything I can do. Drive you anywhere, shop for you.'

'I will, thanks. You be careful on these roads.'

Elsie returned to her room, washed the tea things and prepared another small pot which she carried downstairs to Hillier's bedroom. At this time on a clouded day the room was almost dark in spite of the snow. She switched on the light, drew the curtains, bustled her tray to the other side of the narrow bed.

'That's more cheerful,' she said, lighting a table lamp. Hillier groaned. 'Sit up now for a cup of tea.' She manhandled him, straightening his pyjama jacket, and then combed his short hair. 'Better. Can you pour it out, or shall I?'

No answer. His eyes remained half-shut, his posture spineless.

'Oh, well.' She poured. He paid no attention. She sat, hands in lap. 'It won't be so bad tomorrow.' Hillier looked at her now. 'Every day makes it easier to cope with.'

'What day is it?' He chumbled the sentence.

'Sunday. It's not snowing now. Mrs Fowler's gone.'

'Fowler?'

'She came to find out how you were; I told you, while she was here. You didn't want to see her.'

Hillier moaned.

'Have a sip of this tea. Earl Grey.'

He grasped the saucer uncertainly. 'Hot,' he complained, sipping.

'Blow it, then. Good God, man, you've not lost your brains.' Her fierce sentence had no effect; cup wobbled on saucer; the eyes were closed. 'Here, give it to me.' She removed it from him, returned it to the tray. 'Sit up now, while I do your pillows.' With a rush she fetched a soaped and dampened flannel, a hand towel from the bathroom. 'Let's be having you.' She roughly daubed, dabbed at his face, once, twice, concentrating on the eyes. 'That's better. Now your hands.' She straightened his fingers, scrubbed them, dried them with unnecessary vigour, returned to attack his mouth before dropping towel and flannel to the carpet. 'Up again.' She pummelled the pillows behind him, dragged his jacket and the duvet straight, flattened his hair with her hand. 'That's better. You look more like a human being.' She presented him once more with the cup and saucer. 'Drink up.' She spoke all the time as to a reluctant child or animal.

Adrian Hillier opened his eyes, sipped at his tea.

Mrs Mead disposed of towel and flannel, and returning found him holding an empty cup.

'You drank it. Good! Have a biscuit.' He groaned a refusal and she poured out a second time. 'Mrs Fowler was upset to hear how ill you were. I didn't know what to tell her. "Have you had the doctor?" she asked. Natural questions, but I couldn't answer them.' He turned his face towards her, swollen eyes in

81

a mute, bloodshot appeal. She bent over him. His breath smelt sour in the sweetness of scented soap. 'If you're not better tomorrow, I shall ask Dr Ryder to come to visit you. He's generally sensible. So's that young woman assistant he has now.'

Elsie Mead sat on the bed with her back to the patient, and gabbled. She did not make much sense to herself; it did not seem to matter, as long as the stream of words gushed. Hillier made no answers but did not slump. His hands rested palms down on the bedclothes.

'Shall I come in with you for a bit?'

His eyes opened wide, as if he did not understand the significance of what she said.

'Make up your mind, will you?'

He nodded sadly at the snappish tone.

Mrs Mead unbuttoned her blouse, removed it, folded it carefully and placed it on a chair. Her arms were strong and white, and as she stood by the bedside looking down on him she remembered how he'd complimented her once: 'You shed your years when you shed your clothes.' As she reached for the fastening of her skirt the front-door bell pealed. She cocked her head comically, questioning his wishes, without success.

She frowned, picked up her blouse, and donning it moved towards the door. As she left the room the bell rang again.

Valerie Fitzjames stood on the doorstep, prettily wrapped against the cold.

'May I see Adrian?' she asked.

'He's not very well.'

'I wondered.'

'You'd better come in. It's cold.' Mrs Mead closed the front door. 'He's in bed, I'm afraid.'

'What is it? The 'flu?' The housekeeper shrugged, unwilling to help out. 'Is it possible to see him?'

'Wait here.'

The tone was hard, but on her way upstairs noticing that a button of her blouse was undone she grinned.

'It's that Valerie,' she announced. 'She wants to see you.'

He squirmed, but did not answer.

'Is she to come up? Do you want her?' Again nothing. 'I don't mind keeping her waiting, but you'll have to make your mind up.'

'All right.' Barely audible.

She straightened pillows, patient, duvet again, combed his hair. 'We might as well have you beautiful for your lady friends.'

Down below she switched on more lights. 'He's not well. Don't stay too long. He tires easily. Ten minutes, I should think.'

She led the way, placed the chair on which her blouse had rested close to the bed. Miss Fitzjames unfastened the astrakhan collar of her coat, but did not remove the matching cossack hat.

'I'll leave you to it.' Grimly.

Elsie Mead sauntered back to her room, drew the curtains and took up a Sunday paper. It was wrapped together still; he had not asked for it, though he had joked often enough that his hour with the 'Sundays' was his equivalent of church-going. She read carefully of government plans for health, of the murder of children, of an actor's life. To her in this warm room these were messages from an alien planet. She smiled at her fancy, consulted the clock. Miss Fitzjames had occupied twenty minutes of Mr Hillier's time; she allowed five more. A house falling into pit-workings; a letter from a dentist about apples and teeth easily occupied the short interval. She refolded the newspapers, extinguished her lights, tiptoed downstairs.

She did not tap at the door, but slid swiftly in. Hillier had slumped, but Valerie Fitzjames was holding his right hand with both of hers. Her gloves lay on the duvet.

'Are you ready?' Mrs Mead asked sternly.

The younger woman continued to caress the hand she held. 'I think it will all work out as you wish,' she whispered. 'In the end. Really as you want it. It would be sensible.'

She spoke fast as if to pucker in a sufficiency of crucial promises before Mrs Mead swept her from the room.

Adrian Hillier made no response, not even looking at his visitor. His colour was bad and the hair ruffled again.

'Say goodbye to Miss Fitzjames,' Elsie instructed him, distinctly, as to a child. 'Perhaps she'll visit you again.'

He made some sort of effort. The girl stood, ducked to peck a kiss and snatch up her gloves. She walked quickly from the room and did not speak until she was in the hall, where she pulled on her gloves with military jerks.

'He's not very well,' Miss Fitzjames said.

'No.'

'We had a disagreement at the Phoenix Theatre. It was about policy. Mr Hillier was outvoted and he resigned. I think that's at the bottom of what's wrong. But I expect you knew all this?' Mrs Mead made no answer. 'It will sort itself out in the end, I expect. We can't afford to lose him.' Again no answer. 'Have you had the doctor in? I would if I were you, though I know Adrian can be awkward about these things.' This time Mrs Mead reassured her. 'It was sad,' Valerie continued, 'that we all became very excited. There were high words and table-banging. It was stupid really.'

'You supported Mr Hillier, did you?'

'Well, no, not really.' Abashed.

'Was there anyone on his side?'

'Only one: Mr Gidney, the chemist.' She glanced up, guiltily. 'And he doesn't say much.'

'So you were all on at Mr Hillier?'

'Not personally. It was a matter of policy. About what sort of productions we should choose for next year. I mean, these are often matters of controversy in theatre clubs like ours. People hold ideas strongly and are prepared to argue them out. That's how progress is made.'

'But Mr Hillier wasn't prepared to put up with the changes?'

'No. He resigned.'

'Yes. It sounds as if he's better out of it.' Mrs Mead spoke woodenly. 'Much better.'

'But there's no need to make himself ill. That's what I came to tell him. I'm sure we can compromise, accommodate his point of view. He's very highly regarded even by those who don't share his principles.'

'You mean now that he's resigned you can see that you'll miss all the time and money he puts into the club.'

'We appreciate all he has done, but I tell you: this is not a one-man show. If he goes, he'll be badly missed but it won't be the end of the Phoenix.' She sounded defiant. 'I'm sorry that

84

it's had such a terrible effect on Adrian. I, for one, didn't realize he felt so tender about these things. You'll have the doctor in, won't you?'

'If he's no better.'

'Do you mind if I ring tomorrow?'

'No, why should I?' Mrs Mead sounded awkward.

'I don't know. You don't seem to like me very much; I don't know why.' Now Valerie Fitzjames spoke angrily, fluttering, ready to quarrel.

'You can ring. I said so.'

Mrs Mead moved to the front door and grasped the knob. Miss Fitzjames completed the fastening of her collar.

'Did you come by car?' Mrs Mead, opening the door.

'No. I walked. I only live in Clumber Avenue.'

'Is it bad underfoot?'

'Not if you're careful.' Miss Fitzjames was making her way down the front steps. 'These are very slippery.'

'I'll put salt down, but we don't expect many visitors.'

The housekeeper closed the door and leaned against it. She felt weary. The Fitzjames woman was too sure of herself, knowing who acted sensibly and who did not. The girl was pretty, no doubt of it, and dressed well, made the most of herself. It was no wonder Mr Hillier found her attractive. Mrs Mead eased herself away from the door and walked thoughtfully upstairs. In the bedroom Hillier was flat again, with eyes closed.

'She's gone.' No answer to that. 'They thought better of it, did they?' He did not move. 'They won't be in such a hurry next time with their fancy ideas.' She straightened his bed. 'I'll bring you something to eat. Do you want the radio on?' The silence hurt. She sniffed and went out.

85

9

Over the next six days Adrian Hillier showed signs of recovery, pottering round the house.

He dressed, came downstairs and went out of the front door for the first time on Saturday as the last of the snow melted. A five-minute turn in the garden left him shivering, but scornful of his weakness. Mrs Mead led him into the kitchen for coffee and a tot of whisky. Peter Fowler already occupied his place at the table with bright face.

'Are you better, sir?'

'I think so. Thank you. Give my apologies to your mother about last Sunday.'

'She'll be glad you're improving. She particularly told me to inquire.'

Hillier smiled at the formality and sipped his whisky. He lifted it to the light, then waved it as a toast towards housekeeper and Peter.

'I often wonder what the vintners buy
One half so precious as the goods they sell.

Do you know what a vintner is, young man?'

'A wine merchant?'

'Well done. Not that this is wine.' He examined the yellow liquid. 'Though it's warming, I feel guilty about toping so early.'

'Treat it as medicine,' Mrs Mead ordered.

'I will. I will. Are you sorry the snow's gone?'

'Not really. I like it when it first falls, but after that it's dirty ice.'

'Do you go tobogganing?'

'No, sir. I haven't got a sledge.'

'We have one somewhere, haven't we, Elsie?'

'Not that I know of.'

'I'll institute,' he matched Peter's vocabulary, 'a search. If it's not too late. We may not have it any more.'

'I hope not,' Mrs Mead said. 'Where would it be, if it exists outside your imagination?'

'I'll look in the loft.'

'You haven't the strength.'

They both laughed, but he found the sledge later in an outhouse and slowly, painfully cleaned it up. The runners were rusty. Adrian Hillier seemed slow, weak, his mind untidily elsewhere; he pecked at his food still, but ate enough to keep alive. His conversations with his housekeeper were marked by a polite brevity.

Miss Fitzjames made another visit, was shown upstairs to the study, stayed for three-quarters of an hour and emerged crying. Mrs Mead could barely hide her triumph, but gave Hillier twenty-five minutes before she took in his evening drink and asked for instructions for the morrow.

He sat, white-faced and smiling, one thin hand resting on his knee. They decided without argument on meals. No, he was not thinking of going out in the next day or two, at least. There was nowhere he really wanted to go. He said this slyly, goading her curiosity.

'Miss Fitzjames didn't seem too pleased with herself,' she said.

'How do you mean?'

'She was crying. Don't tell me you hadn't noticed.'

'I had. She's easily moved to tears.'

'Had you quarrelled?' Mrs Mead asked, doggedly, expecting a rebuff.

'No. It's not my style to pick quarrels with ladies.' He drew in his lips. He's improving, she thought. 'I told her that I wasn't thinking of withdrawing my resignation from the Phoenix.'

'Was that wise?'

'What do you mean by that, Elsie?'

'If you're not there you'll be somewhere else. Perhaps somewhere worse.'

'At home.'

'But you were so keen on the theatre?'

He nodded gravely, sagely, like a puppet.

'So I was, so I was. But what I regard as good theatre the

majority don't want. I've done my best to promote my kind of thinking since I've been here, and to some extent I've had my way. But not now. They have had enough of my élitist theories, and said so. "Bums on seats" is their pragmatist motto.'

'It maybe only a battle you've lost, not the war.'

'I'm not staying to find out.'

'If I may say so, it does seem silly to give up what you so much enjoy. You're cutting off your nose to spite your face.'

'There's some truth in that.'

'Especially as these jumped-up Harries will be off and away somewhere else if I know them.'

'You don't, Elsie.' Hillier spoke gently, but that ended the conversation.

Next morning she received a letter from Stephen Youlgrave. The note was short, not informative, but made its text a remark of hers: 'You can't hurt some people.' This had set Youlgrave thinking about, and then writing, a series of sonnets, 'rather free', to prove the opposite. He felt, he said, the need to warn her that his views and hers did not coincide, but he hoped she would be glad to be the beginning of poetry if not wisdom. The piece he had begun at The Firs was still in tatters, 'fully-clothed, but much patched'. He hoped she and Adrian Hillier were well.

Slightly flattered, she decided to reply. She could not, to tell the truth, remember the conversation, though she recalled some remarks about the thick-skinned nature of two people who had taught with her. 'Hurt', she was sure, was a word of Youlgrave's own providing.

At coffee-time she produced the poet's letter for Hillier, who showed polite interest, humming aloud, making the moment last.

'I don't know why he's written,' she argued, 'I can't remember saying anything of much importance.'

'He thinks so.'

'But why?'

'Ah, there now, Elsie, we're in the realms of imagination.' He raised a policeman's hand. 'Perhaps it is that he expects in time to publish the poems, and wants documentary evidence of their origin. So, Elsie, you must preserve this and earn your mention in the histories of literature.' He smiled, sweetness

88

itself. 'On the other hand, it may indicate more personal involvement. Stephen feels drawn to you in some way and therefore wants to re-establish communication. This is his excuse.'

'Why should he want that?'

'Elsie, you constantly underestimate yourself. It may be, and notice my caution, a preliminary intimation,' he coughed comically, 'of Stephen's interest in you, curiosity about you, even love for you.'

Mrs Mead flushed with anger. 'It's all very well for you to talk.'

'Now I've hurt you.'

He put his arms round her and kissed her on the mouth. At that moment, though troubled, she realised that he was recovering. She wrote a reply that evening, rather stiffly, giving little away to Stephen Youlgrave, surprised at the care she took. It would mean nothing to him, she had decided. That night Adrian Hillier made love to her, not altogether successfully, but he demonstrated his need and his convalescence, and as she cradled him in her arms she was fulfilled.

At the weekend she invited Alice Fowler to the house. Peter carried the message; Alice immediately telephoned to say she could come round that evening, but not on the Sunday when they were visiting relatives in Watford. Elsie had no intention of venturing out, and gave the word.

'I hate February,' Mrs Fowler began. 'You always think the worst is over, and it isn't.'

Mrs Mead's room glowed with light; she must have installed at least three new lamps.

'You're cosy up here. Does Mr Hillier come up?'

'No.' A flat lie. 'When I told him you were due to visit me, he suggested we use the small drawing room, but I said, "No". I care for my independence, really. I bet it seems daft to you, but I don't want to be beholden to Mr Hillier – or not to any great extent, anyway. So it was "No." '

'Is he better?'

'Yes. Much. Though it's difficult sometimes to know what he thinks. He's not very forthcoming. Courteous and considerate, but always hiding his face behind his hand, if you know what I mean.'

'That French lady, his ex-wife, do you ever hear from her? Does he, I mean?'

'Not a word. They were in bed together, and yet he's not had a line from her. I always pick the mail up.'

'Nor a card thanking him?'

'No.' The word snapped like the closure of a well-made casket.

'Why's that, d'you think?'

'They never quarrelled openly while she was here. But then the whole thing was a mystery to me. Why did she turn up? They never corresponded as far as I knew.'

'Curiosity, perhaps?'

'You may be right. I didn't like her much. There she was dressed up to the nines, and very correct about meals and behaviour and saying the right thing and next minute, she's lying stark naked in his bed. No, Alice, there are some things and some people I don't fathom. Not that I'm bothering my head over much about her.'

'But you're fond of him, aren't you?'

'In a way . . . yes. More than just employee and employer. I don't want him damaged. I've seen what can happen, and I don't want it again. These last few days I've been on tenterhooks wondering if he really has come round.'

'Do you think he'll stay here? At The Firs?'

'There you have me, Alice. Now this theatre business has happened he may well decamp, go elsewhere. There's nothing to stop him. I know he has a house in Chelsea, I believe it's let out to somebody, and a flat. Or he could chance it abroad. I thought that while he was so engrossed at the Phoenix he'd remain here. But now that's over and done with, it's anybody's guess. I bet that set down at the theatre are kicking themselves. Talk about killing the goose that laid the golden egg.'

'Do they come up to see him?'

'The precious Valerie, but she went away with a flea in her ear. And one other man. They're mad, in my view. Thought because he's so quiet and polite that they could do as they liked with him. But that was their error.'

Mrs Mead sat red-faced with triumph.

'He knows his mind?' Mrs Fowler asked.

'I don't know that he does. It's hard to say. He was in

business, so presumably he had to make decisions there. But . . . If you had seen Frank, my late husband, in his school you would have been impressed by his certainty. He'd give an answer straight away, without a pause or hesitation. But get him at home out of the public eye, and ask him if he preferred tea or coffee he'd dither. He wasn't very interested; that's the first thing. And I expect it's much the same with Adrian.' She used the Christian name for the first time and Mrs Fowler noticed it with a small shock. 'He can be obstinate. The difficulty is to decide what he'll be obstinate about.'

'This theatre? He was serious about that?'

'Well, I can't say. He'd play about with electricity and stage sets for them. No, I don't know.'

They heard steps on the stairs, a finger-nail tap on the door. It could only be Hillier.

'I'm sorry to intrude,' he began. He looked shy, schoolboyish. 'I'm presuming on your indulgence towards an invalid.'

'Are you better?' Mrs Fowler.

'Thank you, yes. Very much so. Mrs Mead has done me proud.' He coughed. 'I wondered if you ladies would care to join me in a drink?'

'Alice is driving,' Mrs Mead almost snapped.

'I didn't specify the nature of the beverages.' He laughed at his own phraseology, his pale hand grasping the door.

'If Alice would like . . .' Mrs Mead said. Her companion nodded. 'Very well. We'll be down in a minute. Where are you suggesting? The study? The small lounge?'

'Which do you prefer?'

'You tell us.'

Hillier removed his hand from the door.

'The drawing room.' Mrs Fowler thought he'd bow. It was like a scene from a play. He withdrew. They listened to the retreating footsteps.

'That's unusual.' Mrs Mead, laconically.

'Perhaps he's lonely.'

'I'm damned sure he is.' Alice had never heard the other swear before. 'That's what I'm everlastingly telling him. If he jettisons his job, then his hobby, he'll be left to himself. And you'd be surprised how few people are capable of occupying themselves.'

91

The women did not hurry, tidied their tray, washed cups and saucers. Mrs Mead made some slight adjustment to furniture, perhaps to demonstrate how free she was from Hillier's thrall.

He waited for them in an already warmed room. First he made them comfortable, then poured out orange juice for Mrs Fowler, gin for himself and Elsie. Upstairs as he stood half in, half out of the door, Alice had not noticed what he was wearing. Now she ran her eye over his polished black shoes, charcoal-grey flannels, black high-necked pullover above which could be seen a thin rim of white shirt. The effect was clerical, parsonical. The serious, smiling mouth, the slightly tousled hair, the hovering, colourless hand confirmed the impression. 'Oh Lord, open Thou our lips,' she thought to herself. 'And our mouth shall show forth Thy praise.'

Her glass was heavy; he had been generous with ice-cubes. The drink was delicious, fresh on the tongue.

'Are we sitting comfortably?' Mrs Mead, grinning.

'I'm glad you're here,' Hillier began, 'because I'd like to ask your advice.' He adjusted his position. 'It might do me good to take a holiday. Where should I go?'

'You can answer that better than we can.' Mrs Mead spoke without sympathy.

'If I were in your position,' Alice gabbled, to cover her companion's criticism, 'I'd go on a cruise.'

'My friend, Stephen Youlgrave, Elsie knows him, did just that when he had retired and become a widower, and he picks up some lady and makes a hasty, ill-advised marriage. And on the whole he's a sensible, well-adjusted man.'

'He's a poet.'

'Genius and madness . . .' Hillier murmured.

'He's like you,' Mrs Mead answered, 'thin-skinned and impulsive.'

'What a character you're giving me!' He smiled warmly at Mrs Fowler. 'Do you think she's right, there?'

'I'm in no position to say.'

Her reply seemed as daunting as Mrs Mead's. Immediately Alice described last year's holiday in Cornwall, which had proved sunny but boring. The housekeeper remembered with warm affection a holiday she and her late husband had spent in a cabin in the Scottish Highlands, and immediately afterwards a trip to relatives in the Rocky Mountains.

'Do you keep photographs?' Hillier.

'We took a few. I still have them . . . somewhere. But I don't need them. What happened is in my head.'

'Did you go abroad?' Alice asked Hillier.

'Every year. We had a little cottage in France. Suzanne often went across on her own. She loved the Dordogne. Or so she said.' Saddened now, he drooped over dangling hands. 'I know,' he said, brightening, 'I'll take a photograph of the three of us in here.' He leapt up, ran out.

'Is he a keen photographer?' Alice, sociably.

'Not that I've heard of. I don't like these crazes.'

It was some little time before he returned with equipment. 'Separately, first,' he commanded.

He fiddled with his camera, consulting a card, before photographing Mrs Mead. 'Now again, smiling,' he begged.

'The flash makes me shut my eyes.'

When he had photographed the two women, he chased out of the room again to return with a tripod.

'All three together.' He skipped about, rearranging chairs. He was to set the camera, and sit between the ladies. He told them how long they had to straighten their skirts after the depredation of his descent.

'I hate waiting,' said Alice.

'My face will look like a wet week.'

'Trial run, now. Pleasant expression, ladies.' He fiddled at length, then dashed between them. 'It's not so bad, is it? Number two.' He adjusted the controls. 'Slightly shorter this time. No chance of frozen fear.'

'I love old photographs,' Mrs Fowler claimed, while he stowed and carried away his equipment. 'They are so lively.'

'They are wrong more often than not.' Mrs Mead made no concessions to pleasantry. 'I wonder where he's got to now. Invites us down here and then spends his time playing with his camera. Men.'

Adrian Hillier returned with a framed photograph and a small pack of postcards.

'There we are,' he said, passing the picture across to Mrs Fowler. 'On holiday.'

'My goodness.'

Mrs Mead had risen to join her friend. 'How old would you have been?'

'Nine or so. Early fifties, I guess.' He drew himself up. 'In a hotel in Bournemouth.'

The black and white portrait of a family group had a more antique air. Mother and father sat stiffly on ornamental chairs while the young Adrian stood between, dressed in an old-fashioned blazer with brass buttons. The mother looked young and thin, slightly worried, pretty. One expected her to speak, to issue instructions through those slightly open lips. Father leaned back in his chair, above the combat, hands clasped, thumbs together pointing upward, hair neatly parted, eyes and nostrils arrogant.

'Your father looks very sure of himself,' Alice said.

'He hated holidays. He was beginning to make quite a lot of money at this period, and resented any time wasted away from work.' He joined the women. 'John Vernon Hillier,' he pronounced, like a flunkey.

'How old was he?' Mrs Mead.

'Thirty-three or four. And my mother a year or two younger. She trained as a French teacher, did two years, married my father and I was born twelve months later. We . . . she . . . lived with my grandparents.'

'Did she mind?' Alice.

'She was glad to leave; she wanted her own home. It was wartime and so she had no choice, I suppose. Father was away for three years, North Africa and Italy. Once they were established, she insisted on a family holiday for a fortnight once a year.'

'She ruled the roost, did she?' Mrs Mead, cackling.

'By no means. But to her, and perhaps even to my father, the idea of a holiday seemed immutable, like the law of gravity, unavoidable. My father hated it. He didn't know what to do. He'd no time for games, golf, or anything else; ten minutes' walk by the sea was all the exercise he needed. He'd as soon have lain on a bed of nails as sit in a deck-chair. He didn't want to read, or talk, or watch me. He didn't see sense in theatres, or cinemas, or amusement arcades. He enjoyed the meals.'

'Why didn't you and your mother go on your own?'

'He suggested that, but she insisted that he needed a rest. It wound him up like a spring. He used to get somebody at his office to call him back and he'd drive off to London for a couple of days.'

'Did you and he always see eye to eye?' Mrs Mead pursued.

'We didn't have much to do with one another. He worked long hours. I might meet him Sunday afternoon or evening. I guess he thought I was feeble. He was short-tempered.'

'With you?' Alice.

'With everybody. He'd bawl at my mother, but she'd answer, "Don't shout like that, John. It's uncouth." She was a match for him in some ways. I think he wanted to impress her, to bring all this money he was making and pour it out in front of her. But she was . . . oh . . . distant. She was proud of him, but wouldn't make a song and dance about it.'

'She's still alive, isn't she?'

'Oh, yes. She's only sixty-eight, and very energetic. She lives partly in Sidmouth and the rest of the time not far from Périgueux. When my father retired, she carted him off to France and they lived there. My father used to tramp about as he'd never done before and talk about horses. I think he'd made enough by that time. He was only just over sixty when he sold out his main holdings.'

'So your mother won in the end?'

'I wouldn't say that, Elsie. He'd done what he set out to, and more, and he saw I wasn't going to follow him in that way, so there was no point hanging on for my benefit. I could hold down a job and look after myself, but I wasn't going to set the financial world ablaze.' Hillier stopped, stared down at the photograph which Mrs Mead was now examining. 'It was a disappointment. I was a disappointment, I suppose.'

'You took after your mother?' Alice asked.

'No. Not really. She was as ruthless as he was inside the limitations of her life.' Hillier smiled, shuffled the cards in his hand like a conjuror. 'I'm a drifter.'

'Rubbish.' Mrs Mead, in strength.

'Compared with them. They both had ambitions. In some ways these aided and abetted. She was proud of him, made him spend on what she wanted. He'd have lived in three or four rooms as long as he was comfortable and not far from his office. But my mother put up with the disadvantages of his sort of life: the long hours, the frequent absence, the uncertainties, the demands for hospitality at short notice. She saw to it that he lived in a place that befitted his income. He could understand that a first-rate car was necessary, but not an estate in the country.'

'Do you inherit your love of the theatre from your mother?' Alice asked.

'Not really. She took me there from childhood, but it wasn't until the end of my school-life I saw that there was something in it for me.'

'Was your wife, Mme Lemercier, interested?'

'To some small extent.'

Hillier now handed out the postcard-sized photographs. He as a member of a cross-country team, he as a small boy lying by the side of a sandcastle, his mother with a tennis-racket, with a class of children, at the wheel of an open-topped car, and one of his father, head and shoulders, a formal portrait for a company prospectus, perhaps.

'You're none of you alike,' Alice gave her opinion.

'Pretty legs,' said Mrs Mead of the child on the sand. 'You don't look very happy, though.'

'I suited neither of them. My father was demon-driven, always occupied, obsessed. My mother liked the best in whatever sphere, clothes, food, houses, hotels. The best of the worst even. If I had been a cat-burglar I'm not saying she'd have actually approved, there was no need for such a choice, but if I was she'd have wanted me to be outstanding. But I was never like that. Middling. Too easily satisfied. I was near the top of the class at school; I did quite well at the university; I was very efficient at my work, but they saw me as run-of-the-mill. At least that's how I thought they saw me. My temperament was wrong.'

'Ah,' said Mrs Mead, a long-drawn-out, minatory sound.

'And what does that piece of pantomime mean?' Hillier sounded positively gleeful.

Alice Fowler felt relieved. Their interrogation had an uneasy effect on her, as if it might develop into a bullying session, hectoring and overbearing. Hillier's cheerful question dismissed her doubts, for the moment. The man kept his poise, would not easily be driven by them into confessions he'd later regret.

'It's you,' said Elsie. 'You're always running yourself down.'

'So you say. What do you think, Mrs Fowler?'

'I don't know you well enough.' She stopped. 'But Elsie's a very sensible lady.'

'I'm sure she is. But she's like my mother. She doesn't exactly approve of what I'm doing, but . . .' He broke off, charmingly.

'So you say.'

Mrs Mead spoke in a hurry, as if she also felt uncertain about the direction or content of the conversation. She seemed to protect her employer, but roughly, with verbal cuffs, not kisses. They settled to talk of the theatre, and Adrian Hillier outlined his difficulties at the Phoenix. Always in control, he made his points strongly, like a lawyer, determined to impress by his clarity. He frowned, sniffed, pointed, once even clapped his hands as if summoning a genie. He interested Alice Fowler, convinced her of his right judgement. She admired him, saw in him something of the relentless quality he'd described in his parents.

'How will it all end?' she asked.

'As it began,' Mrs Mead said dismissively.

'I shan't go back. They'll miss the work and cash I put in, but the society's strong enough to continue to thrive without me.'

'And your principles: that they should only perform the best? What happens to them?'

'They disappear with me until somebody else convincing enough comes along and puts them up for consideration again.'

'When will that be?'

'God knows. Never, perhaps.'

Now Hillier looked tired, vulnerable, old.

'Can I offer either of you another . . .' He waved vaguely towards the decanters. Both women refused. He drank the last of his gin. 'It's been good to talk to you both. Thank you for listening to my grouses; I'm a bit obsessive.'

'Like your father?' Mrs Mead.

'You wouldn't say that if you'd known him. No. I'm tired. If you'll excuse me, I'll retire.'

He held a hand out to Mrs Fowler, and as he passed Mrs Mead gently stroked, very briefly, the housekeeper's upper arm.

'Sit down,' said Elsie, when he had disappeared.

'I mustn't be too long. They don't like me out.'

'Peter, or your husband?'

'The pair of them.'

'Will Peter get himself to bed?' Mrs Mead asked, helping herself to more gin.

'Yes. He'll have a bath and put out his clothes for Sunday. He takes less looking after than his father.' They smiled together, reminiscently. The housekeeper reset her face.

'How did you find him?' Mrs Mead nodded upwards.

'Troubled.' She had no difficulty. 'He's not himself yet.'

'You're right there.'

'He seemed fanatical, the way he talked on and on about Ibsen and Shakespeare. He was so quiet; I mean, he didn't shout, but he was tense. You could see it. His mouth and lips were tight.'

'What can we do about it, Alice?'

'We? I don't know that we can do anything. He ought to go away, have a holiday, forget it, put it behind him.'

'Do you think he could?'

'He could try, at least.'

'You don't know him, Alice.' Mrs Fowler nodded agreement. 'And yet you knew him before I did . . . years before. That seems odd. Was he nice as a young man?'

'Yes. I liked him. But I was frightened of him as well.'

'In what way?'

'Sexually, I suppose. He seemed dangerous.'

Mrs Mead narrowed her eyes.

'I know what you mean,' she answered. 'He's not all milk and water, not by any means. When I was talking about the theatre business, he said, "It's a good job it's drama, not politics," and he went on about some branch meeting here where people were punching and kicking each other. "At least we never descended to the sticks and stones," and then, "Perhaps it would have been better if we had." I don't know.' She sighed. 'I ought not to ask you this, but do you still find him attractive?'

'Oh, yes. Very. But I shan't be leaping into bed with him. Not at my time of life.' She giggled at her own frank speech.

'You're a young woman yet.'

'Don't you believe it. Forty this year.'

'That's when life begins.' No lightness in the grim tone.

'I wish it felt like it, then.' She waved a hand. 'You should know.'

Mrs Mead offered no reply, and the conversation languished. Both women backed away from revealing too much of themselves. When Mrs Fowler spoke of leaving, Mrs Mead did nothing to detain her. In the hall they stood together, briefly held hands.

'I wish Spring would hurry up,' Alice said. 'I hate Winter.'

'At my time of life I hate everything.'

'No, Elsie. Don't say that.'

'Why not? It's true.'

'It isn't. It can't be. You're very comfortable here. You've said so yourself.'

'But I shall give it up. I know I shall.'

'That's not sensible.'

They kissed, clinging to cloth, both shaken.

10

Gerald Fowler heard nothing about promotion.

'It's typical,' he grumbled to his wife. 'They're all of a bloody rush, and then you hear nothing for months.'

'Keeps you up to the mark. And besides, you don't know you'd accept a move even if they offered it to you.'

'You're right. I don't until they say where they want me to go.'

'Would you be disappointed,' she asked, 'if you didn't have an offer?'

'It's up to them, isn't it? I can only take what's there. Do you think it would be worth while to have another word with your Mr Hillier?'

'You are keen, then?'

'Don't you start. Once somebody's dangled the carrot . . .'

She wished he'd finished his sentence, designated himself a donkey. He had on these occasions a rough joviality that did not altogether conceal his serious intentions, or his unease.

'Mr Hillier's not well.'

'What's wrong with him, then?'

'Nerves. Depression.'

'Not enough to occupy himself; that's his trouble.'

'How do you know that?' she pressed.

'Stands to reason, doesn't it? When a man of his age has no job and nothing to do but maunder round the house all day, it's asking for trouble. Why did he give his work up?'

'You ask him.'

'He's your friend, not mine. Presumably his father left him too much to make it worth his while going on earning.'

'If you say so.'

'Sometimes, Alice, I wonder what you're up to. I ask your advice, and I get these prods and gibes. I hope you're not the same with our Peter when he asks you something.'

Mrs Fowler looked at her husband.

'I know you're worried about this, Gerry. Anybody would be. But there's nothing you or I or anybody else can do about it. You can keep your present place going at a smooth speed so that if they drop in on you, everything's as it should be, or better. You realize that as well as I do, and I expect you're acting on it. You've made a success of that place, but I can't see what else you can try, except to make sure nothing slips there.'

'It's not right, keeping me hanging about.'

'It's nothing to them. I imagine their shops are all in profit. Let me say they did promote you, and that you were very successful, what real difference would it make to them? A few thousands every week.'

'Hark who's talking. A few thousand runs into a million inside ten years. But I guess it's not only that; they want a staff that's satisfied and amenable.'

'On the pay they earn?' Alice asked.

'Exactly. They don't get king's ransoms. So it's up to me to see that conditions of work suit them, holidays, breaks. A contented work-force is important. And, moreover,' he raised a finger, 'the Board wants managers in who are flexible. There are all sorts of fluctuations in sales patterns that we need to accommodate to. And there speed is of the essence.'

'I'm not surprised you do well in interviews.'

'If only I get them.'

Alice was proud of her husband. He was sharp, nobody's fool as he read the copious literature the firm provided, acquired the jargon. She wondered how the girls on his cash desks saw him, those re-stocking the shelves, the supervisors, the under-manageress, the young graduate spending a month there learning the ropes. She knew his nickname, 'Creeping Jesus', because he'd told her, laughing. It had worried her; if he was unpopular then there might be trouble, and the firm was ruthless with those who failed to come up to expectation. Gerald knew this and protected himself. The work girls did not look for a friend, a soft touch, except at times of personal crisis. He was exactly their idea of a manager, but he'd been good to one whose baby had died, and constantly put bargains in the way of all of them.

'You'll have an interview,' Alice asserted.

'I'm a small cog in their machine.'

'But indispensable. Keep yourself well oiled.' He'd see no pun.

Gerald had much more on his mind than Mr Hillier, and yet he always seemed smart and personable, punctual, not afraid to exert himself. The Corporation's action in putting the small grocer out on the street had given him an opportunity he would not otherwise have found for himself. He had been lucky. So had Adrian Hillier, but he had made the inheritance from his father an obstacle, a millstone.

On the two or three times she rang The Firs she received no answer, and this surprised her. Peter had attended on Saturday as usual.

During March, driving along the main north road out of the city, she noticed Hillier striding, briefcase in hand. She drew ahead and stopped, leaned over to lower the window.

'Mr Hillier,' she called.

He paid no attention.

'Mr Hillier.' Louder.

This time he stopped, bent to peer, not recognizing the kerb-crawler.

'Would you like a lift?' she asked.

He started back, then opened the door, bundling himself in. 'Are you going home?' He was. 'I'll run you back.'

'I've been reading in the library.'

'Don't you take your car?'

'Never. I walk whenever I can. Besides, it's Spring.' He laughed upwards at the cold, blue sky.

Rush-hour traffic crowded them in.

'You drop me here,' he ordered at a red light.

'No, I'll take you home.'

But he slipped from seat-belt and car, and waved thanks from the pavement. She had found out nothing from him. At the next traffic signal he caught up and waved again, ironically cheerful, in no need of technology.

That evening she tried, again fruitlessly, to telephone Mrs Mead. On the Saturday Peter reported that the housekeeper had 'gone away', and that Mr Hillier had told him to get on with what he usually did. The boy had made coffee for them both; Mr Hillier had been playing the piano most of the morning, and had not appeared put out in any shape or form.

102

'Was Mrs Mead on holiday, then?'

'He didn't say.'

'And didn't you ask?'

'No.'

'She might have been ill.'

'No. He said "gone away" plain as a pikestaff. I can understand English.'

Three days later a postcard, the picture of a railway engine, arrived from Mrs Mead in York: 'I am staying with Professor Youlgrave, and enjoying it. Weather rather cold. Thought Peter might like this photograph. E.A.M.'

By Saturday, according to Peter's report, she had returned and normality reigned.

'What was she doing in York?' his mother demanded.

'Having a holiday.'

Mrs Mead had visited the Minster, the railway museum, the university, and had tried one day in Scarborough which had been 'brisk'. She had spent her first honeymoon there, hated the place, but had said nothing to Professor Youlgrave, not wanting to spoil his pleasure. She had told Peter all this, in bits and pieces through the morning.

'Did you see Mr Hillier?'

'Once.'

'What did he say?'

' "Good morning, Peter. How are you?" '

The boy had joined the conspiracy to plague her. Alice determined to curb her curiosity, did not telephone her friend. Mrs Mead seemed in no hurry to make contact. No message was received until the following Saturday when Peter brought an invitation.

'Perhaps you'd like to go up for a cup of tea tonight or tomorrow afternoon. Give her a ring, she said.'

'I don't know that I've the time,' she groused, but immediately telephoned to make the arrangement.

'I've something to tell you,' Mrs Mead confided, 'but it can wait until tonight.'

The housekeeper was in no hurry with her confidences, describing her holiday, commenting on trains, city traffic, the restoration of the Minster, the difference that minutes of latitude made to the garden. Matter-of-fact, cheerful, she seemed both content and confident. Mr Hillier was out at the theatre, not the Phoenix, at a performance of *Henry V*. Mrs Mead spoke about the film, of her admiration for Olivier, for Walton. This somehow led to a disquisition on Bernard Shaw. Energy flowed from the woman, but her face was set, unsmiling; she might have been teaching in a classroom, when the children were excited on Guy Fawkes' Day or with the onset of snow, and keeping a tight rein, making sure work was done, nothing skimped.

In the end she settled to break the news.

'Do you know,' she began, 'Professor Youlgrave wants me to go up there?'

'To stay?'

'To stay permanently.'

Alice Fowler assumed an expression of pleased anticipation.

'To be his housekeeper, you mean?'

Mrs Mead breathed deeply, an athlete about to attempt a record.

'It's more serious than that.' Both waited. Alice knew better than to interrupt. 'It was a kind of proposal of marriage.'

Silence.

'You perhaps think it's an odd way of putting it. He invited me up because he'd so much enjoyed our company when Adrian and I were there. I knew it would be a kind of working holiday, that I'd have to prepare some meals, but I didn't mind. And, as a matter of interest, we had a main meal out every day. It all went well. He's a very learned gentleman, his house is full of books and he talks in a most fascinating way, very slowly, as if every word counted. But in the last hour, I was packed, and we were waiting for the taxi to take me to York, he suddenly blurted out . . . You won't breathe a word of this, will you, Alice? Not to your husband or anybody? He'd been saying, but in an ordinary sort of way, how much he'd enjoyed my visit, and how he hoped I'd come again before too long, just the sort of things you always repeat when people are leaving whether you mean it or not, when he suddenly said, "I don't know how to put this, Elsie," and he'd never called me that before, always very old-fashioned and polite, Mrs Mead, "but I wonder if we could come to some sort of arrangement. You'll want to know what I understand by that. I don't mean what you think, a post, a job, but a kind of engagement, a betrothal." I was flabbergasted.'

Mrs Mead rose in triumph, flourished her tea-pot. Alice accepted another cup and the pouring out, the replacement of cosy, of milk-jug with its beaded cover, the positioning of cups seemed to both women properly ceremonious, a fitting prelude to the important exposition.

'Well, now. Where was I? Oh, yes. A betrothal. Then he went on like this: "I don't want to rush you, any more than I want to hurry myself. I made a bad mistake over my second, and I don't want any possibility of error with the third. Three times is not too many, is it?" I said, "It would be my third as well."' Alice could imagine the grumpy certainty of that. "'I don't want to harass you, but I think, I thought so when I came down in the winter, in January, but . . ." He went on like this for quite a while, wandering, if you know what I mean, repeating himself. It was not his usual way at all; he's so precise, and concise. Anyway, the upshot was would we seriously consider, both of us, what he'd proposed. The taxi arrived, dead on the dot. I said I would, and that's that.'

'Have you heard from him since you came back?'

'No. But I didn't expect to. He's gone away to do some examining, and to see a publisher, but he did send me a postcard.'

'What did it say?'

'Nothing about proposals.' Mrs Mead took up her cup. 'What should I do?'

Silence.

'If you need to ask me,' Alice Fowler replied, 'you can't be very keen.'

'It's not a matter of keenness. It came as such a surprise. He was quite right when he suggested I thought it was a job he was talking about. His housekeeper would have been more in keeping.' A wicked smirk twisted her lips. 'I know what you're thinking, Alice Fowler.'

'Oh, what's that, then?'

'A housekeeper costs money, a wife's free.'

'Is he so mean, then?'

'I don't think so. He's careful. But he's out of my sphere. After all, he's a professor and a famous poet.'

'I hadn't heard of him.'

'You and I are a pair of ignorant sows, Alice.' The noun surprised, revealed unbalance.

'You speak for yourself.'

This short passage of blunt exchanges cleared the air so that both women sat more at ease. They could laugh now, Alice hoped.

'What are the drawbacks?' Mrs Fowler began.

'I hardly know him, for a start. Apart from my first visit with Adrian, these three short periods are all I've seen of him.'

'You know, surely, whether you're attracted or not?'

'Of course I am. I like older men. As I told you, my second husband, my real husband, was my senior by twenty-eight years. Perhaps I'm looking for another father all the time. My first marriage was a catastrophe, but I don't think that had anything to do with age. I'd chosen a madman. Frank used to say, "This is quite different from my first, Elsie," and I'd pull his leg. "Better or worse?" "Better," he'd say. "More peaceful. More stable." I don't know.'

'And,' Alice probed patiently, 'the other snags, if any?'

'Well, there's . . .' Mrs Mead thumbed towards Hillier's quarters. 'I'm worried about him. He's not himself, and if I announce that I'm . . . well, you don't know how he'll take it.'

'But . . .'

'No, Alice. He gave me a hidey-hole when I was in trouble. I'm grateful for that.'

'But you've told me more than once that he might very well go off to London and leave you to find your own way back into teaching or . . .'

'It's now, Alice, *now*, when he is as he is.'

'And you think this will have a bad effect on him?'

'I'm frightened that it will . . . in the state he is.'

'But you can't put that before your own happiness, Elsie. That would be totally wrong. Are you sure it's what you want?'

'I'm flattered, and attracted. Let's put it no more strongly than that.'

'I see.' Alice Fowler obviously did not. 'Well.'

'And then I'm not certain about him, Stephen. He may come to the conclusion that he's spoken out of turn.'

'Why should he?'

'We'd enjoyed our little trips out. Voyages of discovery, he called them.' Mrs Mead's face showed nothing like the animation her words expressed. 'And he's a lonely man, so that when it was my time to go and leave him, he perhaps said more than he intended or meant.'

'Did he seem upset?'

'No. Neither of us. No. I could have done with a few extra days.'

'Why didn't you stay, then?'

'I had told Adrian when I was coming back, and anyway I can't go inviting myself, can I?'

'Oh, Elsie.' Alice braced herself as Mrs Mead sighed. 'How will you let each other know? Who breaks the ice first? Do you write or what?'

'I don't know. I can't let him hear anything from me until I've made my mind up. If he wrote a firm proposal, then that would make a difference.'

'Swing the balance?'

Mrs Mead rose, walked about the room, touching objects as if to reassure herself of the existence of solid dimensions.

'I expect this seems all very silly to you,' she said. 'People of our age acting like schoolchildren.' She weighed a large glass paperweight internally bright with red, yellow and green flowerets on her flat right hand. 'I had more sense at eighteen than I have at forty-five. I knew my mind better, didn't you?'

Alice considered, fluttering.

She remembered Adrian's sexual advances, her fearful pleasure. 'No, no,' she had sobbed. 'No' to the fingers between her legs. But he had mastered her, and at midnight she had stealthily crept home into her bedroom – sore, terrified, deflowered, saying nothing, dry-eyed, never to be the same girl again.

She straightened herself, adult, assured, giving nothing away. 'No,' she answered, 'I didn't.'

Mrs Mead looked up suspiciously, sniffed in contempt. Almost immediately she relaxed and spoke with unaccustomed softness.

'Stephen is an unusual man,' she said. 'He's very modest.' Mrs Mead searched her walls as if to emphasize the height and depth of Youlgrave's virtues. 'I was talking to him one day

107

about poems. We had quite a number of these little exchanges, at meals, while we were washing up or sitting reading, and one or the other of us would say something that started us off.'

'That's a good sign.'

'It's as may be. We shall see. But this day I mentioned his poems, and he looked at me and clasped his hands, arms straight down between his knees, right down almost to his ankles, very low, as if he were struggling or wrestling with himself, and then said, after a while, very quietly, "Do you know, Mrs Mead," he called me that, "I've worked on my poems now for fifty-five, nearly sixty years, on and off, and I've never managed to put down what I'm trying to. I don't mean that my poems, taken separately, fail to say what they set out to. They do, a few of them, satisfactorily and sometimes even surprisingly. But behind these local successes and, I guess, failures, there is some sort of central mystery that I have not expressed." "What do you mean by that?" I said. And he looked at me and he writhed, and wrung his hands. It was almost comical, if I hadn't been so sure he was trying to force the truth out of himself. You think I'm exaggerating, don't you?'

'I do not.'

'I said to him, "Do you mean God?" And he shook his head straight away, dismissing it. "No. Nothing like that. It's in humanity somewhere." I was baffled, but I could see he was, in some measure. And then he sat up. "It's as though there was some fundamental hollowness in the final understanding." It's odd how I remember his words, even though I'm not sure what they mean. He went on to tell me that it was symbolized by a little clip of film he'd seen on television. It was an old black-and-white, he said, rather like a home movie, and it showed the sea at Aldeburgh, and the shingle, and then Benjamin Britten walking along and sitting down, on a boat or box, and then you saw his face. It didn't take long. And that somehow encapsulated the mystery.'

Mrs Mead paused.

'You have me there,' Mrs Fowler admitted.

'And me. But Britten represented for him a man of genius. It could have been Mozart or Beethoven or Wordsworth or

Shakespeare, but we haven't got any films of them. But there was somebody who could move you beyond telling, walking along the beach like an ordinary man. "I can see that isn't clear to you, Mrs Mead. It's not clear to me either. It's emotional rather than rational. If I could understand it rather than feel it," he said, "I could perhaps put it into words. But then it might not be poetry." He wriggled as if he couldn't squeeze the words out of himself. "There's at the heart of us humans," he said, "something . . . well, if I can use another metaphor, like 'deep calling to deep', and that's the puzzle. And I have never been able to explain it, or even approach it very closely with words. It disappears; it dissipates itself, and I'm left longing, dissatisfied with a hole in my writing heart. I expect I shall die with this feeling, but then, perhaps it won't matter to me." And he sat there shaking his head, on and on and on.'

'It didn't frighten you?' Alice asked.

'No. Why should it?'

'I wondered if you thought he was . . . well. . .'

'Off his head? I never heard a saner man. Or a more convincing. There's a great difference between "unusual" and "mad", you know.'

'You're in love with him, Elsie.'

'If you say so.'

'You don't deny it?'

'I don't know what to say, or do. Why do you think I love him?'

'It just came out off my tongue. It's the way you spoke of him, as if he was so attractive, so far out of the ordinary. And it's not like you to be going off at the deep end. So.'

'You think it's true?'

'Do you think he's physically attractive?' Alice powered her question.

'Well, you know he's thin, skin and grief, really. But he's tall, and well dressed, and has this iron-grey hair parted and cut like a schoolboy's.'

'Do you think he's handsome?'

'His face, you mean? He's lined, wrinkled. And he squints at you with these brown eyes and pushes the short hair from his forehead. His nose is big, and his ears even bigger.' She laughed.

'Has he still got his own teeth?'

'I don't know. They're even. And a bit yellow. What do you think?'

'About his teeth?'

'No. About me.'

'You're tempted. Is he in good health? Would you like to live up there? What about friends down here?'

'Don't you worry yourself, Alice. I shan't rush into anything. We've both made bad marriages, me at the beginning, Stephen at the end. There's no bursting hurry.'

'He's not young.'

'No, I suppose not. Seventy-five. Still . . .'

'If you were suddenly convinced, would you write and tell him so?'

'If, if. Yes, if I was, I would. But I don't think I shall be. I'll wait for him to make his mind up.'

'And not say anything to Mr Hillier?'

'No. Not for the present. It wouldn't be sensible.'

The two women resettled themselves, unwilling to relinquish the topic.

'I sometimes thought . . .' Alice Fowler began.

'There are too . . .' Mrs Mead started exactly with her companion. 'Go on,' she continued. 'Tell me.'

'I thought Mr Hillier might propose. I did really. The way he looked at you sometimes.'

'I've told you, Alice, he's a ladies' man. He can't help it, even with an old frump like me.'

'You're neither.'

'Anyone would guess I was sixteen years older than you, not six. I'm no oil painting.'

'You underestimate yourself.'

They talked on at length. Alice Fowler, arriving home more than an hour late, found her husband grumbling. He had had to see Peter to bed.

'I don't go out often, Gerald. You can't accuse me of that. You're spoilt. That's the trouble.'

'And what were you mother-Hardying about all this time? A. W. H. Hillier, Esquire? "Dead 'oss and donkey-buyer"?'

'We mentioned him.'

'I bet.' He completed his rhyme to his own satisfaction.
' "Cocked his leg over a telegraph wire / And pittled all over
Nottinghamshire." '

As the days moved towards Easter, early this year, the weather became more clement. Alice Fowler found herself rushed off her feet; the rise in temperature had coincided with a burst of illness that had left her struggling to cope with the work of absentee typists. Oddly her husband and Peter reported no depletion of numbers in either supermarket or school, but over the past fortnight her office had not had a full complement for a single day.

Her temper suffered. To her surprise, Peter had entered himself for a lecture- and a poetry-speaking competition at a festival and harried her to listen to his remarks about 'A Victorian House', a description of The Firs, historically placed, with accounts of some of the families who had lived there, and interesting financial details obviously taken from the deeds. Mrs Mead and Mr Hillier had helped him, he said. The boy delivered his three minutes of information slickly, even gracefully, with no lack of confidence; his harassed mother was delighted.

'That's excellent,' she said. 'Ask your Dad to listen to you some time.'

'It's no use bothering him.'

'Why not?'

'He's not interested. He wouldn't know what to say to me.'

'You underestimate him, Peter. Your father's not without brains.'

'I didn't say he was. He just wouldn't be interested in this.'

'Have you asked him?'

'As a matter of fact, I have.'

She wondered at his grown-up poise. 'And what did he say?'

' "Ask your Mum. I've a lot on my mind at present".'

Alice raised this with her husband, huffily, in rebuke.

'He was on to me the night I was doing my monthly return. I just hadn't a spare minute.'

'And that's more important than your son's educational progress, is it?'

'It pays for his keep while he's at school, learning.'

'It helps towards payment. What do I go to work for? Be fair now.'

Gerald knew this was no day for argument, kept quiet.

'What's the poem he's chosen to recite?' she pressed.

'Poem? I thought it was a lecture he was doing.'

'You live in a little world of your own. Why don't you pay attention to other people?'

He mumbled excuses, crept off, acknowledging to himself the justice of her complaint, but knowing she made it out of her own troubles.

Peter reported on Saturday that he had practised both pieces on Mrs Mead.

'What did she say?' Alice asked.

' "Good. Confident and fluent." '

'She's a teacher; she should know.'

'But I mustn't appear too cocky. The poem must move you, she said.'

'How do you manage that?'

'By altering the timbre of the voice.'

'The whatter?'

'Timbre . . . the quality, she said. "The ruined spendthrift now no longer proud/ Claimed kindred there and had his claims allowed." ' The boy's voice brooded, with a darker, parsonical tone quite unlike anything his mother had heard from him before.

'Marvellous. Did Mr Hillier hear you?'

'No. He's in London again.'

'Doing what?'

'Enjoying himself. Spending his money.' She recognized Mrs Mead's sharpness.

They laughed together, but Alice was too busy to ring The Firs to learn her friend's news. She was surprised to receive a telephone call one evening from Adrian Hillier. She had just had a further exchange at the end of supper with her husband, who seemed depressed and sour after a poorish month at Top Fare and blank silence from the Board.

'What can you expect with the weather we've been having?' she asked.

'Listen. Our customers are car owners. Bad weather doesn't put them off.'

'Not snowy roads? Especially as they're also freezer owners, and can afford to miss a week or two. They'll stock up again now the weather's on the mend.'

'You don't know anything about it.'

That sounded unlike her husband, whom she could usually cheer.

'Wait until you see returns from all over the country, and then you'll know whether to blame yourself.'

'That'll be months.'

'All the more reason not to be down in the mouth about it.'

'Alice, sometimes I could bloody hit you.'

He realized at once he'd gone too far. She rose, began to clear the table, though his coffee-cup was full. He did not speak, but sat like a chidden schoolboy at the end of the table, cheeks red, eyes concentrating on the cloth. While she noisily washed the dishes, he took himself to a sheaf of papers which he rustled, glowered at but could not read. When the 'phone rang both sprang to action. He arrived first. 'For you,' he gritted. She took it without a word of thanks.

'Oh, Adrian Hillier here. I wonder if you'd favour me with your advice some time.'

'Certainly.' She answered his old-fashioned request with spryness.

'It's about Elsie, Elsie Mead.'

'I haven't seen anything of her for the last fortnight.'

'No. She's up in Yorkshire again.'

'With Professor Youlgrave?'

'Yes. That's what I want to talk to you about. If you don't mind. But not on the 'phone. Do you think you could come up some time?'

They arranged to meet the next evening.

'What did he want?' Gerald snarled.

'Nothing.' She relented. 'He wants to see me.'

'About me?'

'Afraid not. About Mrs Mead.'

'What's wrong with her?'

114

'I don't know that anything is. Not until I've seen him.'

Alice marched smartly away to rattle at unnecessary tasks in the kitchen.

The following evening Hillier led her in to the small drawing room where she refused alcohol, told him not to worry about entertainment. The quarrel with her husband was still unmended, so that they had barely exchanged half-a-dozen words over breakfast and the evening meal. Peter had observed them knowingly, with superior distaste, she thought, and this had done nothing for her comfort. She tugged at the heel of her shoe, crossly.

'I won't beat about the bush,' Hillier began. 'I'm worried about Elsie Mead.'

'So you said.'

'I thought perhaps you could shed some light. You seem to be her friend, the only one, as far as I know.'

Alice was in no mood to rid a man of embarrassment so she sat primly waiting for him to continue, to make a fool of himself.

'In the last week or two she has been up to York three, four times. Once for two days, the rest day-trips. She has a little Peugeot now, you know that.' Alice did, but could see no sense in the information. 'She visits Stephen Youlgrave.'

'And neglects her work here?'

'Oh, no. I couldn't say that.' He sounded affronted, and now spoke with diffidence. 'She's not on duty seven days a week with me. She can take time off whenever she pleases within reason. And whenever she does go away, she sees to it that I've plenty to eat.'

'What's the trouble, then?'

'It's only recently that she's taken to going off like this.'

'So she has been working seven days a week, and now you don't like it when she's seen sense.'

Hillier smiled ruefully, and answered without vigour, thoughtfully, within reason.

'I don't think that's the case. Of course, it must come into consideration, because I'm as fond of my creature comforts as the next man. But it's Mrs Mead I'm thinking about. When I first came here I appointed a housekeeper who was unsatisfactory, so that I had to get rid of her pretty quickly. Mrs Mead

115

applied. I was uncertain about her. She was over-qualified. There must be compelling reasons, I told myself, why a woman of her education should want to leave teaching, drop salary, work here. If I judged her properly, she ought to have applied long ago for headships and so forth. I'll cut a long story short. What it boiled down to was that her husband had died, and she found herself deeply dissatisfied with her life. Again I put it to her, for my advantage as much as hers, in that I didn't want to make another mistake, that this would almost certainly prove just as unsatisfactory. She would not have it. This would remove her from the house, the school, the way of life that reminded her constantly of her husband. He committed suicide. You knew that? I was very doubtful, but we arranged a three-month trial. At the end of the period she said she wished to continue. She had let her house, was comfortable in the flat, enjoyed the work. For my part, I was delighted. She seemed ideal, thoroughly efficient, an admirable cook and organizer, good company but not intrusive. It could not have been better.'

'And . . . ?'

'She showed no signs of emotional unbalance, which was what I had feared. She had lost a partner whom she deeply loved and admired. Though she never said as much, she must have blamed herself to some extent for his death. But nothing of this showed.' Hillier smiled sweetly, brushed flat-handed at one knee, and concluded, 'She had, as they say, got her act together.' He coughed drily. 'But now she seems to be showing an undue interest in Stephen Youlgrave.'

'Undue? Is he trying to tempt her away from you?'

'Has she said as much?'

'She said how interesting Professor Youlgrave was, they'd had little talks on this and that. This was the occasion when you took her there.'

'Yes. She did not tell you that Stephen had offered her a job?'

'No.' Alice was prepared to lie for her friend, but this was the strict truth.

'I see.'

'Have you any sort of contract with her? Would she have to work out her notice?'

'No. It was . . . all informal. She could leave tomorrow if she wished.'

Alice did not answer. Hillier was now on his feet, restive.

'It's for her sake rather than my own,' he confided, voice flat. 'She has been through a difficult period, I put it mildly as that, and I can't help thinking that meeting Stephen Youlgrave has revived some of those traumas.' Hillier was walking now, somewhere behind her, up and down. 'Stephen was much the same age as her husband, well, within a decade, and perhaps shared other characteristics, if I'm to judge from what she has said. And that means,' she could hear the quiet, deliberate footsteps, 'she perhaps regards this as an opportunity to allay guilt, to make up for her shortcomings at her last attempt; to look after the old man properly this time.'

'You mean she wants to marry Professor Youlgrave?'

'Is that possible, likely?'

'She's a personable woman. You should know that. And interesting. I don't know him at all, but I guess he could do worse.'

'Yes.' The pacing had stopped, he now stood behind her chair. 'I had never thought of that.'

During a long, awkward pause, Alice Fowler dared not look round. Silence hung absolute.

'Would she marry him, do you think?' Hillier began.

'I don't know him. You should be able to answer better than I can. She has never said to me that she had any objections to marriage.'

Hillier had placed both hands with extreme gentleness on her shoulders.

'That puts a different complexion on it,' he said.

'Why?'

'I was thinking in terms of employment, not matrimony.' The pressure of the unmoving hands seemed more important than any words. 'This has taken me aback.'

'You underrate Elsie Mead.'

The sentence told on him. With his right hand he began to stroke her cheek. It comforted her, she thought, ready to check him.

'That's altogether too possible. I've been wrapped up in my own concerns.'

117

'Like all men.'

The hand did not cease from movement. It touched her hair, with warm and delicate strength. She did not want it to stop.

'I suppose so. But women can be selfish.'

'Is she in Yorkshire now?'

'No. She came back this afternoon, having stayed there overnight. She has gone off to call on an acquaintance in Alfreton; she's restless, you see. Feels cramped, perhaps.'

'Did you tell her I was coming?'

'Yes. I think so. I'm almost sure I . . .'

He took a half step forward and bent to kiss her on the lips. She was taken by surprise, but did not pull away. Even at the moment of contact, of shock, she realized how skilfully he had brought off the awkward movement. He had to bend and at the same time tilt her head backwards, and this he had done with artistry. The warm wetness of his mouth rested on hers; his hand touched her left breast. Alice did not move, enjoying the moment, marking up a small score against her husband, but alert, shrewdly calculating.

Hillier drew his mouth away.

'You're very beautiful,' he said.

She neither spoke nor moved. He lowered his face again to hers, his hand more urgent at her breast. She caught a faint perfume, after-shave, hair lotion, soap, she did not know what. His face was smooth; he had shaved for her visit. Now his left arm was behind her back, lifting her forward from the chair.

'Alice,' he breathed. His lips touched her cheeks, her temples, while hands played masterly on her body. 'Dear Alice, dear Alice.'

Suddenly she pushed him away, and stood up.

'You can stop.'

'Alice.' He made towards her again; she side-stepped.

'And what has this to do with Elsie Mead, may I ask?'

'I love you.'

'I don't believe that any more than you do. Just sit down, and calm down.' She felt strong now, in charge, rough.

He obeyed, but unruffled. 'You were enjoying that,' he said.

'You were, you mean. One of these days you'll find yourself in trouble.'

'With you?'

118

'With others as well. You should have learnt by this time to behave yourself.'

'But, Alice,' he pleaded, 'have you no feeling for me?' He waited, winsomely.

'Contempt,' she said.

'This sounds exactly like a scene from a Victorian novel. I should have thought that . . .'

'You do too little thinking. You're self-centred, that's your trouble. No woman can resist you. It's not true, by God, it's not.' Her ill-temper burned.

She was surprised at the ease of his posture, his smile, his lack of embarrassment. Very gently he scratched at his left wrist. There was no bravado about the man; she might have just refused the offer of a cup of coffee.

'I thought you felt something for me.'

Alice stood, picked up her handbag.

'I'd better go, thank you very much.'

'What about Elsie? What am I to do about her?'

'Let her go her own way.'

Alice had opened the door, moved into the hall. Hillier took down her coat and scarf. She donned them without his assistance.

'I'm sorry about all this,' he said. 'I oughtn't to . . .' He frowned, attractively. 'I suppose this means we shan't meet again.'

'Look,' she answered almost angrily, 'I'm not a child. I know what sort of man you are. I knew before, and I'd been warned anyway. But I shan't cut you; I'll speak to you in the street, if that's what you're worried about. No. I'm annoyed. I feel dirtied; you misjudged me, but . . .'

'But what?' He eased the words out.

'But nothing.'

Now he waited, feet apart, wanting to talk still, but unthreatening.

'What about Peter?' he asked. 'Will he be allowed to continue here?'

'If you want him.'

'Yes. He's useful. Besides, I like the boy. I enjoy talking to him. He's sharp.'

'I shall say nothing to him. Nor to anyone else.'

119

'Are you angry with me, Alice?'

'You can't expect me to be otherwise. I don't understand you. You seem to be two people. It's a pity.'

'I could not help myself, Alice.' He sighed. 'You're a beautiful, superior woman. I'm about to annoy you again, but in my view you have married a man who's not fit to clean your shoes. And don't think I don't recognize his virtues. But he's way below your class.'

'You won't talk yourself back into favour like that.'

'I know; it's crude. But I'm afraid you'll open that door at any minute and be outside.'

'So you must blackguard my husband before I go. Is that it?'

She wondered, raggedly, why she prolonged the conversation. They stood, the pair of them, in a hiatus of irresolution, dissatisfied, but uncertain of the next move. At that moment keys rattled in the front door, startling them, and Mrs Mead entered. She stared about her in surprise.

'Hello, what are you doing here? Did you come to see me?'

'No.' A mumble.

Alice had heard no sounds of a car in the drive; perhaps she had been too intent on her passage with Hillier. Mrs Mead looked round accusingly.

'Oh.' She did not like it.

'I invited Mrs Fowler,' Hillier said, very clearly, deliberately provocative.

'Knowing I was out?'

'Of course.' He laughed; the housekeeper did not.

'I'll leave you to it, then.' Mrs Mead, dour.

'I'm just going.' Alice.

'Don't rush on my account. I've things to do.'

'I'll give you a ring in the next few days.'

'Thank you.' Snapped.

Mrs Mead moved upstairs at speed but with composure. They heard her high above, close the door of her flat.

'That's done it.' Hillier pulled a comical face.

'She's jealous?' Alice suggested.

'I doubt it. I very much doubt it. But she doesn't like anything happening on her territory without her foreknowledge. She's a typical schoolma'am. It doesn't do to annoy her.'

Alice pulled at her gloves. 'Good night,' she said.

'I hope you'll forgive me.'

As he made no attempt to open the door for her, she did it for herself, yale lock and handle together. Hillier followed her out to the top of the steps.

'Good night,' he called.

She did not answer, quickly slithered into her car, where she sat for a moment fiercely gripping the wheel, angry with her showing, uneasy. She hoped Hillier had gone indoors, but could not see from where she was parked. Light shone in the windows of Mrs Mead's flat, but behind drawn curtains. Alice pumped her accelerator, and hammered the steering-wheel with a gloved, clenched fist.

Glad that her engine started first time, she fastened her belt, turned on her headlights and cautiously negotiated the dark drive, muttering.

Gerald Fowler had been waiting for his wife.

'Would you like any supper?' he asked. The kettle throbbed. She refused, darting about. 'Did he say anything about me, or the job?' She made cocoa, as though the task was difficult.

'No. I'm afraid not.'

'No hint, or . . . or . . .'

'No. Nothing.'

Alice realized what it cost her husband in pride to ask these questions. He had annoyed her, had not apologized and now wanted the favour of information from her. She did not judge him harshly as he sat at the other side of the table, but compared him with Adrian Hillier. Her husband was aggressive even when, as now, he tried to show politeness; he seemed to bristle. Years of shopman's courtesy, assumed or not, had never quite served to cover his self-assertion. The layer of servility was thin. On the other hand, Mr Hillier's good manners were ubiquitous. Whether he passed the time of day, rebuked, flattered, instructed or attempted to seduce, he appeared quietly urbane, unforceful, unmindful of his own standing. He had bent to caresss her with a diffident gentility. This could not be true; his delicate fingers, warm lips had shown no respect, only a lack of awkwardness. As he had tempted her to adultery he had shown nothing of either oaf or bully.

She looked over at her husband.

The hair at his crown, thinning slightly, but untouched with grey, sprang upwards. He needed little provocation, especially now when he felt uncertain. She owed him a few words, she decided.

'I'm afraid he didn't mention your application,' she began.

'Why was that, do you think?'

She shook her head, unwilling to rile him.

'What did you talk about?'

'Mrs Mead. He's worried about her.'

'Is he, by God? What's she been doing?'

'Nothing much. She's taken a few days away just recently, and he wondered if she was beginning to feel unsettled. He thinks very highly of her, and doesn't want her hurt.'

'Are they having it off together?'

The question shocked her, not only because of her husband's form of words but because she had half suspected something of the sort, without allowing herself to put it so bluntly to herself. She felt again the exploring hand exciting her breast, remembered that Hillier had nakedly bedded his ex-wife.

'What makes you say that?' she asked with chill.

'They're human, aren't they? Together all day. Plenty of spare time.'

'Couldn't people suspect the same of you and one or another of those young women in your supermarket?'

'Whatever else they suspect, plenty of spare time wouldn't come into it. I see to that.' He laughed, not loudly, to himself, a man justified. 'I just wondered. She's not all that old, is she?' Alice told him. 'Um, about my age. She has a very good figure and legs, in spite of that solemn face.'

'You've sized her up, I notice.'

'Yes, I have. I have to set women on to work, and how they look counts in my business.'

He could not resist the temptation to reminisce. His anecdotes demonstrated his shrewdness, and the lengths to which some women would go to land even poorly-paid work. As he warmed to his task, disappointment fell away. 'And there she was up this ladder in a mini-skirt, didn't mind who saw what, and yet she was quite a respectable girl ... young married woman. I don't know, these days.'

Alice made no attempt to interrupt. She felt as calm, as contented as her husband. Pleased that she had repulsed Hillier, she in no way now resented his attempt. She attracted him still; she was a full woman. She smiled. Gerald talked.

On the Saturday after Easter Peter appeared in the final of the speech-making and poetry competition, and won both prizes. He had been at The Firs in the morning, and Mrs Mead had given him a last rehearsal. 'Polished' was the word of commendation he brought back from her. His mother attended the competitions, held in a comprehensive school on the other side of the city.

Peter seemed nervous, kept close to her, hardly spoke while they listened to early items. When the time came for him to slip away for his turn, he touched her arm and nodded. 'Good luck,' she had whispered.

The standard was not high. Out of fifteen competitors, only Peter and three girls had memorized the piece so that there was no hesitation in delivery. Her son, she decided, was outstanding. His voice was strong, carried without being forced, and worked through a wide range. There seemed no doubt about it. Fortunately the adjudicator was of a like mind, and admitted he had been moved by the recitation.

In the smaller lecture competition half an hour later the boy scored an even higher mark, in the nineties, and was invited to repeat the poem in the concluding concert of winners in the evening. They ate pale buns and drank urn-tea together, pleased but with a sense of anti-climax. Peter did not win the Grand Challenge Bowl at the concert; that went to a striking young woman who sang Handel's 'He was despisèd' with a rich, throbbing intensity, but the boy did not disgrace himself and received his two medals and tokens from the Lady Mayoress with aplomb.

Gerald questioned and congratulated them, pleasing Alice. She had rung him at the supermarket to tell him of the afternoon's success and to warn him that he would have to forage for his own supper. He took pride in the boy's performances, said so without qualification, produced a packet of chocolate bars and a pound coin.

'Do you ever think of being a lawyer?' he asked his son, jovially.

'No, Dad.'

'You can think of it now, then.'

Next morning, Sunday, Alice Fowler made her son ring Mrs Mead with his news. She listened from the next room. Peter, as she expected, spoke modestly, gave an excellent précis of the adjudication, described the evening concert with considerable verve.

In answer to a question she heard him say, 'Oh, yes. But I

knew my Mum would be pleased if I did well. You can see she's nervous, as if she were doing it herself. Yes, my Dad was. But Mum would have told him to say something nice. He said perhaps I'd make a lawyer. That's something. He brought me chocolate. Thank you for all the help you gave me. No, you showed me how to understand that poem, and how to make the lecture exactly the right length.' Reciprocated congratulations were cautiously spoken, it appeared.

That afternoon, in fine weather, Gerald Fowler set off for a walk. He invited Alice and Peter, but both refused. The boy had homework to complete, after yesterday's outing, and his mother felt, she said, like putting her feet up. Dashed, but superior, the father set off, dressed to the nines.

Later that evening Gerald informed his wife that he had met Mr Hillier.

'Where was that?' Alice displayed interest.

'I was just coming out of the top end of Manthorpe Park. To tell you the truth, I thought he was going to walk past me, but I spoke and he stopped. He knew quite well who I was. He said a bit about Peter and this festival yesterday. Apparently he'd given him a hand with some information about his house in Victorian times.'

'You knew that.'

'I did not. It was news to me. Nobody tells me anything here.'

'You don't listen, you mean.'

'That's your story. Anyway, Mrs Mead had filled him in with how well Peter had done, and he was "delighted". He thought Peter had plenty going for him.'

Alice encouraged him to talk on. The two men had discussed the boy's future, and the subjects he should study. Hillier had been very interesting outlining the various qualifications one needed to follow university courses and thus careers. At the end of a long disquisition, and a close interrogation from his wife, Gerald had paused, as if the climax of the passage approached. 'Do you know what else he said?' He waited for an answer, wasting nothing of the moment.

'No.'

'He asked me, "Have you heard anything about the promotion you put in for with Top Fare?"'

'And you said?'

'I said, "No"; I hadn't. He hummed and haa'd, but I didn't leave it at that. I asked him if he knew anything, and he just said he didn't. He looked embarrassed, kept shifting from foot to foot.'

'He's always a bit like that.' Alice.

'But I wasn't having it. I wasn't going to leave it there. I came straight out with it and said, "That means they're not considering me any longer?" He shook his head, looked a bit dazed. "No," he says, casual as you like, "I don't think it means that at all." And he went on with some rigmarole about how he didn't really know much about their methods. He usually turned up for the Annual General Meeting, and any special conference or what-have-you, and, he admitted it, read their financial statements before he handed them over to his accountant, but he *knew* as little as I do of the day-to-day transactions of the Board, probably less. For all he understood, there might be a standstill on jobs; it sometimes happened with the firms he'd worked for. They decided against promotions for a year, let's say, so that they could make a very much larger alteration the year after. It had its drawbacks. They might lose somebody of quality who thought he wasn't being properly treated. Or they might fail to appoint somebody really capable to a profitable niche and so lose money. "This is the sort of matter any company's dealing with all the time," he said. "I often thought it was like a game of cards, where luck played a part as well as skill." It was interesting while he was talking like this, but he wasn't interested in it one bit. He could see I was, and so was willing to say a thing or two, but his mind was elsewhere.'

'And there you left it?' Alice pressed.

'No, I didn't. "Is there no way I can find out?" I asked him.'

'And what did he say to that?'

'Usual humming and haa-ing for a start. Then, "I suppose I could inquire for you. Perhaps I should have done so, as they asked me to sound you out in the first place. I will, I will. I'm going up to town again this week, and I'll let you know. That is, if you want me to. It's not always advisable to stir the waters. It sometimes sets them on to give you the answer you don't

126

want." I told him I'd take the risk, and he wished me good afternoon.'

Alice smiled, pleased with her husband's attempt to mimic Adrian Hillier's nervous, quietly staccato tone. Though nothing like accurate, it caught something of the man's diffidence and was certainly quite unlike Gerald's usual voice.

'So you feel a bit more satisfied, easier in your mind?' she asked.

'I put him the questions I wanted answering, I think. There's nothing else I could have said. But whether he'll do anything's another matter. He has this damned vagueness. I don't mean he's slow or stupid, just distant, as if he's occupied with something more important than your business. It annoyed me. When he talked it was as if he'd learnt it out of a book. He's not in the same world as you and me.'

'I shouldn't be too sure.'

'Why do you say that?'

'I found him clever. Once you get behind the manner.'

'I found myself wondering,' Fowler said, wiping moustache and chin hard with his left hand, 'what he *is* interested in.'

On Friday evening Hillier rang the Fowler home, but Gerald had gone back to brood in the supermarket.

'I saw your husband last Sunday; did he tell you? And he inquired about this job at Top Fare Associates. I've been up to town, and I asked the MD's personal assistant about it. Made the excuse I'd sussed him out for them, and was interested. She said her impression was that they'd done nothing, but she wasn't sure. There'd been so much to-ing and fro-ing recently with middle management she didn't know exactly how things stood. She scouted around on the computer, and then in some special file, but still couldn't come up with anything definite.'

'I see.'

'It all seems very ramshackle to you, I expect. I imagine in your office things go by default, and it's exactly the same at the top of the ladder. It never seemed sensible to me, but I guess they don't much consider the feelings of people round about your husband's grade. That was my own level, so I can speak with feeling.'

'So what would you advise him to do?'

'Hang on. It's all he can do, isn't it? He likes his present job, doesn't he? Well, if he continues to make a go of that it'll do him no harm. If he wrote to headquarters to inquire, he'd get a smooth, non-committal answer, at best. No, there's nothing he can do except keep his nose clean and work hard.'

'I see. Thank you. I'll tell him.'

'Good.'

'Is there anything else I ought to have asked you? He's bound to come up with something that was quite obvious in his mind that I should have put to you.'

She heard him laugh. He thought, she thought, clicking his tongue.

'No, I don't think so. You've said it all.'

'And made a shorthand note.'

'Would you like to read it back? Alice, I want to see you again.'

She was momentarily breathless, but steadied herself.

'Would that be wise?' she asked.

'The height of sagacity.'

'We'll leave it there, then.'

'I shan't let it rest. I'm a determined man.'

'You'll get nowhere with me, Adrian.' She used the Christian name forcibly, into his teeth, against the world, in her husband's mould.

'We shall see. But it will be your choice.' He paused, 'hummed and haa-ed'. 'Did you know that Stephen Youlgrave had proposed to Elsie?'

'When?'

'By letter two days ago.'

Alice waited for him to continue, but he kept silent.

'What is she going to do?' she asked.

'What would you do in her place?'

'I can't say.' The spurt of anger again. 'I don't know what he's like.' Still nothing from him. 'Has she made up her mind?'

'She has not made a formal announcement to me. Nor to him. But my guess is that she will have decided to accept him.'

'You'll miss her.'

'More than you know.' He sounded cheerful enough. 'I'm thinking of giving this place up. It's very large for one man.'

'It always has been.'

'That's not very sympathetic.' Again the wait, while he

128

gathered energy or mustered thoughts. 'When I came here I saw the house as a centre where people of like mind could meet. There's need for cultural patronage these days, and I was fortunate, or so I thought, with the leisure and the cash. But I've been disappointed; it hasn't worked out as I imagined it.'

'Is that your fault or other people's?'

He hesitated. 'That's a hard question. And you're not kind to ask it. Of course, I blame myself. I can't help it.'

'I see.'

Conversation petered out, since she made no effort.

Peter reported on Saturday that Mrs Mead seemed exactly as normal, neither moody nor cheerful, but busy, though with time to inquire about his performance at the festival. She had presented him with a prize, a 'World's Classics' edition of Palgrave's *Golden Treasury*.

'Did she tell you to read it?'

'She had it, at school and at college. She said it had brought her more continual pleasure than any book she knew.'

'This is a brand-new copy.'

'Yes. She bought it for me.' On the flyleaf she had written: 'To Peter Fowler, with congratulations and best wishes on his well-deserved success, from E. A. Mead.' And the date.

'Good. Have you shown it to your Dad?'

'Yes.'

'And what did he say?'

'He looked at it, and said, "Uh, it's poetry." But then he had another glance through it.' The boy held the book closed. 'He didn't seem to know what to say. Do you read poetry, Mum?'

Alice felt the strength of his condemnation.

'No. I haven't time. I used to. I used to enjoy it, especially at school. You grow out of the habit.'

'I'll leave it on my shelf, and you can borrow it if you want.'

She thanked him. A strange formality stood between them.

'She said Professor Youlgrave was a poet.'

'Yes. And anything else about him?'

'No. Just that he was a poet.'

'She didn't show you any of his books?'

'No. She said, "You remember Professor Youlgrave who was here? Well, he is a famous modern poet." That's all.'

129

'And what did you say?'

' "Yes." What else could I?'

Alice made the prize an excuse for ringing up her friend. They talked easily enough, and though Alice thought Youlgrave's proposal would never be mentioned, she waited.

'I've news for you,' Mrs Mead said in the end.

'Good, I hope.' Brightly.

'Stephen Youlgrave has proposed to me.'

'Congratulations. When did all this happen?'

'Last week. By letter.' Intake of breath. 'I haven't accepted him as yet.'

'Elsie, you've not kept him hanging around all this time.'

'Give me some credit. I got in touch immediately, thanked him, said I was honoured, but asked for a few days' grace. I said I would give him his answer this week-end. He understood exactly.' Both were silent. 'Can I come round to see you, Alice?'

The appeal in the voice was undeniable. Elsie did not hide her anxiety.

That morning when she took his coffee to her employer's study the housekeeper had been invited to sit down.

'I know you're busy,' Hillier had said. 'I shan't keep you long. I just wondered if you had made up your mind yet.'

'No, not really. I said Saturday, and I shall decide then and not before.'

'I see. That seems rather arbitrary.'

'If I decide I want to marry again, it will be because I've studied it. I'm not going to be rushed into anything.'

'Isn't that rather hard on Stephen?'

'He can wait another week. It will do him no harm.'

Hillier coughed.

'So you honestly don't know?' he argued mildly, as with himself. 'But you must have some inkling, or inclination.' He smiled at his choice of words. 'Surely?'

'Yes, I have.'

'Will you tell me?'

'No, Mr Hillier, I will not. You may think me foolish, but I will leave my mind open until Saturday. If I tell you now, then it's decided.'

'What's likely to happen between now and Saturday to change your views?'

'Nothing that I know of. But there may be a thousand-to-one chance.'

'Such as?'

'Such as... I don't know. You may say something. Something may happen in the world. Stephen might wish to withdraw.'

Hillier knitted his brow, handled his face as if testing the efficacy of his morning shave.

'I'm sorry, Elsie. I don't wish to bully you.'

Now he stood up, put a hand on her shoulder as she sat, and bent to kiss her. She did not move. Now he stroked her face, very gently.

'Do you want my advice, Elsie?'

'Please yourself.' She answered woodenly in spite of the continuing caress.

'You should marry him.' Hillier bent again and kissed her cheek. The silence in the room loomed huge, both calm and oppressive, difficult to break. 'You will be good for him.' In no hurry, he stood behind her, resting both hands lightly on her shoulders. 'He is a distinguished man. A fine scholar. His reputation as a poet is growing, both here and in America.' He paused frequently, as if frightened of error. 'I don't understand his poetry, I've admitted. It's too learned, or dense, or obscure for me. But experts are impressed. Some American professor is bringing out a book on it, but I expect he's told you.' Again he stopped, not removing the warm hands. 'You may think this is not anything to do with a man about to marry. But it is. He is lonely, and adulation may turn his head. He's made one bad mistake about marriage. It surprised me; I thought he would have had more sense; but there it stands, a blot on his copybook.' Silence overrode. 'He needs somebody like you. To steady him.' The hands did not relent, pressing her shoulders.

'Thank you,' she said. He did not know whether or not she spoke with irony.

'He's recovered sufficiently now. The second, bad marriage shut him in, but he's escaped. He's an odd man, though I guess you're beginning to know him better than I do. He's concerned with what's larger than life, at least in his verse. He writes in myths, if you understand me, universals. You and I squeal if we feel a pain, but we can't be heard next door; he creates worldwide cataclysms, or tries to. It doesn't suit me; it's all too grandiose for its own good. Can't be done. Not these days at any rate. But then . . . I make nothing up. I stew here in my own juice.'

'Why are you telling me this?'

'I'm describing Stephen for you as I see him. As an outsider. Perhaps even I'm jealous. He does his thing while I sit silent on my behind, a nobody producing nothing.'

Now the right hand stroked her cheek.

'We've had a good time here, Elsie. Together, I mean. Very quiet. I tried to do my theatrical bit, small as it was, but it got me nowhere. You have kept me sane.'

She took his hand from her face and kissed the palm, once, then again.

'Stephen says he doesn't know what he's about,' she answered. 'He doesn't know why he's here, and the poems he writes don't satisfy him, don't say what he intends.'

'They say something.'

'But if it's the wrong . . .'

'Some of us are dumb. At least he has found a voice.'

She released his hand. 'If I marry Stephen,' she asked, 'how will you manage?'

'I'll stagger on. I'm not telling you this to make you sorry for me. I'll find my way through. I'm a survivor. I'm like Scotch mist and when that breaks it re-forms. No, I'm saying what I think about Stephen for your sake. So you'll know him. Or see him more clearly.'

'Thank you, Adrian.'

His hands were on her breasts, exciting her. She stood, kissed his mouth, embraced him. They made love there and then on his carpet, quickly, almost as if they expected to be interrupted, but satisfactorily to both, intensely.

'You should have given me warning,' she said, dressing.

'Elsie Mead, Elsie Mead.'

'That has put your lunch back half an hour.'

He shook his head, dazed. He looked lost.

· —— 13 —— ·

Alice, busy with Saturday morning chores, waited for Peter's return from The Firs.

Elsie on her visit had given a strictly censored account of the interview with Adrian Hillier, without mention of sex, concentrating on her decision to make up her mind on Saturday.

Peter flourished a sealed note.

'Here you are,' he said, "Hand it over as soon as you get back." '

'Did she seem pleased?' Alice did not immediately open the envelope.

'No more than usual.'

'Did you see Mr Hillier?'

'Yes. He stayed down to have coffee with us in the kitchen. He sounded pleased, at least. He was talking to me about algebra.'

'Does he know anything about it?'

'I'd say so.'

Peter tramped away to his room, cheerful once he had ascertained the time she'd serve lunch. Alice opened the letter with a paper-knife, as befitted its importance. No address; no date. The paper was lined, mean, of poor quality unlike the envelope. 'I decided to accept Stephen's proposal. It is best. E. A. M.'

That seemed little enough and increased her appetite for information. How had Hillier taken the decision? Had he been told? Had Elsie informed Youlgrave yet? When would the wedding take place and where? Alice, rushing about, had lunch on the table early. Her husband did not appear for the meal on Saturday, his heaviest day at Top Fare. She questioned Peter, but he smilingly averred that the morning at The Firs had been utterly ordinary; he had done the usual jobs. True, Mr Hillier had been in for coffee, but only because he happened to be downstairs when it was percolated.

'Doing what?'

'He'd been outside. In the garden. Or the garage.'

'Were his hands dirty?'

'He washed them. He always does.'

Alice tried to believe the boy was not deliberately exasperating her. She declared her hand obliquely, with a question.

'Do you know what that note you brought said?'

'No.' Peter concentrated on his plate.

'Guess, then.'

' "See you next Friday. Love, Elsie." '

'Oh, rubbish. It was much more important than that. She's going to be married.'

'To Hilly?'

'No, not to Mr Hillier. Professor Youlgrave.'

'Oh, him. When?'

'That I don't know. It's probably not fixed yet. She only made up her mind today.'

Peter played the trencherman, keeping his eyes away from his mother's.

'What happened to her last husband?' he asked.

'He died. She's a widow.'

'I like her, Mrs Mead. She was cross-looking, I thought at first, but she's not stern once you know her. In some ways she likes a joke. I wonder who Adrian will get next.'

'You mustn't speak of Mr Hillier like that, Peter.'

'She does . . . recently. Perhaps she was told to. Is Professor Youlgrave rich?'

'Quite well off, I'd think. I mean, I don't know. We've never discussed it.'

'We shall have to look round for a wedding present,' the boy said.

'I'll consult your father.'

'Will he know?'

'Your Dad's not short of ideas. He looks in shop-windows a lot more than I do. And the two of them will have all the normal things, towels or bed-linen or crockery. I'll have to ask her.'

'I'd buy them something unusual.'

'Such as what?'

'A pair of silver candlesticks.' Peter answered without hesitation.

134

'Whatever for?'

'To light them to bed.'

'Oh, our Peter!'

They sniggered together, each uncertain what the other understood. He helped her with the pots, then went over to a friend's home. They were trying to make a telescope, he claimed.

'Don't be a nuisance,' she warned as he whistled his way out of the house.

She rang Mrs Mead, but the 'phone buzzed unanswered.

Later that evening, about nine o'clock, after Gerald Fowler had been fed and had gone off for an hour at the Newstead Abbey and Peter was in the bath, Elsie Mead called.

'Is it convenient? Are you busy? I don't want to be in your way.'

'You come in.'

Alice threw her arms about her friend, who seemed slightly taken aback at the enthusiasm of her reception.

'Congratulations! I'm delighted, I really am. Oh, Elsie.'

They sat down on agreement, to a glass of sweet sherry. Mrs Mead still failed to smile.

'I don't know whether I'm on my head or my heels.'

'That's just as it should be. You make the most of it.' Alice, determined.

'Of what?'

'Oh, Elsie. Don't give me that. This day. This big day. How did you let Stephen know?'

'By 'phone.'

'Come on, now. I'm excited. At what time? What did you say? And him?'

For the first time Elsie's mask cracked, at either Alice's delight or her grammatical error. She lifted her glass.

'At eight o'clock. As soon as I was up and dressed. He was still in bed. I knew he would be. But there's a 'phone on his bedside table.'

'Don't stop there. What did he say?'

'It's what I said, first. "Stephen," I said, "I've made my mind up, but before I tell you, have you had any second thoughts since you wrote?" "No," he answered, very very slowly, "I have

135

not." "Then I accept your proposal. I will marry you if that's what you still want." '

'Just like that?'

'Exactly like that. How else would you put it?'

'And?' Rising inflection of pleasure.

'And he said, "Thank you, Elsie. I'm delighted." Very dry, as if the juice had gone out of his voice. We arranged that I should go up Wednesday and Thursday.'

'Have you told Mr Hillier?'

Mrs Mead nodded.

'What did he say?'

'He put his arms round me, and hugged me and kissed me. "I'm pleased for you, Elsie," he said. "Really, really glad." '

Though Alice quizzed her friend there was little information to be culled. To her surprise no mention had been made of the date of the wedding, and Elsie did not seem much concerned. They'd discuss it on Wednesday, yes. She'd drive to York where they'd have lunch, and then back to Stephen's place. He had a beautiful ring, diamonds, which had belonged to his Aunt Edith who had died recently. It really was beautiful, and in some way, he had claimed, it would suit her exactly. If if did not, they would go round the jewellers' shops in York. Elsie announced this with a kind of stiff pride.

She did not stay long. Alice kissed her as she left, again to the slight consternation of her friend. The younger woman shook her head.

On Wednesday Elsie met Stephen Youlgrave exactly as arranged. His letter had spent much longer on instructions about where to park than on love or wedding preparations. She had arrived at the trysting place ten minutes early, but he was already there, very well dressed in a new lightweight overcoat and a green tweed suit. He had kissed her in the street and they had walked arm in arm to the restaurant which was almost empty at midday. There he had produced a black, velvet-covered box and the engagement ring which had a great cluster of diamonds. It was heavy and obviously expensive. 'Pompous,' she thought.

'With my love,' he said, slipping it on to her finger. They kissed awkwardly again in the restaurant, leaning over the table. No one had seen the giving of the ring; the waiter had disappeared with their order.

'It's very beautiful.'

'Do you like it?' he asked, almost bashfully.

'Oh, yes.' She admired the sparkle, the grandeur. 'It's far too good for me.'

Then he had extended a finger in rebuke.

'It is not,' he said, stately, rather loud, as if he didn't mind who heard. 'To my mind it is exactly right.'

In her eyes it looked ostentatious on the humdrum hand.

He lowered his voice to give her the history of Aunt Edith, his mother's younger sister who had died a year ago aged ninety-five. A handsome woman, she had married the owner of the factory where she worked and had lived in a large house outside Huddersfield, the only one of her generation to be anything like wealthy. His mother had thought she had done well when she had snared his father, a three-pound-a-week clerk. 'They were good-looking, the Branson girls, all three, but not fertile.' He was the only offspring. His aunt left him money, jewellery and a set of six Yorkshire water-colours, very fine in his opinion. The painter had loved Edith when they were young, had never married; she had bought these pictures at an exhibition years later. He had been there when she made her imperious entry; they had spoken to each other, but nothing had come of it. They made no attempt to meet again. 'A real talent,' Youlgrave said. 'Ought to be better known. Taught art in Bradford somewhere.'

The pictures were hanging, gold-framed, with wide white mounts, in his sitting room; he had had them re-set. Two were of streams, two of heathery landscapes, one of a cottage in a garden and the last a terrace of dark grey stone houses on a hill. Skies were magnificent, blue or cloud-huge, except for the street where a wash of thin grey topped slate roofs.

'The composition and the conception are faultless,' Stephen said to her, tracing shapes with a finger-nail on the glass. She thought she understood him. The pictures seemed an offering, a sacrifice in her praise.

She could not help glancing down at her engagement ring, which heavily dwarfed her thin wedding ring. She had considered removing that, but had decided against it. This stirred her imagination with its solid splendour quite unlike the tall, thin, grey man who was to be her husband. They talked of the date of the wedding, but did not make up their minds. She had to consult Adrian, she claimed; it was only fair.

'Haven't you talked to him already?'

'Yes,' she answered. 'Vaguely. But I would say nothing definite until I'd seen you in the flesh. It didn't seem real until now. You might have changed your mind.'

She glanced down at the potent ring.

They spent the rest of the day in talk. They would be married here or in Beechnall, quietly, in a register office. She would decide what little furniture she would bring. If she did not care for the bungalow, they would look round for something more suitable. Early summer, June say, would perhaps be the best time for the wedding. She must decide where to spend the honeymoon. If it were left to him he would choose Iceland, but he could see that she.... His sub-junctives fell about. She promised to consider.

Sunshine spilled and they walked in the garden hand in hand.

He had not yet completed the poem he had begun at The Firs, but had started on two more. He had been spending too much time reading the proofs of an edition of Ælfric for a distinguished former student. He had completed the task, which had taken a long time – 'I was very rusty' – and could now turn to something more congenial.

'Why did you do it?' she asked.

'I wanted to see that I still could manage it. And, in my puritan way, I can't help imagining that I shall be better prepared for my own verse by slogging through this scholarly farrago. Don't tell John, if you ever meet him, that I called it that. He'd think any confusion there was provided by me.'

She enjoyed these exchanges. They spoke of the former successful marriages: his to Anne, his first; hers to Frank, the second. The failures went unmentioned. He showed her his treasures: Anne's necklaces, lockets; a gold medal for poetry presented on his seventieth birthday, three rows of signed first editions. As on her earlier visits, she was surprised how simply he lived; he ought to have invested in antiques, but to him tables were surfaces where one could eat or write, not beautiful objects. He showed her the room he would clear so that she could fill it entirely with her own furniture; it had been her bedroom when she came to stay.

'And what happens to these things?' She pointed round.

'I've plenty of storage space. Or some charity will take them off my hands.'

After breakfast on the second day they drove into York and stared at shop windows in pleasant sunshine. They had decided on a pub lunch on their way back and then she would leave for The Firs at about four o'clock. Both were content, laconic and happy. They spoke to nobody, met no one they knew, though the streets were thronged.

'How do you fancy those pictures?' he asked with a kind of giggle.

They were looking into a second-hand shop with shelves full of bric-à-brac, rubbishy brass shoes, figurines and windmills so crowded she could not see any pictures.

'Over there. On the wall.'

Her eyes accustomed themselves to the dimness. There were two largish five-foot-by-two panels each with an outline painting of a woman, naked except for transparent scraps of floating drapery. The hair-style and expression on the faces seemed Pre-Raphaelite, but the execution was Art Deco. Mrs Mead was surprised as she stood with the sun graciously warm on her back.

'I look at them every time I walk along this street. They've been there ever since I came. Perhaps he doesn't want to sell them. I've never inquired.'

'Do you find them attractive?' she asked.

'No. I wonder what they are. That size. I wonder if they were painted for a restaurant, or something of the sort. Two of the four seasons. Spring and Autumn perhaps.'

'I hope they put more clothes on for Winter.'

'I've never been inside to look closely, or to ask about the subject or the price.'

'Let's go in now,' she said, boldly.

'No. No thanks. I prefer to keep my mystery.' He took her elbow, moving her along. 'They weren't very good, were they?' he asked, hesitantly.

'I wouldn't give them house-room, certainly,' she answered,

wondering why he had drawn attention to these objects. 'Not that I know anything about it.'

Back in his bungalow they sat over a cup of tea. Elsie had already packed; her cases were stowed in the Peugeot. Though sunshine splayed bright in the garden, the rooms seemed dull, chill, empty of interest, extraordinarily silent. The visit, the anticipations, the promises were over and done; now they had nothing to say to each other. They drank China tea, feeling uncomfortable, wanting a few days to think over their exchanges. Only the ring on Elsie's finger struck any note of drama. Stephen clasped his cup high as if he depended on it for body-warmth.

'I had a dream,' he began, and stopped.

'Ah have a dream,' she mocked, and checked herself. 'Go on. Tell me about it.'

'I was in a theatre audience, in a place like a church hall or garrison cinema, with another man, and he had a gun. It was an odd weapon, shortish with sights, not that I'm expert, quite unlike the Lee-Enfields we had when I was in the Army. We were together, but I was in charge and we were there to shoot one of the young princesses; I cannot say which, it seemed neither Princess Diana nor the Duchess of York, though who else could it have been? The princess was on the stage with other people, not acting, making a presentation perhaps, I can't say. Another curious facet was that while my companion was a young man, I was both young and old. I felt as I do now in every way, but then I'd switch and be in my twenties again.'

Youlgrave stroked his chin, in no hurry, pondering.

'Yes?' She spoke softly, worrying about him.

'We didn't succeed. While we sat there, three-quarters of the way back on the left, lining the gun up, nobody in the audience paid any attention to us at all. Nobody seemed suspicious. But we were arrested somehow, somewhere. Later. Elsewhere. And I felt dreadful, not that we hadn't succeeded but that I, and I was myself again, as I am now, a retired and respected university teacher, a poet, had been involved in such a cruel, pointless exercise, trying to murder a young woman carrying out her public duties. I was deeply depressed and ashamed.'

'Why were you . . .?'

140

'I've no idea. We were dressed in camouflaged combat outfits, a uniform of some kind, with those American peaked caps. But who or what we represented I do not know. Nor do I know why I did not give the order. Nor do I remember the moment of arrest. Only my shame.'

'Does it tie up with anything you have been thinking about?'

'No. You mean these madmen running wild in the streets? Or terrorist murders? I suppose I must have been concerned with them. We all are. But here was I, with the same moral concerns and counter-balances I have now, finding myself involved. And, in a way, the gaps were worse. Why did I not know the reason for the assassination? Why did we not make the attempt? Were there compunctions I felt, but have forgotten or dismissed? The whole thing was too fragmented to make sense, but I was left with this terrible sense of degradation, even when I awoke.'

'Aren't dreams always like that? Broken and illogical?' she asked.

He shook his head. 'I felt so bad,' he whispered.

'It was a nightmare.'

'Putting a different name on it doesn't alter anything. No.' He shook a helpless head. 'No, Elsie.'

'It wasn't connected with our marriage, was it?' Mrs Mead pressed. 'You're not worried by that?'

'I don't see the connection.'

'Not taking a step that can't be reversed?'

'I don't think so, Elsie. I can't think that. The real mystery is that I can't connect it in any way with myself. I'm not anti-royalist. Those young ladies wouldn't have much to say to me, I suppose, but I in no way resent that. It was all utterly irrational, yet with a vaguely sensible framework, and I was taking part. Why should I be part of this murderous attempt, even in a dream?'

'There's more to you than you're aware of,' Elsie laughed.

Stephen shook his head, again and again.

When she left he had not quite recovered, though before he had begun to describe the dream he had seemed normal, quietly content.

'I'll decide on the date of the wedding,' she said, robustly, 'and let you know. You can choose the venue.'

'Do you want to make something memorable of it?' he asked. 'In a church? With friends? A wedding breakfast? Speeches?'

'No, thank you very much.' She put her arms round him. 'It will be memorable enough as it is.'

· —— 14 —— ·

Back in Beechnall Gerald Fowler received a letter from the
Board of Top Fare offering him the post of manager of their
store in Leicester. At his first glance at the envelope (and he
waved it frowningly for some seconds), he had thought it would
hold an invitation to an interview in London. He slit the
envelope with a knife, and snatched out the short letter and the
enclosure, a cyclostyled job specification. He read one, then
the other, once, twice, biting at his left index finger near the
knuckle-joint. His wife and Peter watched him in silence. He
passed the letter on; Alice read it, and handed it to her son.
The father looked angrier at that.

'Well?' she said, at length.

Fowler's face grew red and he worked his lips as if to prepare
them for an outburst of ill-temper.

Peter carefully refolded both sheets of paper and replaced
them in the envelope which was passed back, formally, via his
mother. The father dug into the envelope and crumpled the
papers he scrabbled out. Straightening them on the tablecloth,
he reread them. He glared at his wife, tapped the letter with his
fingernails.

'What the bloody hell . . .?' he burst out.

'Gerald.' She did not mind his swearing, even in front of
Peter, but wanted to warn him to be careful, reasonable,
prescient even in what he thought.

'What do they mean by this?' he blustered.

'They say it's a promotion. "Your invaluable service," ' Alice
quoted.

'Some promotion. It's a rise of £150 per annum. The place
will be much the same size as this one. I have to uproot myself,
and you and Peter; and there's no mention of help with moving
expenses, solicitors' and house agents' fees. They must think
I'm simple.'

'Is it a kind of test?'

He looked startled, snatched up the papers again.

'To find out,' she queried, 'what you are prepared to do or not to do.'

'Would you accept this?' Gerald challenged her.

'I don't know,' she said. She did not.

He buttered his toast with irascible vigour.

'Promotion. Three measly quid a week.' He bit into his bread with animosity. 'You give up your job. Peter changes the school where he's doing well. No.'

'Think about it first.'

'It doesn't bear thinking about. It's a cover. They can always say they've offered me promotion and I refused it.'

'Give yourself a few days. They don't mention a date for reply. What do you say about changing schools, Peter?'

'Might be for the better,' the boy answered, 'though I'd miss my friends.'

'Not for this you wouldn't. I'll tell you that for nothing.' An angrier father.

Fowler groused and raged for his ten minutes at the breakfast table, and thereafter his wife observed him. He saw no advantage in this move, but could not convince himself that the firm did not intend some great advancement once he'd demonstrated obedience or commitment. Alice allowed him two days of fuming indecision, then made up his mind for him.

'It's not worth moving with all the commotion and upset for that money,' she said.

'Shall I tell them that?'

'Yes. The truth. What else? Very politely, but exactly.'

She knew he was grateful though he did not say so. He'd shortly be boasting: 'I told them what I thought about their offer. Straight to their faces. No ifs and buts about it. If they didn't like it they could lump it.' She would have to support him, keep on repeating her conviction that he had acted for the best. Within reason she was prepared to do so.

'Will you mention this,' Fowler asked, 'to your friend Mr Hillier, or his housekeeper?'

'I don't know whether I'll see them, but I'll tell him if I do.'

'The bloody cheek of these people.'

But she admired the restraint of his letter of refusal.

*

144

Life at The Firs seemed uneventful. Adrian Hillier had agreed that a date in June or July would suit him. He had not made up his mind about moving, and he would advertise for a housekeeper, though he could never hope to match Elsie. If the worst came to the worst, he'd employ Peter Fowler two or three days a week in his summer holiday, and failing that he'd call in one of these professional firms. She had decided on the first Saturday in July as the date for the wedding, and had instructed Stephen to make arrangements for the ceremony. He had invited Adrian to be best man.

Exchanges between Mrs Mead and her employer were minimal. Though they ate together they did not talk of anything but provisions, news items and a visit that Youlgrave proposed to make in a fortnight's time. Elsie judged that Hillier felt debarred and was sulky. Polite as ever he spoke distantly, would not be rushed into inserting an advertisement in the newspaper, nor be drawn into conversation about the future, either his or hers. She did not feel guilt, and had so much to mull over in her mind that any reproach in Hillier's behaviour was wasted on her.

One evening after she had cleared the dinner-table, he said he would take coffee in the large dining room, and invited her to join him there. When she arrived he was already cradling a brandy glass.

'Will you . . .?' He pointed at the large array of bottles. She smiled. 'Drambuie or curaçao?' She chose the latter, and poured out coffee. 'I ought to propose, formally, you know, my congratulations and best wishes for your happiness.'

'Thank you.' Elsie Mead had chosen her seat on the settee a good five yards from his armchair by the hearth.

'I'm not quite certain how to express my feelings.' He floundered, speaking with slow hesitancy. 'I wish for nothing but good fortune for you, and yet . . .'

Mrs Mead waited, unable to help him out.

'It is not as if . . .' he began and broke off. 'I don't want to suggest that you may be making a mistake because I don't believe that you are, but . . .' He sniffed. 'Perhaps it is jealousy or annoyance on my part that this move of yours will disturb, will end the amicable arrangements under which we lived together here. I must seem very grudging to you. Is it chagrin? I greatly dislike change. When I finished my job I felt lost, and so came up here.'

'This will give you the chance to move again.'

'Oh, yes. I've considered that. But it is you that . . .'

He looked at his coffee, his brandy, and signalled towards them as if they held the secret he could not convey.

'Are you trying to tell me something?' she asked brusquely. 'About Stephen? Something I should know?'

'No.' Long, anxious hesitation. 'No. I am not.'

'Then why all this fuss?'

'Fuss.' He repeated the word, as if it were unfamiliar, then translated. 'What my father called palaver.' He stroked chin, lifted cup, touched glass.

'I admire Stephen,' he said. 'You can be sure of that. Whether you and he will suit each other is in the lap of the gods. I don't see why not. But you, Elsie, have done me good. I came here in uncertainty, in a mess, and lost my way again over that wretched theatre. Still, the Phoenix passed my time, saw me into retirement proper without any fearful trauma so that when the second break came I wasn't, for all you may think, completely demoralised. You too, Elsie, were there holding me steady, wiping my eyes, keeping me fed. I'm very grateful. Come now; all this seems to be leading us nowhere. You may think I don't know what I'm saying, and there's some truth in that. I don't. I'm struggling, not understanding myself. Do you follow me?'

'No. I'm sorry, I don't.' She sounded half amused.

'I have every reason to be grateful to you, Elsie. And I don't want you to be hurt. That's why I'm not singing and dancing in celebration. If you want to withdraw, this is the time.'

'Why should I?'

'You're sure marriage is what you want?'

'As ever I shall be. What is it you're trying to say? If there is something, come on out with it. I'd see that as sensible.'

'No. There is nothing. Nothing at all. I just wanted you to be sure in yourself.' He raised his coffee-cup. 'To the good health and fortune of both of you,' he proposed.

'Thank you.' They sipped their coffee. 'Talk to me about Stephen, will you?'

'I've done that before. But I'll do my best for you. It's not as if I've known him all my life, or even for a long time. Only over the last five or six years. He's an interesting man, who came from a poorish family and worked himself into a good academic position by his own intellect and assiduity. He married either a student of his or a girl he met at university, I've forgotten which. Her name was Anne, and it lasted forty or so years until she died. She was diabetic and died in hospital after an operation, rather unexpectedly. It was about the time of his retirement. He married an American, Shirley Anne, but that barely lasted a year and was a complete fiasco. He'll talk about it, though, tell you quite cheerfully what a fool he made of himself. It's left no lasting scars. There's a son of the first marriage, Hugh, who must be getting on towards fifty now. But you'll know all this; he'll have told you. He was a lecturer and professor in various universities, here and abroad. A very respected man, I'd guess. Clever and conscientious, did his stuff on committees and at the same time kept his research and teaching on the go.'

'Yes.' Elsie Mead sounded grim. 'Don't stop now.'

'There was this other side of him.' Hillier paused, twisted the cup and saucer.

'What does that mean?'

'Nothing bad, nothing for you to worry about. It's the poetry; that holds the mystery for me. As far as I can make out from my observation and from what friends have told me, Stephen Youlgrave is ... or was ... a successful academic, a good husband and father, citizen and neighbour for all I know. But outside this, or inside, yes, better inside, is this other thing, this desire ...' He broke off and mused, tapping the arm of his chair.

' "The desire of the moth for the star," ' she quoted.

Hillier frowned, not looking up.

'Say it again.' She complied with the order. 'Who wrote that?'

'A poet. Shelley.'

'Why did you come out with that all of a sudden?'

'Because of the word you used. "Desire".'

'Did I?'

'You did.'

Again the brow-knitting and leg-crossing, as if he tried to

147

wrestle himself back into sense. He breathed heavily, clenched his fists, fidgeting.

'That just about sums him up,' he began. 'Wanting something that is not to be obtained. Your poem meant that, didn't it? Most of us would be satisfied with a successful career in a respected profession which we have chosen for ourselves. But not Stephen Youlgrave. He must edge further out. He must be a poet.'

'He's studied literature all his life,' Mrs Mead answered. 'He admires poets, thinks them important. It would be surprising if he did not want to join them.'

'That sounds sensible, but I doubt if it's the main consideration. There's some gap, some wound in him. He's a misfit in some way.'

'How do you mean?'

'I can't say, Elsie. I would if I could. I don't understand. I've questioned him from time to time because I'm inquisitive, but I've got nowhere. God knows, he's secretive about it. That's his trouble as a poet, that he doesn't come out with what he means, but whether that's because he can't or he won't. . . .'

'Do you ask him about that?'

'Not really. I hint. Always the diplomat, that's me. I'd like to be able to say to him that he is perfectly capable of making his meaning clear when he's talking or writing prose, but as soon as he's poetic he loses me, and everybody else.'

'Daren't you ask him?'

'No. Because in my view, and I could be wrong, I'd be probing into the very heart of his trouble, and he won't talk about it except in the disguised, esoteric language of his poetry.'

'Have you no idea what he's trying to say?' Mrs Mead felt sorry for him.

'No. I look through a poem of his and I admire the elegance, the choice of words. But I don't think that's what he's aiming for. It's an important part, but not the message itself, if you understand me.' He paused, pawing the air.

'What is he saying then?'

'I'm not sure. That's the problem. But if you force me into a corner I'd say . . . guess . . . suggest . . .' each verb emerged slowly as if he postponed the ending, ' "Something is rotten in the state of Denmark." '

'In everything he writes?'

'Everything I can come to terms with. He goes out into the mountains; he's fond of the Highlands and the Alps, and he's overawed by the staggering beauty of the scenery. Nothing untoward about that, you might say. So are we all unless we're blind or stupid. And to express this in fine words is not unusual either, is it?'

' "The sounding cataract/Haunted me like a passion." '

'That's Wordsworth, Tintern Abbey? It is understandable, and admirable, and expresses in language quite beyond the reach of any but a genius something of what we all feel in our small way. But with Stephen it is as if those mountains and waterfalls are there to highlight his own inadequacy, not only the inability to express their towering beauty, but the sense that all human effort is doomed to failure and that the grandeur of nature was created expressly to reduce, to diminish, to extinguish even all that humanity is.'

'That's pessimistic,' Mrs Mead said in a flat, unconvinced voice.

'It is. But there's a heroism in pessimism sometimes. A man placed in circumstances which are bound to overwhelm him, fighting impossible odds, standing against implacable fate, can act so courageously that we admire him, know we should not be so valiant. But that's not Stephen. There is built into man a ruin, a completeness of failure, an inevitability that everything serves to underline. Man is nothing, four score years of ephemerality, without prospect of eternal life, with remembrance of him on earth at best, at greatest, a thousand or two years in the millions of years of geological time.'

'In other words, we are nothing, even compared with pebbles.' Mrs Mead's face seemed long, pale, blank, dismal.

'Yes. We are distinguished only in that we are the sole creatures capable of recognizing our intrinsic littleness. That is the tragedy of mankind. Everything large or small, grand or microscopic, grave or jocose, lovable or hateful, exhilarating or depressing, brilliant or dim, everything serves to remind us of our own worthlessness. That is the only lesson to be learned. You fall in love, you earn millions, write a supreme poem, make

149

a scientific discovery that seems to revolutionize the world, live well, die greatly, but for all the good you do ultimately you might as well write your name in water in the desert, and spell it wrongly to boot.'

They sat, failing to see each other. Cups and glasses were unobserved. If Hillier had set out to sadden his hearer, he had succeeded. Finally Mrs Mead drew herself up, sat straight-backed on the settee.

'That is what his poems mean?' she asked, strongly.

'Yes, though I don't think he'd admit as much straight out.'

'He deceives himself?'

'Yes. We all do in order to make life comfortable or bearable. That is part of this inbuilt failure. Just as some people promise themselves an afterlife, or immortality for their products on earth, or instant fame or physical satisfactions. These hide from ourselves our utter inadequacy.'

Mrs Mead argued; she and Francis, her second husband, had enjoyed polemics.

'If we live,' she said, 'only seventy or eighty years and that's the end of it, we can still be successful inside that short period. And we can still have ambition and strive to rise above ourselves and impress other people or influence them, or even kill them, I suppose. That's not nothing.'

'I expect Stephen would agree. I'm not telling you he lives a life of constant depression. He tries to excel, I'm sure, as a scholar and a poet. He'd be a fool otherwise. He can't radically alter the nature of our condition, so he makes the best of it. But it does not shift this immovable bedrock of belief that man is bound to failure, cannot be other.'

'Do *you* believe that?'

'No, I don't. I'm agnostic in religion, and see man as a tiny speck in a vast universe. But what he is, he is, and that in itself is worthwhile, even great, or capable of greatness as well as failure. Stephen would argue that I don't regard it properly, *sub specie aeternitatis.*'

'And he's wrong?'

'Badly, in my view. His personality leads him to this view; some defect, or perhaps some virtue, makes him decide as he does.' Hillier rubbed his chin, desperately, slowly. 'As in my case. But what makes it worse in my eyes is that he won't come out with it plainly. A poet's job is to be clear: difficult he may be, but not opaque. I think he daren't admit what he believes, but I may be wrong. Or cynical.'

Hillier reached for his brandy. 'To the good fortune of both of you,' he said, too loudly.

'Thank you.' Mrs Mead spoke with an equal irony and touched her mouth with curaçao. 'Now I know what he's on with I'll be prepared. Perhaps.' She narrowed her eyes. 'I've been reading "In Memoriam E.L.B.", his friend Eric Butterworth. He admired him.'

'Yes. Stephen is capable of admiration.'

Hillier waved his hands in capitulation, not wishing to argue further. They finished their coffee and liqueurs; Elsie refused more, saying she'd be tipsy, and clearing the tray left him to his silence.

Downstairs, preparing briefly for the morrow, she considered the conversation only to conclude uncertainly that Hillier had said more than he intended.

Half an hour later as she went upstairs to her room, he came out of the study and took her in his arms. He pressed his mouth on hers in desperation, groaned, attempted to lead her from the landing to his bedroom.

'No, Adrian.'

Taken aback by his unexpected foray, she spoke without conviction.

'Elsie.' He held her strongly close, attacking her mouth with kisses.

'No, Adrian.' She tried to break away. 'It would not be right.'

'Right?'

'I have given my promise to Stephen. We can't continue with this.' The sentence seemed inadequate to her. 'I have given him my promise.'

Hillier still did not release her.

'Let me go, Adrian. That's enough.'

They staggered together into the balustrade.

'Steady,' he warned. 'You'll have us over.'

'Leave me alone.'

He did not answer, kissing her mouth. She jerked her head away, awkwardly powerful.

'Elsie,' he chided now. 'What's wrong?'

'You know. I've given my promise elsewhere.'

Adrian stepped back.

'You made love to me before, just before you accepted Stephen, even though your mind was made up.'

'I hadn't given my word.'

'That's splitting hairs. It won't harm Stephen; he won't know. And it will give us great pleasure, as it always has. We have loved each other, Elsie.'

'That was before. If you don't see the difference, then I feel sorry for you.'

'I could tell Stephen: "Elsie and I were lovers." '

'That's up to you.'

'He probably suspects it already.'

'I don't know. Tell him if you like.'

'He's an old man, Elsie, seventy-five. He might not want a sexual relation.' Hillier waited in vain for comment. 'Don't our times together mean anything to you? Do they?'

'Yes.' She whispered.

'Well, then.' He spoke as if to a reluctant child.

'It does not change my mind now. Now is different from then. I thought you at least would understand that. I have given Stephen my word.'

'So you feel differently about me?'

'I must do. By the nature of what I've promised.' Schoolma'am.

'I'm sorry, then.'

'So am I, Adrian. You must try to see it as I do. I'll go now.'

She pushed past him and he made no attempt to detain her. When she had closed the door to her stairway very quietly and with tact, he gripped the banister-rail and stared down. He tried after a time to shake it, but the spindles were too well made. No sound came from above. He bit his lip and made for his study and the whisky bottle.

152

·—— 15 ——·

'Invite your friend Mrs Fowler over when Stephen's here,' Hillier ordered the next day with a cheerful bluster. 'I'm sure she'd like to meet him again.'

'Thank you.'

They were wary of each other now.

Youlgrave rang most days, and occasionally wrote long, odd, straggling letters explaining himself. He had already cleared a room in the bungalow for her use, and hers alone. He would enter it after their marriage only on invitation. She could bring her own treasures, or they would furnish it from the shops, at his expense and her choice; the decision would be hers. The ceremony would be at his local register office. If she wanted a service of blessing in the village church, that could easily be arranged. He had altered his will in her favour. Stephen wrote in a smallish, neat hand, 'something like runes' he described it, and seemed both thorough and naïve. Expressions of affection for her were temperate, but letters and calls interested and excited her. She felt, she confessed to Alice, not as a prospective bride but as a child looking forward to a seaside holiday.

'Will you miss Adrian?' Alice Fowler.

'Yes. He's been very good to me.'

For the moment, at least, both believed it.

Alice came up to The Firs one midweek evening for a candle-lit dinner. The occasion was not altogether easy at the start. Elsie was busy with the preparation of the meal and Stephen sat preoccupied, disinclined to talk.

Giving her friend a hand between courses, Alice questioned.

'They seem to get on. I can see no reason why they shouldn't.' Elsie Mead.

'Adrian's not jealous?'

'You must be joking.'

153

Elsie brushed her reddened face with her fingers as she produced two delicious puddings, a crumble and a trifle.

'Fattening them up for the kill,' she said, unflatteringly.

Both men drank wine sparingly and the women not at all.

'We're all very sober,' Hillier chided.

'We're all getting old,' said Alice, the youngest.

'We've reached the age, at least, where happiness need not entail noise. I feel very comfortable. I am amongst people I like. I have just enjoyed a meal that was both plain and excellent. I have not overeaten. Elsie and I will marry shortly. I feel physically well. But I don't wish to shout about my good fortune, or make a public fool of myself.'

Alice was impressed and said as much to her friend. Elsie nodded, but did not commit herself. 'It doesn't do to boast.'

One afternoon later in Youlgrave's visit Mrs Mead and her fiancé were sitting on a seat in the nearby small park. They came out most afternoons, walked or drove and chatted. Lovers' weather enveloped them: sunshine, big clouds white as cotton-wool, a warm western wind. Sometimes Stephen dozed, but though his head dropped his back was stiff. If she raised a point in conversation he leaned out and bent forward as if to catch what she was saying with more interest from that awkward position.

'Adrian has a theory about your poems,' she told him.

'Adrian has a theory about most things,' he replied, not altogether pleasantly, so that she was uncertain whether to continue.

She outlined her ideas plainly once she'd set about the subject. Adrian believed, she said, that Stephen thought failure was inbuilt in man, but dared not say as much; hence the difficulty of his poems.

He asked a quiet question or two which she was able to answer. Now he did not seem displeased. His eyes twinkled and he rubbed his fingertips together as if he had some clinching argument ready.

'You find them hard to understand?'

'Yes, I do.' Then she added, as in pity, 'I keep reading them.'

'With no enlightenment?'

'Not yet.'

He scratched his face with great deliberation. Both sat

silent. Stephen appeared to her both content and nervous, as he cracked his fingers or disturbed the grey stubble on his cheeks.

'Well,' she broke in, firmly enough, 'Is he right?'

'One part at a time,' Stephen answered. 'In one sense, man is a failure. "The time of life is short," even given the few hundred years' extension of public remembrance. And this troubles serious people.' He smiled gently as if at the antics of a beloved grandchild. 'But no. I don't think that is the main drift of my poems. To be fair to him, there is some pessimism, I'd agree. I think I know the poems he has in mind. But,' here he held up a finger as if instructing an impatient crowd, 'what he says is more typical of Adrian's own view than mine. He sees all life, all endeavour, all success even as inevitable failure in the long run.'

Again there was a silence as Stephen stared down at the gravel between his feet.

'All critics concentrate on aspects that particularly appeal or refer to them. That's not improper. A poem consists not only of my words but of the experience brought to it by a reader. Therefore a depressive like Adrian will seize upon matters, ideas that apply to him. I don't altogether complain. Though the opinion will be limited, not dealing with the whole, it may be enlightening if the critic is a sensitive or learned or talented reader. So, no, to question one. It reflects more on Adrian's personality than on my poems.' He moved his body, shifted the bones. 'Of course I could be wrong.'

'I see. Don't you know?'

The finger for silence pointed again.

'And your second observation that my poems are written in a way that is meaningless because I am afraid to say outright what I believe.... You know, I don't find that offensive, as perhaps I ought. I don't think Adrian is arraigning my honesty. No.' Stephen seemed in no hurry to continue. 'No. But a poem is not like an order for a pound of pork sausages. There one can be simple because you and the butcher have agreed on a code that will make the transaction quick and painless. One could order the sausage in a way that the butcher would fail to understand: in grammes or in terms of chemical or physical analysis; but there would be positive disadvantage in that. But

155

poetry has more than a straightforward commercial exchange in view. It speaks of complication of emotion. It is expressed in words that will echo and re-echo. It has magic. Oh, yes, I know there are great poems of the utmost simplicity that also have these effects, but we are sophisticated these days. We are even sophisticated in the old Shakespearean sense of "adulterated". And my Alexandrian verse tries to take that into account.'

'Alexandrian?' she queried, in a murmur.

'Learned, erudite, dependent on other books, other poems.' He coughed, took her hand, leaned back. 'I do my best to make my poems statements of emotional importance, and if they need to be read and re-read time and again so much the better. Any messages as complicated as those I send are rightly not immediately available. I know the argument that will be levelled against my poems, that I am either too inept or too idle to work them out properly, but such is the fragmented nature of modern society and thus modern verse that I cannot do otherwise. Given my sort of talent, I would not expect anything else.'

'Will poems never be simple again?' she asked.

'They have never been simple, but I know what you mean. Yes, they may. The arrival of a change of sensibility or an outstanding genius, or more likely both together, might bring it off. Some people, not fools either, have expected it through the development of what we could call serious pop-music. I don't believe that.'

They sat together in Spring sunshine. Behind them in the back gardens of houses camellias, magnolias, flowering cherries, pear trees and yellow berberis massed multicoloured blossom. The air leisurely moved leaves, and warmly. The sun clung to walls; friendly shadows spread across new grass. The foliage on the avenue of lime trees tentatively appeared. Birds fluttered and twittered. A fresh, new world began to thrive.

'I like the sun on my back,' Stephen announced. They walked without hurry towards the car park, hand in hand. 'It doesn't worry you that Adrian criticizes my poems, does it?'

'No.'

'You don't think he was trying to warn you off marriage to me? On the grounds of my acute pessimism?'

'I don't know. I think he tried to describe you as you are, as

156

honestly as he could. And he made you seem that much more interesting to me.'

Youlgrave's visit succeeded beyond Elsie's imagination. Arrangements for wedding and honeymoon were easily made; every day the couple fell into discussions, not only about verse but music and theatre and politics and religion. To Elsie it was like the first months of her marriage to Francis Mead, a ferment of excitement. The two men were different. Stephen knew a great deal more, but was less confident in his assertions. He had a humbling contempt for all but minor certainties, but he surprised her, quoting the first Old Norse poem he had ever learnt at the age of eighteen, something about the howl of the wolf being unpleasant compared with the song of the sea-bird, from a wry tale of a woman who chose a husband from amongst the Gods by looking only at their feet. Her foolish choice fell on the sea-god because he had the cleanest toes, but neither husband nor wife could bear the home ground of their spouses.

'I hope that's not meant as a warning to me,' she said.

'Not really. Besides, my feet are nothing to write home about, washed or otherwise.'

Meals at The Firs were pleasant; Adrian Hillier went out of his way to make his friend's stay memorable. They saw a Priestley play at the theatre: *An Inspector Calls*; and went to a concert of Haydn, Debussy and Ravel that the men enjoyed and Elsie found dull. They took coffee one morning at the Royal, dined one evening at the Albany; and drank abstemiously, the males half-pints of beer and Elsie a fancy orange juice at a public house, the World's End, out in a village. The men chaffed each other; when Adrian referred to Stephen as the bridegroom, the older man judiciously declared that it was time the younger tried his luck again.

'Don't despair,' Hillier laughed.

'Despair is not my field just now.' Youlgrave put his arm round Elsie's shoulder in full public view; she stood proud.

On the dull day after Youlgrave's departure, Adrian said at lunch, 'You told Stephen what I had said about his poetry.'

'I did.'

'Why did you do that?'

'It seemed to come up naturally in the conversation.'

157

'It might have affected our relationship. Did you never consider that?'

'I told him,' Elsie answered slowly, each word counting, 'what you had said because I knew you were his friend, and that your opinion would have been honestly reached and was therefore worth considering.'

'People are very often touchy about their own bits and pieces.'

'He said he wasn't angry.'

'But was he? He didn't seem altogether pleased when he spoke to me.'

'Then I'm sorry.'

'I don't mind, Elsie, and I don't want to create trouble between you. I played it very lightly, but I could see that he wasn't exactly chuffed to be informed that he daren't write down what he meant. Is that what you told him? It's a very rough expression of my view, if you did. Almost a parody.'

Adrian sounded annoyed, not impolite, but wanting to hurt her, or making certain that he set her in her properly low intellectual place. 'Still,' he claimed at one point, 'the very difficult nature of his views possibly makes their unintelligibility a vital part of the message. The ineffable is, if I understand him properly, the result of absolute accuracy.'

'And how did you answer him?'

'I told him I'd need to think about it.'

'And did you?'

'I did. But I won't tell you my conclusion, or you'll report it to him.'

'In that case it must have been unfavourable.'

Adrian pursed his lips and dismissed her with the subject.

The exchange typified their present relationship. Adrian resented the forthcoming marriage, but continued to congratulate her on it. Mrs Mead walked the house uncomfortably, kept out of his way, dreaded the next hooded, sharp word. Frequently she called in on her friend, Alice Fowler.

Alice and Peter were to attend the wedding. Gerald Fowler, after much hesitation visited edgily on his family, had decided against a day off from Top Fare.

'It's not my sort of thing,' he told Peter. 'Besides, I don't know either of them very well.'

158

'There'll be champagne and claret,' his son informed him.
'I'd either drink too much or too little. I'm that sort of man.'

'You'd enjoy it once you were there.'

'I know.' Then, grimacing, 'Peter, you're getting to sound more and more like your mother.'

Elsie Mead seemed genuinely grateful for her friend's advice. Alice accompanied her round the shops to choose the wedding outfit.

'I'd wear my navy costume,' Elsie worried herself, 'but I feel I ought to dress myself in something completely new.'

'So you should.' Alice.

'Something new, something blue.' Peter, who unboylike loved to be in on this sort of conversation.

'It will all be very quiet,' Elsie said. 'I've no relatives, and Stephen's son is away. His two sisters will be there, and you and Peter. That's the sum total.'

'Not Adrian?'

'Well, yes. He's the best man, or the chief witness, or whatever. But he seems distant from it all, as if, as if . . . If he decided not to go at the last minute, well, it wouldn't surprise me.'

Their second topic of conversation was Gerald Fowler's refusal to transfer himself to Leicester.

'He sent them a very good letter,' Alice pronounced. 'It was very plainly written, and he laid it out exactly why it was neither to his advantage nor theirs to take up this "promotion".' Her voice made a mockery of the word. 'It surprised me. It was so very good.'

'You didn't need to alter it?' Elsie, sly.

'Just here and there.'

'And what did they say in reply?'

'Not a word. No acknowledgement. Nothing. Not polite really. You'd think that they'd have a standard note of thanks. They aren't good employers, at least in that respect. A few fourteen pences isn't much to them. It would be worth it in terms of saving on suspicion or resentment.'

Gerald's reaction had been much as she had predicted. For the first week he had been on the lookout for the morning mail, even postponing his departure for work when he spotted the postman down the road. Then followed a period of boasting, of bolstering his ego. Soon after this doubts began to appear; Gerald demanded to know, reasonably, what she thought, then more and more openly voiced his misgivings. The firm had it in for him now; they would be on the look-out for opportunities to make him redundant, to replace him with some young whizz-kid graduate more willing than he to toe the line.

'If that's the case, then you'd be better off with somebody else. Besides, they have to be careful these days. You could take them before a tribunal on the grounds of unfair dismissal. They'd have to pay compensation, and the publicity would do them harm.'

'It wouldn't do me much good, either.'

'But what advantage is there for them in giving you the sack?' she persisted. 'You've made a commercial success of your shop; it's a model of its kind; their inspectors have said so. You put in a great deal more time than they pay you for. They must realize that. You have good relationships with the staff. The Board gets a fat profit and not much trouble from your place, and they won't want to upset that. They're not stupid, Gerald. They know which side their bread's buttered.'

Alice realized that she'd have to repeat these consolations day after day. Insomnia and chronic dyspepsia troubled Gerald, but he set off smartly turned-out and on time each morning. She gathered that he feared now that the notice of redundancy would appear amongst the post delivered at the supermarket, but he opened up at eight-thirty with a clean well-shaven face. Though Alice did not like the disquietude this fear aroused at home, she felt admiration for her husband. He had not, like Adrian Hillier, retired to bed. She brooded on the effect of money. Tired herself, she woke more than once in the small hours to find her husband sitting by the bedside in the dark.

'What's wrong?' she had asked.

'Nothing. You go to sleep.'

'You'll catch cold.'

'I'm all right. I'm coming back into bed in a minute.'

These whispered colloquies frightened her. She decided to ring Adrian, choosing a time when her husband was out.

'Yes, yes.' Hillier sounded bored as he heard her out. She read him a copy of Gerald's letter of refusal and he hummed as if in appreciation. 'Yes, yes,' he repeated. 'They haven't replied? I'm not surprised. Not that I know anything specifically about this case. But most large concerns treat people of your husband's level in this way, like dirt. I know; that was my own status when I was working. They tell you nothing until it directly affects you. If they want you to make some changes they let you hear soon enough, but your job is to keep your small corner bright and efficient.'

'That's not altogether sensible, is it?' She remembered a former conversation.

'They must know what they're about. Advantages must outweigh disadvantages in their eyes. Or it makes so little difference they won't exert themselves.'

'Gerald's worrying himself that they haven't received his letter.'

'Unlikely. He can claim, in return, if anything happens, that he didn't receive their offer.'

'That's lying.'

'Strict adherence to the truth is about as useful in business as it is in politics. But I will ring the managing director's personal assistant if that's what you wish. Not that I shall get anything vital out of her. Nor from the MD himself. If your husband refused this promotion, they'll offer the job elsewhere. There'll be plenty of takers.'

'I'll be glad if you would.'

'Are you sure?'

'I know you said it wasn't altogether wise, but yes, I would.'

'First thing tomorrow morning, then. Will you come round to see me?' His voice sounded more animated. 'Tomorrow evening? I'll be glad to talk to you. Elsie's not much company these days. She has more important matters on her mind.'

'Can't you 'phone me?'

'You don't trust me. Alice, I'm so worn out, weary of well-doing, that you'll be quite safe.'

'It'll be only for a short . . . Half an hour.'

She fixed the time of her appointment and announced it to Gerald when he returned. Her husband frowned, sighed, complained that he'd have to stay in with Peter while she went 'gallivanting around', but she could tell he was relieved.

'He won't tell you anything,' he grumbled next day.

'He didn't promise he would.'

Gerald spoke with a glum, suppressed excitement like a man who had backed a much fancied horse.

Adrian Hillier opened the front door.

'To the minute,' he said, consulting his wrist-watch, cheerfully brisk.

'Isn't Elsie at home?'

'Yorkshire again.'

He led her upstairs to the study, inquiring about her health. He seemed especially cheerful.

'Can I get you something to drink?' he asked, settling her into a chair.

'No, thank you. I shan't stay long.'

'No.' He took up an easy position by the desk. 'Well, now.' He put finger-tips prayerfully together in front of his face. She wondered why he needed these comical antics. 'I rang Carol Spurgin, the PA to the MD.' He giggled at his pronunciation of these initials, but almost immediately straightened his face. 'She knew nothing, as I expected. But she's a remarkable woman, and she and I hit it off rather well.' He sounded self-satisfied. 'She promised me she would do some detective work for me and report before the day was out.'

He smiled at Alice, keeping her waiting. She was repelled by his smugness, but kept quiet.

'She came up trumps,' he continued, 'as I expected. If there is anything to be discovered, she'll find it. She rang round; she consulted the computers; she even quizzed her boss. They had received your husband's letter and as far as Carol and I could make out, took no umbrage. He didn't want that job and they didn't blame him. It was offered to him because they thought he might like a move. These large firms don't understand stick-in-the muds; they think everybody is bursting to be up and off somewhere else. They encourage the attitude. But your husband didn't want to accept, said so, and that's that. It will not be held against him.'

'They'll promote him, you think?'

'If something suitable appears. He's recorded in their books as hard-working, efficient, conscientious, all the rest of it. What he is not is a high-flier. He won't be placed in a key administrative position; they don't see him as a future member of the Board. But he's favourably regarded, and as long as he remains so they'll look after him.'

'Thank you.'

The pair sat in silence, facing one another.

'You're disappointed, aren't you?' he asked in the end. 'You don't think they appreciate your husband's good qualities. Is that it? I've told you what was passed on to me. Some of it, much of it for all I know, must be Carol's interpretation of what she's learnt. But she's very sharp, and has been with John Hancox a year or two now. She understands the way these people talk. If she took over from Hancox for the next month as managing director, nobody would notice the difference. A year now, that might be another cup of tea, but what I'm telling you is that she knows her way about and that's what she reported to me.'

'Thank you.'

'You would have liked something else, something more positive, wouldn't you?'

'I asked you,' Alice answered, 'to find out what you could, what was there. I wouldn't want fiction, however flattering.'

'But you think they underestimate him?'

'Gerald works hard, has made a success of his present place. Their own inspectors have said so. Profits are increasing.'

'That's true. That's the impression I tried to give you.'

'But he's reached his ceiling?'

'Possibly.'

'How do they know?'

'They don't. They guess or estimate. Trial and error. Pragmatism.' She hated the self-assured mockery in the voice. 'You've heard of the Peter principle, haven't you? You promote successful people until they reach a job they're incapable of doing properly, and there you have to leave them, willy-nilly.' He laughed, unpleasantly in her view; he was enjoying her discomfort.

The front-door bell rang. Adrian looked up, surprised.

'I wonder who that is. I'm not expecting anybody.'

'I must go now, in any case.'

They went downstairs slowly, he two steps to the rear. As they reached the ground floor, the bell pealed again.

163

'Somebody's impatient,' he said, back to his tired politeness.
He opened the door and Valerie Fitzjames breezed in.
'I've left my key behind like a fool,' she said and stopped,
seeing the visitor. Alice stared straight at Hillier, but exchanged a sentence with the young woman before the man let
her out. He seemed dumb.
The air on the drive blew clean . . .

When Elsie Mead returned from York she paid a long evening
visit to the Fowlers. Gerald kept out of the way, and Peter had
homework and a model Lancaster to complete.
Elsie sat refreshed. The first half hour she spent on an
account of the final details of the wedding, the honeymoon, her
move northwards. Stephen Youlgrave had proved efficient,
and there were no insuperable snags. She had decided on her
outfits and he had approved. He had invested in a new light
grey suit, 'cost the earth', and six shirts. 'I've been working on
the assumption that they'd see me out, but now there's a new
life coming. It won't do to be shabby.'
'I hope you don't mind, but I've arranged for Adrian to take
you and Peter up on the morning. He'll pick you up here. The
wedding's not until one o'clock, so you'll have plenty of time.
You don't mind, do you?'
Then Alice mentioned the Fitzjames incident, the girl's
remark about the key. 'He had the grace to look shamefaced,
I'll give him that.'
Mrs Mead smiled, nothing could throw her now.
'I'm not surprised,' she said. 'Not one jot.'
'I thought he'd given up his theatrical connection.'
'There's more than acting between that pair.'
She abandoned the ephemeral lovers quickly enough and
returned to her fiancé.
'He's a very interesting man, is Stephen.' She sat up
straight, compelling attention, as she might have done before
introducing an important subject in the classroom. 'He's very
quiet now, but you can tell he's been a bit uproarious. I would
like to have known him when he was a student.' She paused.
'As you did Adrian.'
'I don't connect the young man with the present material-
ization.' Deliberately hard.

164

'No. I don't know what to make of him either. He's like a child looking for his lollipop. Stephen's in a different category. In this last month or two he's started writing a new set of poems. He's very preoccupied by his childhood and youth. He goes back to the street where he was born. It hasn't changed a great deal, in fact, except in colours and doors and windows. Same bricks, same slates, same pavement slabs. And it makes him wonder what has happened to him, what this seventy-five-year-old professor has to do with the lad in short pants listening to neighbours and Sunday School superintendents . . .'

'Is he religious?'

'He says not in any strict sense. He attends the Anglican church now and then. But he's trying to work out what it is he owes, let's say, to his parents, or the chapel, or the very good teachers he was lucky enough to be under. "I have had instructors from primary school all the way to university who exactly suited my state of development." That's what he claims. "Not many have had that sort of educational fortune." "You mean," I told him, "that you knew how to use them." "No," he says, "I did not. They opened my ignorant eyes." He's remarkable, and modest. I could talk about him all day.'

'You're in love.'

Both stopped at that; it seemed improper. Elsie laughed half-heartedly.

'It's not like the feelings I had at twenty; I'll tell you that for nothing. But I'm excited and in a way satisfied, about going to live up there. We'll get on.'

'And is he head over heels in love?'

'No, he's happy enough to work on his poems every day. "I've something to look forward to," he says. "You've made time available to me." And he spends it writing and revising. Somehow it's made clear, "emotionally clear" are his words, what he was doing as a child. "I didn't know at the time," he says. "I went fishing or playing football or doing my homework, or obeying my parents and teachers and walking round on my own, or sorting out God or my bike-chain. I didn't understand it then; I never questioned it. Sometimes I was unhappy or bored or disobedient, but on the whole it was a fortunate, pleasant, successful childhood. I never questioned it. What I

165

did was what most people do; I got on with life, on lines laid down by other people. But now I see these fragments of memory which remain, and I must stress, Elsie, their broken nature, I see them now as preparations for this moment in the life of a seventy-five-year-old bridegroom-to-be." And do you know what I said to him?'

'No.' Both glanced in mischief.

'I said, "The child is father to the man." He was very pleased with that. He rubbed his hands and beamed. I thought, "Well, Elsie, you've hit the jackpot there." '

'And that was right, was it?' Alice.

'Well, no, it wasn't. Nothing's easy with him. He gave me a lecture on Wordsworth and how he lost his early vision. It was very interesting, but not what *he* meant. As far as I could gather, Stephen's every recollection threw light on the present situation, but the present situation was a movable feast, always on the change, and so each remembered piece of childhood – saying the collection piece on the Sunday School anniversary, passing the scholarship, paddling in the river, acting in a play – all led and, if I have it right, predetermined in some way the ever-altering pattern of present life. I wrote all this down in my diary. I was determined to tell you. He'd lost me by then. I did my best to hang on. "Is your death there, then?" I said. "Led up to?" "It must be," he answered, "but I shan't know in what way until it comes, and then my consciousness will have gone, so I shan't have any faculties for knowledge, so that question's finally unanswerable." "Unless there's life after death," I said. "I don't expect it," he said. "Blessed is he that expecteth nothing for he shall not be disappointed," I told him and we laughed, but in a very guarded way, as if a ghost had jumped out of the dark, dark cupboard.'

'And all this is going down into the new poems?' Alice asked, head cocked.

'Presumably.'

'Doesn't he show them to you then?'

'Well, yes, in a way. He does them on bits of paper first. They're like that, kept together by a bulldog clip, for months sometimes, and you never saw such a mess. Alterations and crossings-out, and circles round and arrows; you couldn't make any sense, or at least I couldn't. And then when he's fairly satisfied he copies the poem into a big notebook, an old-fashioned ledger really.'

'And that's the end of it? It's ready for a book?'

'By no means. He'll play about with that, and sometimes that leads to a new bout with the loose sheets of paper.'

'On a new poem?'

'Sometimes. Sometimes not, sometimes just getting the old one right a second time. I said to him, "You need to buy one of those word-processors."'

'And what did he say?'

'That the method could well alter the poem. And I said, "It might be an improvement," and I don't think he was any too pleased. Actually he went tiptoeing out to his study and fetched out a poem he'd done on a word-processor while he was staying with a friend who'd shown him the ins and outs. Of course, since he'd come back home he'd been fiddling with it. But I tell you this, I could at least understand the first few lines. It was about going to the athletic sports as a schoolboy, and seeing the tracks marked out for the hundred yards and the two-twenty.'

'It's all metres now.'

'I suppose it is. But he was torn between excitement and fear, and he knows exactly how far a hundred yards is today because of that.'

'Did he win?'

'*I* asked him, you can be sure.' Elsie smirked appreciation of a well-delivered query. 'He said in his own dry way that he wasn't as good as all that, but he sometimes got out of the heats and into the finals.'

'And that's how he sees himself now, is it?' Alice enjoyed herself.

'He didn't say so. He's sly. Jumps the other way to what you think. What he did finally write was more than I, my poor brain could cope with, but there we are. "Poetry," he said to me, "is like a Spring morning, immediately beautiful in its impact, but full of hidden joys that you have to search for." "What about Winter, then?" I asked him. "One doesn't usually poke about then." he said. "One's not attracted to discovery. It's too cold and grey and hard. Poetry must draw you towards itself."'

'You've had a high old time, I can see.'

167

'It suited me. Yes. I felt, "This is the life, Elsie Hooper. This is what you need." And I really did think of myself as "Hooper". That's unusual. And I think he tried to put things in a simple way for me. I don't think he'd done that before. "I don't mind losing absolute accuracy when I explain something to you, Elsie, because you know how to put first things first, better than I do."'

'That's nice.'

'I suppose it's a compliment. In a lopsided way. Frank, my last husband, loved explaining things to me. He was a typical teacher and missed his captive audience when he retired. Anything new or interesting he'd read, he'd tell me about. He'd be waiting at home all prepared with his bits and pieces. "Have you written them down for me?" I used to ask him. Oh, I'd pull his leg. He didn't mind.' Suddenly her face straightened; she snatched in a great noisy lungful of air and stood, dumb, stricken. 'He committed suicide in the end. Did you know?'

'Yes. I did.' How could Elsie have forgotten her confession?

'Did somebody tell you? Adrian?'

'I can't remember. I'm sorry.' Alice lied with grace.

'I didn't expect it, Alice.' She grimaced. 'If anybody said that to me I don't think I'd believe it, but honestly, it's true. I knew he was depressed from time to time; I knew he resented having to retire. But we were talkers. We didn't hide things, or so I thought. I also prided myself on keeping him going. He was failing . . . oh, only slightly, physically, and his memory wasn't always as sharp as it had been; he mixed things up as he never did when I first knew him. But I did not expect that, Alice. He'd kept this secret from me. Even when I look back, with hindsight, I can't recall hints. Nothing. Nothing. It hit me like a flying brick.'

Elsie's eyes were awash with tears. Her voice whispered steadily, but the face round the shadowed eyes seemed paler, less healthy.

'Frank was my ideal,' she continued. 'I wish I'd known him as a younger man, but then he was married to someone else. He always wore a trilby hat.'

Alice laughed sympathetically; Elsie dabbed at her eyes.

'We had some happy years. Or so I thought. He and Stephen would be about of an age. What a queer expression.'

168

'Frank had no children?'

'No. I wondered sometimes if that's what he had wanted from me. But one has to be careful with elderly parents. Perhaps I was too careful.'

'And Stephen's son?'

'Doesn't say much about him. He's abroad a lot, but they write in a friendly way. He's not married. He's not coming to the wedding, either. Can't or won't. Stephen doesn't talk about him. Makes me wonder. His only child. You or your husband would speak about Peter, wouldn't you?'

'When we're seventy-five? I don't know.'

Mrs Mead grew cheerful, drank her own health, bustled away. As Alice saw the stocky figure down the garden path, she remembered the slim prefect at school, with a fine bosom above the green sash of her gym-slip, issuing orders in the same flat voice, to be obeyed, but not considering her own importance. Once, out of the blue, she had allowed the passing Alice to hold her books while she used both hands to adjust her hair-slide. Did that moment in some way connect or prepare either or both parties for the coming wedding? Alice could have gone to the exact place on the corridor, if it still existed, where the incident took place, where she had stood in proud patience with Elsie's books. She had not dared to look at the titles. 'Thank you,' Elsie had said. 'That's kind of you,' and had laughed and swept away. Oh, the world.

Alice stared down the short length of her back garden. A wind had sprung up, and blossom blew from the trees thick as snowflakes or confetti.

'Don't leave this behind,' Gerald Fowler called out, holding up a cylindrical tartan box of confetti he had brought in the night before. 'First things first.'

Outside the late June morning began to burn brilliantly, and Adrian Hillier's car stood ready to take Alice and Peter to the wedding. The sky stretched cloudless; at eight-thirty the air already shimmered.

'A scorcher,' Gerald informed them all. 'Heard the five-to-seven forecast. No, Peter won't need a mac, even in Yorkshire.' He seemed inordinately cheerful, either at the imminent absence of wife and son, or sunshine, or the sight in the front seat of Valerie Fitzjames, suitably hatted for the ceremony. Alice had not realized that Miss Fitzjames had been invited.

'Would you like to sit at the front?' Valerie inquired, not shifting.

'No, thank you. You'll need to read the maps.'

'I think I can find my way to the A1.' Hillier stood resplendent and smiling on the pavement in a light grey herring-bone suit, slightly dashing for him. The effect was spoilt by an uncleaned pair of driving shoes, to be changed later. He had the air of a major-domo.

'The Great North Road,' Peter said, in excitement.

'Precisely.' Hillier's word sounded like a cheer.

' "O'er the dull plains of earth must lie the road," ' Gerald sang out. His wife had never heard him quote a hymn before in his life. The husband, wreathed in smiles, conducted his own performance.

Mother and son made a stately entrance into the back of the large, cool car. Their present, a kitchen clock Elsie had chosen, was stowed in the boot under Alice's wide-brimmed hat, navy with wide white ribbon and bow.

'Keep sober,' Gerald called, woodenly waving. The under-manageress would open the superstore this morning and milord would arrive half an hour late in deference to the nuptials.

'See you tonight,' Alice called. All four travellers gave perfunctory hand signals and they were away.

Stephen Youlgrave's bungalow was a place of quietness and order. Elsie was not to be seen; she had spent the night in a hotel, following some old superstition. When Stephen made a faintly critical reference to this, he was immediately checked by one of his sisters, a thin, formidable lady not unlike himself with a Manchester accent. 'She knows the proprieties, our Stephen, even if you don't.' The older sister, a stout woman, red-cheeked with bonhomie, a widow it appeared, nodded agreement. Both were a few years younger than their brother and very efficient with cups of tea or coffee, reviving chocolate biscuits for Peter, arrowroot and digestives for the grown-ups. They had laid it down that no alcohol was to be served before the ceremony.

'Lily doesn't trust me,' Stephen ventured to Adrian.

'Lily doesn't trust anybody,' the formidable lady replied. 'Especially on days like this.'

They talked in spasmodic bursts. The stout sister questioned Peter about school, told him how difficult she had found it to draw pictures for her classroom when she was a teacher, and led into an anecdote about her youngest son who had broken his leg on the first night of a scout camp by jumping over a fallen branch into a hole. Peter answered brightly; he had no idea whether Leonard's accident had happened last week or thirty, forty years ago, but he charmed the lady, enjoyed the company, was taken for an arm-in-arm walk round the garden.

'The names of the flowers this boy knows,' stout Mrs Keighley reported. 'It shames me.'

'Naming is about as far as his gardening goes.' His mother let him down.

'You can't expect everything. Nothing's perfect in this world.' The sister put an arm round the boy.

Valerie Fitzjames sat beautifully, talked to Stephen, to Lily, then to Alice. She did not seem to mind that Adrian paid little attention to her.

171

Outside a tropical sun scorched.

'It's just wedding weather,' Lily said. 'Our Stephen was always lucky. It rained at mine.' She wore no wedding ring.

'At least it didn't snow,' said her sister.

'If you will wed in December, what can you expect?' Stephen joining in.

The two women in charge of the catering arrived, donned aprons; a tall, mustachioed man helped them unload a van. The Youlgrave sisters disappeared to adjust their finery, and exactly as arranged telephoned Elsie Mead to say they were setting off to pick her up.

' "All glorious to behold," ' Hillier whispered to Valerie, but loud enough to be overheard by Alice.

When the bridegroom's party arrived at the register office, Hillier found no difficulty in parking. They crossed the road, walked fifty yards, mounted the steps. Elsie and the sisters were already inside, standing and serious. The bride wore a blue suit, a straw hat and carried a bouquet of small, dark red roses. She bowed her head to Stephen in a curious respectful, subservient greeting. The men went off to make inquiries while the women, still standing, clustered together. Elsie had grasped Alice's arm.

'Have you brought the confetti?' Peter asked.

'No. It makes a mess. But don't tell your Dad. We'll get rid of it.'

There was confetti, coloured hearts and flowers about the floor, and in one corner of the largish room a wedding party was laughing uproariously. Their bride, a fat girl, wore a white gown and a veil; her new husband's suit was electric blue. Children ran about; claps of sound swelled and died; their ceremony over, the guests waited for something in hysteric camaraderie; one could smell the alcohol from yards away. The five sober women and the boy tried hard to ignore them. Miss Fitzjames seemed infinitely more beautiful to Peter than that white-clad bride; so did his mother, for that matter. A parakeet screech of prolonged laughter and shouts wrecked ugly faces.

Stephen and Adrian returned.

'They'll call for us,' Stephen said, sotto voce.

'They're running to time.' Adrian. Both men wore carnations, as did Peter.

They had to wait for ten minutes, a period of broken silences, half-hearted sentences that no one seemed comfortable with. The riotous party suddenly upped and went; one moment the room bounced with sound, the next it lay silent, dusty green like an old-fashioned schoolroom in holiday time. Peter observed four other people, three women and a youth he had not noticed before, stranded like flotsam. A man in a trilby with a rose in his buttonhole pushed a wheel-chair into the room; its occupant, a middle-aged woman, hugged a ribbon-tied parcel in her lap.

'Where's our Glad?' the woman asked.

'We're very early,' the man replied.

'We always are.'

He manoeuvred the chair, sat down himself. Sister Lily took a seat, opining they might just as well be comfortable as think about it. Valerie and the boy joined her. All were relieved when the call came. Peter's mother took his arm; they brought up the rear as they crossed a high, dark corridor and into a large, still dim room. The registrar, at the table, smiled and took off his glasses. Lily, Elsie, Stephen and Adrian occupied the middle of the front row, the other four exactly behind them. Peter between Valerie and his mother enjoyed their perfume. Behind were at least three long rows of empty chairs. The registrar looked them over and quietly, quite beautifully, began to join Stephen William Youlgrave to Elsie Ann Mead in lawful matrimony.

'I'll tell you something,' Lily announced, once they were outside and the congratulatory handshakes and kisses had been exchanged, 'it was a lot nearer a proper wedding service than a good many I've attended in churches. Nearer the language of the prayer book.'

'I liked that registrar,' the other sister backed her. 'He saw it was serious.'

'I bet he was married in church,' Valerie said, and blushed as they turned inquisitive eyes on her.

The lady in the wheel-chair had gone but other groups, nervous and buttonholed, occupied the space with shining shoes and Sunday suits.

'They keep these places clean,' the plump sister told Alice. 'They're dull, but they've been dusted. Dust is human skin, y'know.'

'Charming,' said Lily in rebuke.

As they stepped outside the sun struck them with brash, blinding force.

'More like the Gold Coast than Yorkshire,' Hillier murmured.

They kissed, shook hands, patted shoulders again before the bride and groom were installed in the back of the sisters' car.

'Give them a chance to get away,' Hillier warned. In the road heat shimmered from the pavements, so that Peter sought for the shadow of houses. He could not get over the fact that the wedding had taken so little time, had made so dull a display. Those people with their loud laughs, their alcoholic shouts, their jokes and showy, cheap clothes had known better, had signalled the importance of what was happening. The still, small voice might do for God; humans need something noisier.

'Have you been to a wedding before?' Valerie asked Peter as they moved towards the car.

'No. My first time.'

'I wish there had been some music.'

'For God's sake.' Hillier turned round; he had been listening. ' "We'll gather lilacs in the spring again".' Alice walking in front with Hillier laughed out loud.

'You speak for yourself,' said Valerie pugnaciously.

The car's interior throbbed with heat like an oven, the seats almost too hot to touch.

'Leave the doors open for a minute,' Hillier ordered.

Alice and Valerie were conversing together, heads down. 'Do you and Adrian quarrel much?' Peter heard his mother ask the girl; he did not catch the answer. Hillier was fanning himself on the far side of the car.

They hardly spoke on the way to the bungalow. Peter missed the stiff-backed Stephen, although there had been plenty of room for him on the journey in. As the bridegroom had sat between the boy and his mother, he had sniffed from time to time, cleared his throat. His hair had been neatly parted, his suit ideal, his after-shave discreet. Now and then he had smiled uneasily down at Peter, had said something about

174

1oad-mending or town houses, had spoken ordinarily, but had seemed heroic to the boy, a cynosure, different from the humdrum, transcendental. A thin elderly man in a beautiful suit had gone with them, in their company, to his wedding and now was out of their reach. The boy wished he had the words to parallel this transformation, and his own sense of a happening as remarkable as this burning, blistering day. There must be some great phrase in a foreign language, some magnificence of expression to match his response. He crouched deeper into his comfortable corner, in silence, bemused.

'Lost your tongue?' his mother chaffed. 'You don't feel sick, do you?'

'I'm thinking,' Peter said.

White tablecloths glistened in the bungalow. The caterer's women smiled broadly from behind the feast; the Youlgrave sisters were already drinking tea.

'It's cooling on a day like this,' the stout sister said, ferociously red of face. 'You can keep your champagne.'

'Is it a good cup?' the pinafore asked.

'Excellent. Well, for this side of the Pennines.'

They broached the champagne; Peter was allowed a small glass and thought little of it. He enjoyed the popping of corks. They sat down to food that was superior and delicious: soup, cold meats, salad, trifles, cheese, fruits. The banquet was interrupted by a telephone call from Stephen's son in New York. 'It's about eight or nine in the morning there, I think.'

Adrian Hillier rose, said he could not let the occasion pass without boring them to death with a few words. He stood with one hand on the table, fingers splayed and spoke with a shy deference, but he had obviously learnt his speech by heart and for all his nervous manner was determined to deliver it. He congratulated both bride and groom; Elsie was perfect, he claimed, and so fulfilled the poet Stephen's long search for the ideal. Stephen attempted . . . no, worried words, to express his progress from early life to the present moment. Today the exact course of the line had been revealed. The scholar had met his ideal student; the teacher her poet-scholar. Elsie admired no one more than poets, and had lived out the belief by marrying one. He quoted Youlgrave: 'Eye, ear and nostril/

175

Provoke memory. Bravado/Shrills . . .' If Peter lived to be eighty, another sixty-six, sixty-seven years he would never forget this day because something remarkable had happened, Adrian said. He wished his friends much happiness, certainly, they all did, but he suspected something beyond mere felicity had begun, 'something inexpressible'. He coughed. The room expanded silently. Outside, the brilliance of sun tossed thrilling light among the shrubs. Adrian renewed his cough. 'With words like "inexpressible", I suppose I'm trespassing on the portentous, and before I overdo it I'll sit down. But I've hinted. Make of this great occasion what you will,' he said, voice strengthening, glass upraised. 'A marriage of true minds. Their health,' he whispered, and sat down as if suddenly paralysed.

They drank, the guests clapped politely and, impressed, said nothing for a moment. Adrian had done his work to good effect. Elsie Youlgrave bowed her head, meek but pleased, and concentrated on her plate. Valerie seemed removed, virginal, a child of quality. Alice thought the speech, though carefully assembled and exaggerating, eminently suitable. The sisters sat straight-faced, hard to please.

'What has Peter to say?' the stout one shouted out of the blue, breaking the silence.

The boy cringed. He wished to be left alone, but the adults wanted to open a space for him by their unwelcome invitation.

'God bless us every one,' said Lily, rescuing him. 'Is that suitable, Peter?'

'This is a marvellous day,' the boy answered, and made as if to go on.

'Thank you,' Youlgrave said. 'It is. Thank you.'

Valerie led the clapping.

'Well, now then, Stephen,' Lily chided, 'aren't we going to have a word from you?'

'I gave my word at the registrar's.' He leaned back.

'If a professor of English can't put a little speech together, then I for one will go home disappointed.' Lily.

'As usual,' said her sister, and blushed.

'Fill more glasses, then.' Stephen stood now. The caterer's women opened another bottle, and did the lavish honours. On his mother's instruction they did not include Peter. Stephen stood still, pursing his lips, staring into the distance, before recovering himself and placing a hand on Elsie's shoulder. 'We both thank you for your good wishes, your presents and your presence.' Peter thought that rather neat. 'I also would like especially to thank Adrian for his friendly speech. We enjoyed it; we approved its intention, though I do not know how near the truth it struck. He described my wife as perfect.' He lifted his hand to clap the shoulder he held.

Elsie raised her head. 'That's not true for a start,' she said. 'As you'll soon discover.'

'I shall work on his assumption until I learn otherwise.' He smiled sadly. 'He said also that Elsie loved poetry and that is true. Whether it is a good enough reason for marrying a poet I do not know. The words on the paper are not, except in a shallow sense, the man who wrote them. Of that I am certain.' He stared at the dazzle of the garden through the window. 'If we had weather like this through every summer we'd be able to grow Cox's Orange Pippins, but we can't.' He smiled ruminatively, hand still on Elsie's shoulder as if the slowly delivered sentence, protasis and apodosis, had made all clear. He took a minute sip at his champagne, barely wetting his lips.

'I'm with you,' shouted the stout sister, puzzled but pleased, raising her glass. 'Good health to you both!'

Glasses were lifted again to a murmur of congratulation.

'As to his other point that the child led inexorably to the man as one of the main concerns of my verse, I'll make a comment if I may, though I don't know if it is quite decorous to do so on an occasion like this. You must realize I'm an old pedant, and so probably you'll expect no better. I don't know if Adrian's interpretation is right. I would say, rather, if I am to descend to plain prose, that I am interpreting in the light of today, and a particularly happy light it is, those memories that remain.' He nodded round them, pausing at each face. 'Now that is off my chest, I thank you again on behalf of us both for coming, for your good wishes, for your love and friendship. We hope to see something of you here, or elsewhere if we decide to move. Thank you all.'

He sat down and they applauded with their hands without comment, as befitted the dignified tenor of Stephen's speech.

After a short period of silence, the stout sister called, 'I'd like to hear the bride's voice.'

They looked at Elsie, who rose immediately and without flurry.

'Thank you,' she said. 'You won't get much speechifying from me. I can tell you I am very happy, that this my new husband is a good man, but you know all that. The food,' and she turned to the caterer's women, 'is excellent, and I hope you're doing justice to it. I thought I shouldn't be able to manage much above a mouthful, but I've had my share. It shows how little I know about myself.' She looked down at Stephen. 'Is that good or bad?' She put a hand affectionately for a few seconds on his head, a girlish unexpected touch. 'I don't know what I've done to deserve such happiness, but I'm not complaining. Enjoy yourselves. Eat, drink and be merry. Oh, yes, I know how that goes on.' Her face twisted into mischief. 'Tomorrow we'll be sober. Thank you.'

They shouted this time and Adrian banged the table, out of character.

'Rose,' he called. 'How about you?'

'No fear,' said the stout sister. 'I'm too shy.'

'Lily, then?'

'I've more sense. Elsie's said it all.'

They began as was proper to feed again, and then three of the guests wandered out in the garden in the incandescent heat. Valerie and Alice walked slowly together, both now carrying glasses of much-iced orange juice. Peter occupied himself in silence swinging gently on a strong, white wooden gate. Indoors Adrian Hillier talked to the sisters and Elsie, delighting them with his babble. Stephen listened, his chair slightly withdrawn from the rest. He seemed tired, paying as much attention to the caterer's assistants clearing the table as to Hillier's monologue.

When the younger women returned from the dazzle, coffee was ready and they drank, but without panache. Half an hour's cat-nap would not have come amiss all round. The elders were subdued.

Lily now sat by her brother, apart. 'I think this is what heaven will be like,' she said. 'Just a bit too much for me. Too hectic.'

'Do you remember Douglas Whitworth?'

'The son of the minister at the old Wesleyan Chapel on Sale Road?'

'Yes. He was at Oxford two years ahead of me. Read chemistry. He used to say his idea of heaven was singing tenor in "Be present at our table, Lord" to the tune Rimington as the grace at a Methodist choir supper.'

'Is he still alive?'

'No, he was killed in a car accident on the continent not long after the war. On holiday. He held some very responsible job in Boots' research labs. Married a girl from Hunstanton.'

'Oh. I didn't know him all that well; he was a lot older than I was.'

'Anyway, that's what he used to claim. More than once. At an old boys' dinner at Oxford, I remember. He longed for a meat-and-potato pie with thick gravy. Made a marvellous performance out of it.'

'Well, he knows now.'

'Knows what?'

'About heaven.'

'He no more believed in the golden streets than you do.'

'Our Steve.' Lily's tone caressed him; she approved of men who knew and spoke their minds.

'What are you two whispering about?' Rose shouted.

'The dear, dead days beyond recall,' Lily answered back, sharply, 'and the choir at Sale Street Methodist.'

'Good God, girl.' The stout sister's mouth gaped. 'What next?'

Stephen Youlgrave's eyes were half-closed as he clutched the seat of his chair, paying no attention to the rest. Very quietly he was singing to himself:

> Thy creatures bless, and grant that we
> May feast in Paradise with Thee.

His voice was thin, but the words distinct and on 'Paradise' he cocked his head as if to hear again the gently swelling harmony of long-dead tenors and basses.

'Ay,' The stout sister made much of the one syllable, in a silence.

179

'The champers,' said Adrian.
'Ssh.' Lily was having no nonsense. Elsie, alongside now, took Stephen's hand.

'Đaer waes hearpan sweg
Swutol sang scopes,' he intoned.

Then Stephen recovered, nodded at them, reassuring them that his moment was complete, that he recognized rationality again. He laced his arm through Elsie's and looked his guests over with pride.

'Drink up,' he commanded. 'Elsie and I won't know what to do with crates of champagne.'

Again guests took to the garden. Alice Fowler walked round with Adrian who had donned dark glasses.

'Have you enjoyed yourself?' she asked.

'I'm tipsy, if that's what you mean. Don't worry. Valerie will drive us back.'

The garden stretched large and neat but unremarkable. The long lawns were freshly mown with edges clipped; the borders proffered bright flowers amongst taller ordered delphiniums, lupins, roses. At even distances new cherry trees flourished.

'This is well looked after, isn't it?' Alice.

Adrian stared his rueful lack of sympathy. 'He'll have a firm in. Bedding plants. Municipal style. You can see they had the hoses on this lawn yesterday.'

'You don't approve?'

'Who am I to complain? I'm no expert. But what he has here is order and decency, not a real gardener's series of sprung surprises and secret corners. He can walk here, and see his flowers and the swathes in his grass, and not be bothered if the birds do damage because somebody else will sort it out for him. A man will appear with his lorry and his machines. Regularly.'

'I see. I thought gardening was his hobby?'

'He wants a place to walk round and not be violently or unpleasantly distracted so that he can carry on with his real concerns. I doubt if he realizes that he's been provided with the epitome of suburban banality.'

'And his real concerns?'

'Scholarship, poetry. I don't know his order of priority. But don't run away with the idea that he's a stuffed shirt or a pedagogue. He feels with an immense surging power. He's emotionally very deep and very volatile, I'd guess. You saw that in there. But in limited fields. Literature explodes inside him, uproots him. And it needn't be "a chorus ending from Euripides"; that hymn removed him from his wedding to some earlier time, and evoked emotion which expressed what he thinks or feels today's ceremony means. He was transfigured. That grey old man sitting there humming to himself was not only different from me and you, that's not too hard or unexpected, but from himself. Momentarily he was transformed because he brought together the powerful feelings of many periods of his life into one end at one moment. There were a dozen, fifty men and boys, all Stephens, fused into that one old heart. I must be drunk.'

'And what will Elsie do about it?'

'Do? Do? Elsie?'

He took a few comical, staggering dance-steps forward, arms out wide.

'I'll tell you,' he said. He stood like a scarecrow. 'She probably won't even notice. She'll provide him with good meals and a clean house and warmth in bed.'

'And that's not what he needs?'

'I wouldn't say that either. He's so set in his important habits, those that produce the poems, that quiet and calm and order elsewhere can't but do good. And Elsie is not a bad-looking woman.'

'You mean they'll have sex?' Alice giggled.

'It's not physiologically impossible. I don't suppose his libido is as strong as it was fifty years ago . . . and he's been ill. But, yes, it's possible. I would like to think it was.'

'Why do you say that?'

'They are a marvellous pair. You knew Elsie at school, didn't you? What was she like?'

'Grown-up. Or so she seemed to me. Adrian, I thought you'd marry her. You're much of an age.'

'She's a few months older. It never crossed my mind. Quite honestly.'

'Did it cross hers?'

'Ah, now then, Alice. That's a good question, as they say. It's

181

possible, I suppose.' Hillier quickened his pace, turned left at the end of the lawn without slackening, as if to cover embarrassment. 'I'm not the marrying sort.'

'You've been . . .'

'Oh, yes. Once. I did my best. It might have been different if I'd married you.'

'Rubbish.'

'I'm not so sure. I loved you, Alice Hogg. But I was in no position to marry. I had to get through university, make a start somewhere, impress my parents. I was a failure to my father then and through my life. I'd had all the advantages he'd never had, and still made no sort of mark. Perhaps I should have stood up to him. Marrying you might have done the trick.' He breathed comically deep, at a standstill before a staked delphinium, legs a-straddle. 'Made a man of me.'

'You never gave it a thought, even considered it.'

'That's not true.'

'You didn't say a word.'

'How could I?' Adrian spread his hands, then rubbed his thighs. 'I'm a philanderer, I know. And it's quite possible that if I'd been your husband I'd have been the same. It's my way of getting my own back at the world.'

'At the expense of women,' she pressed.

'No. They have found some pleasure.'

'You terrified me, I'll tell you that.'

'Yes.' He half turned away. 'Yes, I'm sorry.' He pulled himself together. 'You wouldn't have put up with my infidelities, would you?'

'I don't know. It would have depended on the circumstances. There might have been children to consider. But certainly I wouldn't have liked it.'

'Any more than Suzanne did. She was a decent woman. I'm a failure, Alice. Everything I touch goes wrong. If there's a choice to be made, you can bet I'll make the wrong one.'

Stephen stood in the distance at the back door. Elsie and the sisters were on the patio. Valerie and Peter walked down the garden together.

'What are you going to do, then?' Alice asked.

'Struggle on. I've put everything off until this wedding. I

182

wonder now if it wasn't in the hope that it wouldn't take place. I shall go home, and sulk. And beg you to come round and comfort me.'

'You're wasting your time there.'

'I do nothing else.'

'Can't you take up some voluntary work?'

'It would come to nothing, like my spell at the Phoenix. I've just enough of my father in me to make me impossible to work with.'

Valerie and Peter passed them, greeting them but not stopping. Alice watched the retreating backs.

'You're not serious about that young lady?' she asked.

'No. She has plenty going for her, but no.'

'She has a lot more about her than I had at her age.'

'I don't think so. You underrate yourself, Alice Hogg.'

'Fowler.'

'Fowler. I have never forgotten you.'

'You just annoy me, talking like that. You made no attempt to contact me after you left the university.'

'I was always a fool.' He waved his arms, hopelessly.

'Adrian, you'll win yourself no credit with me by trying to make out that things were different from what they were. You took advantage of my innocence or inexperience, but you had other girls. I knew about that at the time. I suppose you were learning, but at my expense and that of others.'

'It's done you no lasting harm.'

'That remains to be seen.' She spoke with a subdued vehemence. 'You terrified me, even when I thought I was in love with you. I kept away from men for at least three years. It was eight before I married. You left me in a mess, but perhaps that was your inexperience. I don't know.' Alice pulled herself up. 'We've both had too much champagne, and we're both speaking out of turn. Let's go back.'

'I'm sorry.'

She led the way to the bungalow.

'You two have been having a right old chat,' Elsie greeted them.

'The old days.' Alice smiled back.

'The good old days?' Elsie.

183

'Couldn't be otherwise,' Adrian answered, spirits revived, 'with such a cast.' He bowed exaggeratedly towards Alice.

'There's no end of food left,' Elsie warned them. 'Stephen and I'll be stuffing ourselves for a month before we can go away.'

The newlyweds, Alice knew, were to spend a week and a half at home before they set off on a cruise in northern waters. Elsie had told her, face serious, 'If there's one thing we must not do it's rush ourselves. We've plenty of time. Or if we haven't, we must act as if we had.'

Valerie had disappeared. Adrian was charming the sisters. Elsie and Alice stood silent, solid, undrunk, happy. Stephen Youlgrave crossed to where Peter was crouching to straighten a displaced small paving slab. The boy stood, brushing dirt from his fingers.

'I'd like to thank you for coming, Peter. It must have been dull for you. I don't think you'd have much difficulty in finding more entertaining ways of spending a Saturday afternoon. But Elsie, my wife, is delighted to have you and your mother here on our big day. Old people are just as excitable as young, you know. We're better at covering up, that's all. Or perhaps we are more fearful of consequences. But it's good to see you. I like young faces. Of course, to someone as old as I am, your mother is young. But there's you and Miss Fitzjames . . . Valerie. If I remember anything, it will be the sight of you two striding down this garden, as if your lives depended on it.'

'Yes, sir. She does walk quickly.'

'You like her? Get on well with her?'

'Oh, yes.'

Youlgrave nodded, to Peter's puzzlement as if some difficult problem had been broached and solved. The old man had his hands up, as in prayer, and was moving his chin raspingly between the tips of his fingers.

'It's a scorching day,' he said.

'It's suitable,' Peter answered gravely. 'I don't think I shall forget it.'

'Thank you.'

An ex-colleague of Stephen's called in on the offchance, stood embarrassed when he discovered the nature of the celebration, was made welcome and stuffed with left-overs. A

184

rotund, bald, red-faced man, he played, beautifully, a Mozart sonata movement to them on the piano before setting off to collect a friend from the university. 'A Fellow of the Royal Society,' Stephen informed them. 'A geneticist.' The guests tried to appear impressed. 'He's one scientist, there aren't many, who has in my opinion altered the real quality of our life.' Nobody took him up on that, and the house seemed quieter.

The Beechnall party made the first move to go home.

After kissing and hand-shakings Adrian, now nearer sobriety, pronounced that he had never spent a happier day.

'It's not finished yet.' Elsie. 'It's only four-thirty.' His face fell. The rest gabbled.

Valerie drove; Adrian slumped in the front seat; Alice dozed for a short time, but Peter kept his eyes open for the skimming trees and fields, other travelling cars, the birds, the sun.

Talk was desultory, and when they arrived at the Fowlers' house and Alice asked Valerie and Hillier in for a cup of tea, the man refused.

'Thanks,' he said, 'no. The bright day is done. We can't prolong it, can we, Peter?'

'Funny man,' Alice said from the pavement, watching the departing car. 'I'll be glad to take these shoes off.'

·——— 17 ———·

The summer passed.

Peter continued to trek up to The Firs on Saturday mornings, though the rooms stood dull without the old Mrs Mead, the new Mrs Youlgrave. Often he had to let himself in and work out for himself a rota of necessary tasks; if he wanted coffee or lemonade, he foraged in the kitchen. Once, Mr Hillier had not only left no instructions but no money, but the boy conscientiously completed his duties. Mrs Mead had trained him well, but now the house was gloomy, silent, sombre in spite of sunshine outside, when he had the place to himself.

He excelled in the school examinations at the end of June, soon after the wedding, was top in English and biology, third in maths, and in double figures only in geography. 'Old Bas doesn't like me,' he grumbled. 'Why not?' his father probed. 'Awkward questions he can't answer.' His father nodded in surprising agreement: 'Far too many people like that about for my liking.'

In August the Fowlers had a week in Marbella, swimming and idling. Gerald almost against his will enjoyed himself, talking to people, acting as a kind of hilarious host at their part of the dining table. To his son he seemed a different man, English to the bone, but with a flow of astonishing Spanish, witty, quick with the right word, good at bodily caricature, small, silent flashes of acting which exactly took off waiters, pompous idiots, yobbos, Spanish policemen, English drunks, tour guides, managerial inefficients. Young people eyed him with some caution, but the middle-aged, and not only the staid, sought out his company. He had a word for them all, and in his blue shorts acted like a modest generalissimo after a successful war. Much admired.

'My word, Alice,' one woman confessed, 'your husband's clever. He knows his way about.'

It was no more than the truth.

'We'll have a fortnight next year,' Gerald announced, back home, tanned and ebullient.

'Careful, now. I might hold you to it.'

'Where did my Dad learn Spanish?' Peter asked.

'He did it for "O" level. And I think he went there a time or two before we were married.'

'He's never said anything.'

'There's more to that man than you give him credit for.'

Alice received two postcards from Elsie, Peter one from Stephen, aboard the cruise liner. A long letter from Yorkshire announced that the Youlgraves were flying to the United States, to visit relatives, to see Niagara and for Stephen to lecture in Chicago at the beginning of the new term, much earlier than ours. Elsie wrote as if she'd been a university wife for years. Both were well. The cruise had been everything they expected, though their puritan souls, Stephen had said, felt guilty about the leisure and luxury. They thought they'd stay in the bungalow at least over the winter; it was most comfortable. Elsie had had a real 'row to end rows' with the gardener, but thought she had sorted him out now. 'He saw I was a different proposition from Stephen. He threatened to down tools and leave, but I just told him that was up to him. He's still sulking.'

Mrs Youlgrave was surprisingly open about her husband.

Stephen was a man who was used to working hard, and regretted that he no longer had the energy for a full day's labour. This had led him into a state of hypochondria; he laughed about it, said his doctor encouraged him in foolishness, laid it down that the word was a plural form like agenda, but had a box full of tablets that he swallowed at all hours of the day. ' "It's mere superstition, I know," and he had laughed and tapped his medicine chest. "That's my Kiblah," he'd said. "What's that?" I asked him. "It's the point in Mecca towards which pious Muslims face in prayer." He loves these unusual words. I say to him, "Do you keep going through the dictionary to blind me with science?" and he says something like, "That's a good use of science in its old sense." He's always coming out with bits like that about why we pronounce "schism" as "sizm" and "schist" like "shist". It's a real treat for me. Like lessons from "Pop" Peters at school, without the boring bits.'

She made her husband take a walk with her every day if it

was fine, and they'd had a lovely evening with a bonfire. Stephen had acted like a schoolboy on holiday, dashing about with his stainless steel fork. 'Sometimes I don't think he ever had a proper childhood. I thought I was a sober-sided frowsty old stick, but we laugh and lark about as if we're daft. It's a good job the neighbours can't see us.'

Elsie enclosed photographs of the wedding, and Alice and Peter working through them argued their merits. The mother declared that Stephen was most handsome, but Adrian, as usual, looked as if he was trying to sell somebody something. The bride could not be other than herself, they decided; no amount of dressing up would alter, improve or worsen the substantial figure, the stolid set of head and shoulders. She was her own woman, always. Valerie stood prettily, at ease, very young and happy, but the sisters had become obscure, stereotypes of fat and thin. 'You're the most beautiful of them all,' the boy confessed to his mother, and his mother kissed him, wondering if he spoke the truth or merely flattered.

No address was enclosed, so that Alice could not reply.

'I'd like to tell them about Marbella.' To Peter.

'And the miraculous change in Señor Fowler?' They laughed out loud.

Gerald was ordered south for a three-day management course at Watford in the same week that Peter began school.

'What's this in aid of?' his wife demanded.

'That I don't know.'

'It hasn't happened before.'

'They suddenly get these brain-waves. It'll be some new director of training they've appointed who wants to make his presence felt.'

'Is it a good idea?'

'I shan't know until I've seen what they do.'

He took out the carefully unfolded envelope from his briefcase. The letter was short, not well set out, the signature above the typed name – H. R. Coombes – a foolish scribble.

'They could do with a short course for typists,' she said.

'I agree,' Gerald answered. 'I'll tell 'em so.'

'You be careful.'

' "As wise as serpents, as harmless as doves". The Bible. It's what old Clarkey in the junior school used to tell us in assembly.'

He worried, as she knew he would, about which shirts and ties to pack, which suit to travel in, how much money to carry. He polished the travelling bag and packed all his shoes, three pairs. He decided against a hat, kissed his wife goodbye and shook hands with Peter.

'Surprise and delight them, Dad,' the boy said, quoting one of his teachers.

'When I'm not dodging the flak.'

Gerald slipped away to the station, by bus not taxi, a cunning expression even in the shape of his back. To Alice he looked vulnerable.

When he returned home he acted the unimpressed, provincial shopkeeper.

'Well, it could have been worse. They didn't tell me anything I didn't know or couldn't work out for myself about shop management. The best was an accountant who gave us an idea how they determine the profitability of a store. You'd be surprised at the difference in overheads. Rent and rates in the south are ridiculous. A shop in London of our size, doing our business and charging our prices, would hardly make a profit. In a way we carry them. Well, not altogether, you know. They do all right. This man was very good, I thought. Clever and thorough. "You can see why we accountants get ourselves a bad name," he told me. We had quite a long talk the evening he was there.'

Some stuffed-shirt, who made a poor impression on everybody for a start, had informed them that they had been called on this course, at considerable expense, because they were promotion material: 'We want men of ideas. Don't be afraid of speaking up. But I warn you. You will be watched all three days, and assessed.'

'Did you shape well?' Alice asked.

'Can't say. I couldn't make out what they wanted. I spoke out according to my size, especially in the seminars.'

'Were the others any good?'

'Some were, some weren't. The usual handful of gas-bags poking their oar in. One young chap, in charge of this new DIY centre they've opened in Finchley, was very quiet but, my

189

word, he had all the info at his finger-ends. He gave a very interesting little lecture on shop-arrangement. Impressive. We all had to give these lecturettes.'

'What was yours on?'

' "Display." '

'Did it go down well?'

'One or two said as much afterwards. I told them what we did in Mansfield Road, and what the principles were, and why we couldn't make what seemed obvious improvements, and how I used what I called "local amenities". Jane Keys and her posters; I'd taken some photographs with me.'

'Were they impressed?'

'They seemed to be. The leader of our group asked some awkward questions.'

'Which you could answer?'

'When there were answers to be given.'

'And at the end of the whole course, did anybody say anything?'

Gerald knew what she meant.

'No. A final pep-talk from some headquarters man on the firm's plans for expansion. A cup of tea, and that was it.'

'Was it worth it?'

'Yes. You saw what you were up against.'

She judged he was not dissatisfied.

'Did you know anybody?'

'No. I met the man who had Mansfield Road before me. He has this new place in Hull. From what he hinted, I guess it's a bit of a struggle. He wasn't going to say as much.'

'You don't want to follow him there, then?'

'I don't want to follow him anywhere; his arrangements down here left something to be desired. But we'll see.'

His hopes ranged high. She heard him lecture Peter on the value of solid work, 'the foundation of a successful GCSE', in the middle school. 'It seems a long way off but it isn't. It'll be on you like a thief in the night.' (Clarke again?) 'Acquire the right habits.'

A letter from America warned that the Youlgraves were extending their stay for a further month. Stephen's lectures had been really appreciated. Elsie had been made most welcome, had taken part in some dramatic excerpts from Shaw and Pinter and Stoppard, 'not my cup of tea at all', and all on her own had given the students an evening of readings from Wordsworth, Keats, Tennyson and Walter de la Mare. That had been most successful. They had received a great deal of private and lavish hospitality; the Americans put themselves out, but she missed English gardens. They had plenty of room, but didn't know what to do with it. The weather was superb, and colours of the fall incredible. She inquired about Peter and said she had received a letter from Adrian. This made Alice wonder how he had found the address. Probably he had just banged a letter off to some university Stephen had mentioned and the authorities had sorted it out that end. The Youlgraves would be back about the beginning of November unless they had another change of plan.

Elsie ended, 'I have talked more in this last month than in the last twelve, but I'd give anything to sit down over a cup of tea in those armchairs of yours, with Peter wandering in and out and your husband totting up his books somewhere upstairs, and exchange a few words with you, dear Alice.' The tone made her friend suspect that Elsie was underemployed, or home-sick, or acquiring transatlantic habits of exaggeration, so that Alice sat down after the evening meal for two nights to write a long account of English provincial life.

In November, after three further postcards and a silence, Elsie rang up to ask if she could come down to stay with the Fowlers for two days.

'Good idea,' Alice answered. 'They owe me some holiday. So we can skid about in my car and you can give me all the news. But what about Stephen? We can put him up.'

'Thanks, but he's going to lecture in Scotland. It'll do him good to have a few days on his own.'

The weather seemed surprisingly mild when Elsie arrived about noon. The two women talked hard, ate omelettes, took a stroll round the district, staring into shop-windows enjoying themselves.

'This is what I miss, living in the country,' Elsie confessed. 'Shops. I don't want to buy anything, just feast my eyes.'

She was full of America, a wonderful country. She described the honeymoon cruise, the northern seas, the everlasting air of party-going.

191

'It must make all this look very drab?'

'Not at all. To tell you the truth, it's brighter, more spick-and-span, more prosperous than I remember.'

Stephen was in great form, she reported, had a new lease of life. He could be really funny about people, especially when he'd had one or two. 'I thought he was prim and proper, but, oh dear, no. And sharp-tongued.' She really had enjoyed his lectures. Even if the basic plan was the same, he always varied the content according to the audience. 'The Americans love people instructing them.' They'd queue up, young and old, when he'd given a talk to ask him questions. Stephen wished he'd gone to the New World as a young man to work. ' "You wouldn't have met me, then," I said. "Is that it?" "Elsie," he answered, "I married one American, and it didn't come off." '

Elsie inquired whether her friend had seen or heard anything of Adrian Hillier.

'Not a thing. I had the impression he'd disappeared to London.'

'He's not attempted to get in touch with you?'

'Not a word since your wedding.' Alice grimaced. 'Funny man.'

'At the wedding he said to me, "I should have married Alice Hogg." '

'Well, he's imaginative. I'll give him that.'

'Do you mind if I ring him up when we get back?'

Hillier was at home, and answered. He invited both women up for coffee on the next day. He claimed to be perfectly well, quite happy, not busy.

Gerald Fowler made an unaccustomed fuss of Mrs Youlgrave, though Peter was offhand. Never less than polite, the boy answered the inquisition about schooling, but shortly, as if he had more important concerns. His father was allowed a long period of complaint about the higher management of Top Fare; indeed he excelled himself with sharp malice and innuendo, so that his son stayed behind to hear the philippic. Señor Fowler had reappeared. Elsie encouraged him with some second-hand anecdotes from Stephen about the squabbling over resources or status amongst the university hierarchy, and the pair reached conclusions on the effects of power-seeking. Alice laughed and her husband opened a bottle of good sherry to prolong the atmosphere.

Next morning the two women drove up to visit Hillier. It had been decided that Elsie should stay another night, and that she would leave immediately after breakfast. Alice, delighted if dazed by the profusion of talk in her usually laconic house, felt that she was doing her friend good, sorting her out, allowing her to come to terms with her new life by describing it. She was not exactly sure that Elsie was altogether happy, though why she had such reservations she did not know.

Their exchange on the way to The Firs was typical.

'Stephen says' – too many of Elsie's conversations began thus – 'that one of the great reliefs of growing old is that you no longer have to tell lies.'

'He would be about the last person I'd accuse of being a liar.'

'Well, that's what he says. And also that most people lie out of vanity, to put themselves in a better light. He could forgive himself, he says, for lying to escape from an awkward situation, but to do it for mere cosmetic purposes puts a gloss on his character that hardly bears thinking about.'

'Do you find . . .?' Alice broke off, unwilling to commit herself.

'Find what?'

'That he lies to you?'

'No. No more than I to him. We might polish the truth just now and again.' She giggled, and laid a hand on Alice. 'Just stop here. Yes, anywhere. At the side of the road.'

Alice did so, and they sat under a huge lime tree.

'We have a minute or two.' Elsie sat back, folding her arms. 'My word, it used to be a drag up this hill with my shopping-trolley.'

'Surely you used your car?'

'Not always. If I had time to spare, I'd do it for the exercise. I was always a fool where my own advantage was concerned. It's a beautiful road, this, with the trees. I've seen squirrels up and down in spite of heavy traffic. Stephen has a picture of big lime trees with a mass of cow-parsley, and buttercups and clover, done by some man in a park in Leeds, I think. "It's the end of Spring," he said, "and beautiful." "The end of Spring's the beginning of Summer," I said. "Elsie, you're incorrigible."'

'What did he mean?'

'I think beauty to him is . . . means the ending of something, decline, decay, falling off. It's the sadness that makes the loveliness. "Everything is ephemeral."'

'He sounds a real pessimist,' Alice ventured.

'He isn't, really; that's the odd thing. He's glad to wake up in the morning, and still to be able to do the jobs he's set himself. I think he's grateful to me; he thinks he's looked after now, though he sends me off to York every Friday for a shopping expedition, and he prepares the dinner. No, life holds something for him still. He calls it "a walk down a darkening street". Look, those trees have still some leaves left. He'd love that.'

'You're good for him, Elsie.'

'I hope so. So far. He's glad to talk now and again. And neither of us is afraid to be quiet. And he loves to come in to a meal he likes but hasn't expected. Frank was the same.'

The two women sat in silence.

'I tell you what I am dreading,' said Elsie out of the blue, 'and that's going to see Adrian.'

'Why?'

'I wonder what sort of mess he's in. I ran that house for him like a four-star hotel. And now there'll be dust in corners. I shouldn't be surprised to find the place full of packing-cases.'

'Peter hasn't said anything about his flitting permanently.'

'No. No.' Two sighs.

'And he has that Valerie Fitzjames. She'll do a bit.'

'We'll see.' Elsie Youlgrave's mouth grew thin. 'She'd roll about on his bed with him. That's all he'd require of her.'

'He didn't want you to . . .?' Alice could have bitten her tongue out.

Elsie put a heavy hand on her arm, in warning or companionship. 'We'd better go. We don't want to be late.'

The rest of the journey, two minutes, was taken up with forced, anxious silence. As soon as they drew up in Hillier's drive, Elsie made the effort at reconciliation.

'Peter still comes up on Saturdays?'

'Yes. I don't know how long it will continue.'

'No. He's growing up fast.'

'D'you know, Elsie, he is. I think I shall soon lose him. In five

194

years he'll be away from home. And he's changing. He was really looking forward to your visit, and then when you arrive he can hardly muster a civil word.' Alice tapped the wheel. 'It makes me so cross, sometimes.'

'He's a good boy.'

'You get out,' Alice ordered, 'and then I can lock your door from the inside.'

They looked over the garden without speaking from the top of the steps before Alice touched the door-bell. Hillier opened immediately; he must have been skulking in the hall.

'Welcome,' he said, and kissed both.

They did not move away as the preliminary questions were put and answered. Elsie made no attempt to hide her scrutiny of the furniture, the staircase; she even straightened a gold-framed oil painting of a lake with trees. Hillier, neat as ever, spoke quietly, was most attentive. Finally, and the preliminaries took at least ten minutes, he ushered them into the smaller drawing room and went out for coffee. The place shone well-cared for, smelt of furniture polish, was warm, quiet and comfortable. Coffee appeared on a trolley, with a handsome selection of biscuits on three plates, an ostentation suggesting masculine nervousness to the amused Alice.

The first half-hour was occupied with the banalities, and then more vividly with Elsie's cruise and American visit. Alice, hardly speaking a word, listened and watched as the courteous Hillier encouraged Elsie to talk; he played the perfect host to both women, temperate, interested, interesting.

Elsie Youlgrave who had been loquacious about the foolishness of the pursuit of pleasure on ships, about American learning or roads or television, now settled herself to question Hillier. Her face wore the same smiling expression of enjoyment.

'That's enough of me,' she ruled. 'Now tell us about yourself. You say you're all right?'

'I do my best.'

'Have you found another housekeeper?'

'No. It's difficult after your "Lord Mayor's Show".'

'Is Miss Fitzjames still here?'

'No, she's gone back nearer home. Cheltenham. A job came up and she applied.'

195

'In the hospital service?'

'Yes.'

He seemed almost to appreciate the bluntness of her questions, showed no resentment, answered without hesitation.

'Alice tells me Peter still comes on Saturdays?'

'Yes. And I have a cleaning woman in twice a week. She's adequate.'

'And meals?'

'I eat out sometimes. I cook myself. I keep your kitchen spotless; I'll show you before you go. Of course, I'm not so well looked after as under your régime. Every day reminds me of that. But I'm not starving.'

'You're financially better off. You must be.' Elsie at her sternest.

'That's not a major consideration.'

They paused there. He offered to replenish the coffee pot, was refused and absent-mindedly poured the dregs into his cup. The women watched him avidly, as if he performed some delicate, difficult operation with uncertain outcome. In the end he raised the completed drink as a toast. Elsie allowed him time to sip and replace cup and saucer.

'You're thinking of staying here?' she asked.

'I haven't made up my mind.'

'It's nearly five months since I left.'

'Is there any hurry?' For the first time his voice betrayed a slight alarm.

'Do you have visitors?'

'Occasionally. Not many. I go to town myself from time to time. I'm not uncomfortable and I keep myself occupied.'

'Have you rejoined the theatre people, the Phoenix?'

'No.'

This time the silence seemed awkward, as if both questioner and questioned were momentarily at a loss.

'What do you do with yourself all day?' Elsie in exasperation.

'I read a great deal. I write letters. I'm corresponding with an Irish academic, for instance, about *Timon of Athens*.'

'You should marry.'

'All the best women are accounted for.'

He bowed ironically to both, and began to question Alice

about Gerald's advancement with Top Fare. He obviously knew nothing up-to-date. She described the course at Watford. Hillier rather glumly said it must be good to have caught the eye of superiors so favourably. He then, as if by rote or from an interviewer's invisible clipboard, asked about Stephen Youlgrave's poetry.

When Elsie replied that her husband had written a great deal, for him, in the past few months, he said, 'I'm glad.'

'Why, didn't you expect him to?'

'To tell you the truth, Elsie, no, I didn't. In my mind, and mark you this is only my opinion which might well be wrong, Stephen's poetry thrives on trouble. Verses from adversity.' He pulled a wry face. 'And if you've settled him, and fed the inner man and dusted his picture rails, well now, I thought his Muse might well grow quiet.'

'Or I might be more of a hindrance than a help?'

'Yes. Not in yourself. In his mind. You have perhaps disturbed his habits or his system or something of the sort.'

'Which would be better?' Alice asked sharply. The other two looked at her. 'Unhappiness and poetry, or a pleasant life?'

'I don't think Stephen's like that at all,' Elsie answered mildly. 'I think I agree that he writes from his anxieties, his worrying obsessions, but they would be there whether or not his life was comfortable. On the cruise, in the middle of all that luxury, I'd catch him staring at the sea and wondering what it would be like to sail there in an open boat with the Vikings.'

'The comfort and warmth would strengthen the feeling.' Alice.

'He's a bit of an Anglo-Saxon in my view,' Hillier said. 'A bad-weather poet.'

'I don't know.' Elsie spoke now with a certain confidence. 'I've heard him lecture, and I have the advantage of being able to question him afterwards, and he attempts to imagine the life-style of the people who wrote the poems, but he's a twentieth-century man, keen on central heating and word-processors. I guess he was clever at these old languages when he was young and so got stuck with them.'

'You mean he feels he could have done something more important with his life?'

Elsie sat straighter, stroked her chin almost comically.

197

'To some extent,' she conceded. 'He never finished his book on *Piers Plowman*, and that's unlike him, weighs on his conscience.' She sighed. 'Perhaps he felt that was not compatible with his poetry. Or his *Piers Plowman* would not be as good as his verse.'

'Couldn't he do both?' Alice asked.

'Exactly the question I'd pose,' said Hillier gravely.

'I don't know. He's still energetic enough, but perhaps he felt at the time that the one task would rob him of too much of his strength. I don't know.' She faced Hillier. 'I've often heard you say, Adrian, that you have never taken an important decision in your life and made it correctly.'

Hillier coughed, drily. 'That's what it feels like. It can't be exactly true, or I shouldn't be here to tell the tale.' He spoke unemphatically, like a solicitor explaining why the law seemed to run counter to common sense. 'But I have always regarded Stephen as a very successful man indeed. As a scholar and a poet. Of course there'd be areas where he'd think he could have done better, or where he saw he'd missed opportunities, or where he couldn't complete what he felt he ought. Everybody is like that. Einstein was, they tell me, that great man. But like Stephen he'd have something completed to look on, some outstanding achievement.'

'That could make it worse.' Alice, who blushed.

'How do you mean?' Hillier.

'If you have done it well once, you think you ought to be able to do it again.'

'I see. Yes.'

Elsie stirred. 'Alice tells me,' she began, 'that she's seen nothing of you since the wedding?'

'That's true. I'm often away or caught up at the weekends.'

'Adrian, you don't know your friends.'

'Alice is busier than I am,' Hillier answered. 'She has a job and a family. And Alice is like you, Elsie; she admires success. Her husband is making something of his career; he has been picked out for close scrutiny.' He held up a hand to prevent intervention. 'And he's done it, moreover, with no outside help, without influence. He started late, but he's made great headway.'

'You sound jealous.' Elsie.

198

'You said yourself he's not Board material.' Alice. The women blurted out their sentences together.

'Well, yes.' He waved an ironical hand towards both, as though to indicate that he'd received both communications and would deal with them in turn. 'I'm human. I envy those who outstrip me. I always felt I was appointed to jobs because I was my father's son. And even with that support, I didn't do marvellously well. And as to being material of the highest grade, their number is very, very small. The rest of the Board they make up with the titled, the well-to-do, and accountants. I am consulted because I have shares. No, Alice's husband is doing very well and she's right to be pleased with him.'

'She'd still see you.'

'No, she would not.' They spoke as if Alice was elsewhere. 'For that and other reasons.'

'You're very sorry for yourself, Adrian.' Elsie, uncomfortably.

'You're pleased with yourself, you mean.'

'This is a marvellously attractive world, full of marvels even on a November morning.'

Adrian sang suddenly to himself but clearly, 'I love the wild birds, the dawn and the dew.' He grinned with sudden mischief. 'We only appreciate these miracles of yours when we're happy enough to keep our eyes wide open to see them. I spend my life keeping my head down.'

'More fool you.' Elsie's rudeness shocked Alice.

'Right, but that's the way I am.'

'And are you going to do anything about it?'

'I may. I may.' He smiled with resigned cheerfulness. 'I've decided that I shan't move from here until after the winter. It's sensible. House prices are rising and will, I'm told on good authority, continue to do so. I'll hibernate here.'

'There'll be some woman.' Elsie's rudeness brushed vulgarity.

'There are always women,' he answered. 'That keeps me from despair.'

Elsie slapped her lap but did not pursue the subject.

Very easily Hillier began to question Alice about Peter's future. Soon all three were enjoying themselves. Adrian talked about his university days; Elsie about institutions of higher education she had visited with Stephen.

'I wish I had been made to apply for university,' she told them. 'But my teachers never set their stalls out for me. Training college was good enough for girls.'

'Your grammar-school teachers were all graduates, weren't they?' Hillier.

'Yes. I used to enjoy seeing them with their gowns and hoods on speech day. But they didn't press me.'

'They thought a secretarial course was my limit,' said Alice. 'Don't let them fob Peter off with second best.'

'That will be up to him,' said the mother. 'I shan't stand in his way.'

They talked until nearly one o'clock, when he offered to take them out to lunch, but Elsie refused.

'I've enjoyed every minute of your company, Adrian, but now Alice and I want to round off our girlish confessions.'

He showed them over the kitchen as he had promised, and it sparkled in first-rate, spick-and-span order. The three shook hands and kissed in the hall, but by that time their spirit had departed, they looked furtive.

Once they were in the car, before the ignition key was turned, Elsie said, 'I hope you didn't mind my refusing lunch like that. I ought really to have left it to you.' She listened to Alice's murmurs of agreement. 'To tell you the truth, I'd had enough. He's an interesting man, but he's too full of self-pity. He's one of the luckiest people I know, all that money, plenty of time, very attractive, and yet he grouses, and stumbles about his life like a cripple.'

'But you lived there with him for long enough?'

'I didn't notice so much; I was too full of my own concerns. But since I took up with Stephen, I can't help but criticize Adrian.'

'Does your husband do so?'

'Criticize? Not really. Oh, he'll pronounce his little sentence now and again, but he's less ready than I am to use the rough end of his tongue. No: the more I think about Adrian, the more annoyed I am.'

'What'll happen to him, Elsie?'

'God knows. I just can't make him out. It's a shame, a

personable man like that. Oh, I could hit him. I could feel it rising up in me. I'd had enough. And when I thought of him in a restaurant with the wine-waiter and all the rest of it, and his suggesting this and that while he's throwing his life away, well . . .' Elsie Youlgrave bumped her clasped hands on one thigh. 'What do you think?'

Alice drove away.

'You didn't say what you thought,' Elsie pressed.

'You're making a big thing of it.'

'That's right. I am.' She breathed heavily. 'I loved that man.' Alice concentrated on the right turn at traffic lights. 'Some men need women to bolster them. Frank did. He was successful, a good headmaster, a fine speaker, but he needed a woman to make him feel his success. Stephen is the same. So's Adrian. I think I would have married him if he'd asked me. But he didn't, and perhaps I'm glad now. Adrian's one of my failures.'

'What would you have made him do?' Alice queried.

'Made? That's a good question. He wouldn't have been another Bernard Shaw or Ibsen, but he'd have had my encouragement. That's what he lacks. When the Phoenix committee turned against him, it was his father and mother all over again: "You aren't doing it right. You're a failure." Now I'd have ticked him off, I don't doubt, but he would have been quite sure that I admired him, and he'd have been the better for it.'

'Yes.' Alice cast a judging eye over the small jam in front of her. There was silence between the women, but a hum outside of traffic, pneumatic drills, shouting.

'Do you think I'm boasting, Alice? I failed with Frank. He saw me off to school exactly as he did every other morning, and then he went, he went and . . . I fell short there.'

They were out in the clear, spinning along a minor road.

'You gave him some years of happiness.'

'I suppose I did. That's better than nothing . . . I hope. What did you think when he praised your husband as a success? Did it surprise you?'

'He doesn't know what he's talking about. That's what I thought. Gerald's as uncertain as can be. He's like a cat on hot bricks when he thinks the Top Fare Board is considering him.'

201

'You steady him, don't you?'

'I do my best.'

'Is Peter the same?'

'No. Not yet. But he's not suffered any major setbacks. Not to the best of my knowledge. But we can't be sure, can we? He seems cheerful enough most of the time, and doing the right things to get on. We don't know. But when I think of Adrian Hillier, a millionaire, he must be, envying Gerald, it's just daft. He needs kicking.'

' "I should have married Alice Hogg." '

'You don't forget that, do you?'

Alice Fowler could laugh now as she parked neatly in her drive. She banged flat hands on her steering-wheel as if in applause.

'It never once entered his head to marry me. He was a randy student and I was a silly, fluttery, dancing partner who caught his roving eye. That's all there was to it. "I should have married Alice." Rubbish! "I should have married Marilyn Monroe." And if he thinks otherwise now, he's deceiving himself.'

'Don't we all?'

'Only if we want to. Not otherwise. I shan't lose any beauty sleep over Adrian Hillier, I can promise you that.'

They stood together in the porch of the Fowlers' house.

'What do you think about Stephen and me?' Elsie Youlgrave muttered the question.

'He's lucky.'

'And am I?'

'From what you say, yes.' Alice opened the house, ushered her friend in, locked the door behind them. The hall seemed dark and narrow, walls and stairs crowding on to their backs. 'At least I hope you are. You deserve it.'

Elsie threw her arms about her friend and Alice, taken aback, enclosed the other woman, reciprocating. They laid cheek on cheek as they hugged vehemently as wrestlers. They did not understand either the strength or the motive, but stood swaying and holding together in that confined, dim space.

When they broke apart both were smiling.

· —— 18 —— ·

The Christmas holidays passed happily for the Fowlers. Peter had again done well in his end-of-term tests and Gerald's business boomed. He had ordered beyond reason and sold out. He confessed to his wife that he felt excited: 'there's plenty of money about, and by God we're not half taking advantage of it.' She inquired if these profits would be reported to higher authority, but he answered only cautiously. 'They may be general and so the Board will expect them.' But he was happy, tired, fully occupied, above himself, taking chances which came off, constantly grousing and at the top of his form. He seemed to grudge himself the few days of holiday, but spent generously on wife and son. Alice, delighted, began to see some truth in Hillier's judgement of her husband as one of life's successes.

Of Hillier they heard little.

He had instructed Peter not to come up to the house for the last three Saturdays in December, as he'd be away, and left him a staggering Christmas gift of book tokens. 'What are you going to buy with that lot, then?' Gerald demanded. 'The *Encyclopaedia Britannica?*' The family received a handsome Christmas card, Jan Breughel the Elder's 'Adoration of the Kings'. 'Do you know where he's going?' Alice queried. 'France, I think,' Peter replied. Many of his answers these days, especially the unexpected, were delivered with offhand nonchalance.

Letters from Yorkshire were frequent; Alice conscientiously replied to them. 'Hanged if I know what you find to write about,' Gerald said, watching his wife scribble.

'Your progress, amongst other things.'

'Pah. Bloody women.' Both found life good.

Stephen Youlgrave had now enough pieces for a new volume; his editor had been to see him, and he had twice descended on London where his publishers were talking about

203

a *Collected Poems*. He spent hours every day at his desk, 'playing with commas' according to Elsie, but she said it kept him indoors and away from the weather, 'more severe' than she was used to. 'He eats well, even if he sleeps badly, but I've threatened to move into another bedroom.' Stephen's son, whom they had met briefly in the United States, had spent a week with them. 'He's quite unlike his father, and has a lot more to say to me than to his Dad. I can't make either of them out. I think Stephen was relieved when George went, but he hasn't said so. I asked Stephen if his boy was like his mother, but he wasn't having that. "He's like himself, worse luck." I wonder if he's homosexual, as he's not married, but he has no overt signs, even if I could recognize them. He's also not short of money; as far as I can make out he's connected with the publication of magnificent scientific textbooks and technical manuals. He promised to send me one of a new popular series they're doing. This is about the solar system.'

Elsie's letters were like her conversation, brusque and fluent, with rapid changes of subject matter which demanded second readings. Alice wondered if she wrote her letters in short three-minute bursts, but dared not ask. Sturdy Mrs Youlgrave was more than one woman.

In the wretched weather of January, Elsie reported that Stephen had 'suffered a stroke'. The letter was short, a mere half page. Alice did not know whether to 'phone, or if that would be more of a nuisance than a comfort. She wrote with difficulty, not knowing what obstacles her friend faced or how she coped. Elsie rang. Stephen was in hospital; they were pleased with him; he had not lost his power of speech; he was beginning to get the use back in his right hand. He was, moreover, both cheerful and stoical, joked about his disability, told the ward sister that, like Henry James, he had thought that this was the 'distinguished thing', death. Well, yes, Elsie said, yes, he'd been overdoing it. He was so finicky about his poems he'd spent hours every day altering and retyping, and changing back and forward, and worrying himself sick. I asked him what the hurry was, but he wouldn't listen. 'No, of course he hadn't,' she snapped when Alice asked if he had had a presentiment of the catastrophe. Then Elsie had laughed, and apologized so that Alice had guessed everything was not as straightforward as her friend tried to make out.

At the end of the month Alice spent a day in the Yorkshire bungalow. She had driven in pouring rain; skies loured; every room contracted into darkness and damp. The Youlgraves seemed glad to see her. Stephen moved perhaps more slowly, but otherwise appeared little different. Elsie allowed him to work for one and a half hours in the morning, and one hour after three o'clock. 'She bullies me.' 'For your own good,' Alice chaffed. 'To tell you the truth,' Stephen spoke very deliberately, with gaps, 'this economy with time is a blessing in disguise. I use my allotment properly. Before, I was stirring myself up for hours on end. Now I have to set everything right in the short time allowed.' 'Is it possible?' Alice asked. 'It seems so. I would have denied it on oath before, but, yes, yes, it seems so.'

The Youlgraves made her welcome, pressed her to stay. Winter weather confined them; they did not like that. 'We could do with a place the size of The Firs,' Elsie grumbled. They inquired about Hillier, but Alice had heard nothing beyond the snippets of grudging information which Peter brought back. Adrian Hillier had spent Christmas in Paris, and the New Year in Cornwall. One Saturday morning there were two ladies much in evidence, both beautifully dressed and scented. Their names were Poskett-Smith and Latimer, something like that. No, Mr Hillier had not shown partiality to one rather than the other. Neither had said much to Peter. On another occasion Mr Hillier had gone about upstairs singing very loudly. Something about 'like a refiner's fire'. No, he hadn't seemed particularly pleased when he had appeared down below.

On the last day of the month Alice had opened the evening paper to read with a fierce pang of shock that 'Adrian Hillier (45)' had been beaten up in a quiet road not far from his house. Three young men, two white, one coloured, had attempted to rob him and when he had resisted had knocked him down and set about him. This vicious attack had been interrupted by the fortuitous arrival of a police patrol car. Two men were helping the police with inquiries, a third was being sought. Mr Hillier had been detained overnight for treatment in the university hospital suffering from cuts, contusions and shock.

Alice inquired about the hospital ward, visited him there that night. He lay in bed, his face lacerated, both eyes black, but calm, casual even, in his demeanour. They had kept him in because he lived on his own, but he would go home the next day. He spoke without rancour of the mugging.

Three young men had begged for money; they had been drinking. He refused and made as if to walk on. They had pushed him back against a wall, where he had struggled. All three were bigger than he was. Fortunately an old lady sitting in the house opposite had watched the assault and had immediately called the police. By the time the patrol car arrived, there had been a further round of threats and demands, the yobbos had punched him, floored and searched him, and disappointed that he carried no money had begun to kick.

When Alice expressed her horror, Adrian had put a hand to his puffy, discoloured face and grinned.

'I don't think they knew what to do. I wasn't carrying money.'

'Did you try to run away?'

'Of course. I even made a yard or two. But even though they had been drinking, they were younger than I was. They'd be eighteen, perhaps. They tipped me over in the end, but they weren't wearing heavy boots. I banged my face badly on a stone wall. That was after they'd punched me. I lay there, face down, hoping to God they wouldn't kick my head.'

'And they didn't?'

'I understand they did. I was very dazed by this time. When the police arrived I tried to crawl away, dripping blood all over the pavement. They nobbled two of them there and then and the other one escaped. They've pulled them all in, they say.'

He was very sore, had a badly gashed hand, now stitched, cracked ribs and bruises all over back and legs.

'It could have been worse,' he asserted.

Alice sat with him for half an hour and promised that she would call at The Firs the following evening.

He let her into the hall himself. He wore a pullover, flannel trousers and an open-necked shirt, looking ridiculously neat compared with the grotesque discoloration of his face. His eyes barely opened; his lips gaped distorted; the cheeks were uneven with ugly, flushed lumps. Both hands were plastered, but he insisted he was able to make coffee. She noticed that he limped, opened the door gingerly and once, for no obvious reason, let out a stifled whinny of pain.

Once they were seated and his every movement was awkward, he assumed sweet reason.

'Yes, I'm sore still. They aren't doing anything about my ribs. I have to heal myself. But I'm functioning, if only just.'

She invited him to her house for a meal, but he refused.

'Thanks very much, but I'm not going out while my appearance frightens the horses.'

'Horses?'

'It's what Mrs Pat Campbell said about sexual goings-on.'

'Oh.'

Alice did not stay long. Adrian clearly did not wish it; he was in pain and despite his calmness found little to talk about. The three drunken youths had been caught and charged. All, according to the police, would go to prison. Apart from the constant pain, the glimpses of his smashed face which he caught in the mirror, the police interrogations, it might all have happened to someone else. He spoke to Alice, but it seemed against his will, as if he were ashamed.

She telephoned the Youlgraves, and two days later had a letter which announced that they were coming down to stay with Hillier at The Firs for a week. 'It's the best I can do.'

Elsie called round the second evening after arrival. She sounded satisfied with herself, chaffing Peter, cross-examining Gerald. She held Alice briefly but strongly in her arms.

'I've left my two invalids together, and have come out to cheer myself up.'

'How are they?'

'Better. Adrian's face is nearly normal, and he seems to have recovered from the shock.'

'And Stephen?'

'He's coming round. Slowly. It will take time. But this was a good excuse to get him away from Yorkshire. He wouldn't have gone anywhere else. He can work down here and he and Adrian are company for each other, though often as not they just sit there reading books. They won't venture out much. This weather . . . I hate February.'

Elsie spoke cheerfully, but was uncertain about her husband. 'It's happened once. It might very well happen again. Oh, he's acting sensibly, but . . .'

'How does he feel about it?'

'It's altered him, Alice. I mean, you wouldn't think so if you saw him. He's the same quiet, humorous, learned old man. But it's slowed him up. He's more hesitant now. And . . . and . . . I came on him one morning at his desk, the tears streaming down his cheeks and a book in his hand. It was *Fourteenth Century Verse and Prose*; he calls it "Sisam". "Whatever's wrong, Stephen?" I said. He couldn't speak; he just pointed, with his poor mouth open. It turned out later he'd picked this book up and opened it and it had belonged to Anne, his first wife. She'd written a translation of some of the words in pencil in the margin. She was one of his first students. The writing was as clear as it was when she did it fifty years ago, and it had moved him. I suppose it recalled what she was like. And these pencil scrawls were still there now she was nothing. But it wasn't like him to sit there crying. He's lost his confidence, or his social poise. He seemed ashamed of himself afterwards. "I don't know, Elsie," he said. "I couldn't contain myself." And he couldn't. This seizure has changed him. I tried to jolly him along. "I'll see to it that there's always a good supply of well-ironed handkerchiefs," I said, and he smiled. "You're a good girl, Elsie," he said, but his eyes were watery again.'

'It must be worrying.'

'Yes. But he's improving. And I make him eat and sleep, and not kill himself with his work. And I think he's enjoying it down here. And Adrian as well. They suit each other, they really do.'

'What do they talk about?'

'Shakespeare and Dryden. It's a real pleasure to listen. They sometimes speak very slowly with great pauses in between, and then they'll be going at it hammer and tongs; they can hardly wait to get their words out. It does both of them good, and me with them.'

'And how does Adrian seem? When I went up, I didn't think he was at all pleased.'

'Well, he's very vain. He wouldn't like the idea of your seeing him with a swollen face.'

'But it wasn't his fault.'

'What difference does that make?' Elsie Youlgrave laughed with genuine enjoyment. 'He has to be at his classical best in front of his lady friends. Just because he's quiet it doesn't mean he doesn't think highly of himself. What we used to call "self-regarding" at college.'

'Is he recovering?'

'From the shock, you mean? The two of them are in the same boat. Stephen's much older, and he's had a warning before this one, so that I suspect he's on the look-out for the next attack, whereas there's no reason why anybody should beat Adrian up again.'

'Unless it's a jealous husband.'

'Yes, I see what you mean.' Elsie pursed her lips. 'But they're both finding company and being looked after. Stephen's doctor says he might well live on to ninety, but I don't know if that's good or bad. I couldn't bear it if he became senile and unable to think or talk or write. An old colleague of his is like that, a cabbage, incontinent, wordless and yet worried. Or so he seems. It wouldn't be so bad if he didn't know what was happening; rotten for those looking after him, but he wouldn't grasp the situation. But poor Bertie Moulton's unhappy.'

'Was he a professor?'

'Yes. A brilliant mathematician when he was young. But now he mutters, and swears, and sobs. Stephen doesn't go to see him very often; it upsets him too much.'

'Does he recognize Stephen?'

'No. He doesn't recognize his wife or family or anybody. He's locked up inside this box of aggression and frustration, angry with himself perhaps. He could take it out on his work before, but now he's a nobody and a nothing existing in discomfort. It's awful, Stephen says. I don't think he liked the man much when he was normal, and at work, he was too arrogant. But now, oh, oh God, no.'

'And Adrian?'

'I can't tell, Alice. I don't think he's in much pain now. He said an odd thing to me. "Elsie," he said, "perhaps this is just

209

what I needed to jolt me back to life." And I said, "I was always a believer in corporal punishment." It was a bit of a joke, really, but he didn't take it like that. "I've been thrashed for my lassitude, you mean, my bone idleness?" "Don't be stupid," I told him, but I could see the idea appealed. There are some people who want to feel their slate wiped clean, but don't think it can be done without payment or punishment. I don't understand him, that's for sure.'

'What's he planning to do?'

'You've got me there again. I think he's just been dawdling about, incapable of making his mind up, and this last week or two in considerable pain. And the winter weather doesn't encourage you to change anything very radically.' Wind rattled the windows; through the curtains they heard the fusillade of rain. 'February fill-dyke. Ugh!'

'So what will you do?'

'We'll stop with him a week or so. Stephen's bungalow's all right. The heating will keep it intact, and a neighbour calls in every day to see there's nothing wrong and sends the mail on. I can always run over there and back in a day.'

'Don't you go knocking yourself up.'

'Don't fret. I'm never better than when I'm organizing somebody or something.'

Alice explained about Gerald's annoyance with his employers and Peter's progress at school.

'Peter misses you on Saturday mornings, you know.'

'We suited each other. He's a bit old-fashioned – probably the way you've brought him up. He's sharp, and will speak his mind, but he's very polite.'

'That's from his Dad and the shop.'

'His mother has something to do with it, and don't you tell me otherwise. It's an attractive manner, and it boils down to the fact that he's confident in himself. Unlike Adrian. You've done a good job with your boy, Alice.'

'We ought to have had other children. It's too late now.'

'I don't know. At forty? Biologically possible.'

'Get away with you. I wouldn't know what to do with a new-born baby.' They laughed together. 'And what are you going to do with Adrian?'

'My baby? Keep him interested.'

'In what?'

'In life. He does not know what he's about. Books, sexual conquests, square meals and that's about it. He'll have to change, you know, Alice. "I should have married Alice Hogg" about sums him up. You wouldn't have let him drift. You'd have niggled at him and straightened him out.'

'And put up with his infidelities? No, Elsie. No, I don't think so.'

'That's just his way of getting back at the world, and at his parents. He needs love. And he must dominate somebody somehow.'

'He should have married Elsie Hooper.'

'No. I'm too straightforward for him.'

'Meaning I'm not?' Alice sounded indignant and amused.

'Now, now. You have this sort of mystery about you. He wouldn't exactly understand you and so he'd work to impress you. You're deep, madam. Interesting and, well, not quite devious, but . . .'

'Have you been attending psychology classes?'

'How did you guess? I drive to York on Tuesdays to the WEA. But we don't talk about anything like this. I make it up for myself. You're the woman he never mastered, never came to terms with.'

'There must be dozens.'

'Not named to me, Mrs Fowler. Not named to me.'

They laughed again, and Alice remembered the terrified girl struggling, calling for pity, a halt, knickers pulled down. It did not matter now. Two other people. Adrian had taken her virginity and that she would not forget, but it meant little to the adult woman. Perhaps she could have made something of him, given the chance. More probably she would have gone the way of Madame Lemercier, on to the scrap-heap of experience. She could not become excited. Easily, scarcely blushing, she began to describe the fortnight's summer holiday in Spain she had booked last month.

'I'm attending a class on elementary Spanish.'

'You'll be able to order them about.'

'Gerald does that. He speaks very good, very fluent Spanish. He surprised me and Peter.'

'A dark horse, that husband of yours.'

211

The two women arranged that the Fowler parents should go for dinner to The Firs in a week's time.

'It gives me leisure to sort everything out up there, and it will stop Stephen worrying about going home and Adrian will have his beauty back.'

'Does he mention that Valerie Fitzjames?'

'Not a word.'

'You must come here.'

'We'll see, Alice. But not for the moment. It will depend on how long we stay. Just give me half a chance to settle the conservative club up there.'

Gerald Fowler grumbled about the clean shirt, cuff-links, haircut that the dinner party involved, but his wife was certain that the invitation had pleased him. Peter said he was quite capable of looking after himself, and had in any case been invited to stay for lunch on Saturday after his morning chores.

'Will you know what to say to them?' Gerald asked the boy.

'I hope so. They're only human beings.'

'What will you talk about?'

'They'll ask me questions, I expect.'

'Ay, but will you be able to answer them?'

'Yes. I wouldn't mind being a university professor.'

The father, voicing his own inadequacies, looked with affection at his son.

On the morning of his visit to The Firs, Gerald received a letter from the Board of Top Fare which instructed him to hold himself in readiness for a temporary stint of perhaps three months from the week after next as manager in one of the largest London branches. He was to 'phone his acceptance on the day of receiving the letter so that arrangements could be made. Living accommodation would be provided for him on the premises, and full details would be forwarded to him if and when he accepted.

He passed the letter over to his wife at the breakfast table. The post had arrived early. His toast lay on his plate; the one bite taken out at the corner he had masticated while Peter went to fetch the mail. Gerald read once, then twice, closed his eyes, scrutinized a third time before, oddly, replacing the letter in the envelope and handing it thus to his wife. While she perused it his eyes fixed themselves on the picture-rail above Peter's head, and his fingers drummed lightly on the cloth.

'Will you go?' she asked.

'I think so. Don't you?'

'It will be a sort of test.' He peremptorily signalled her to pass the letter to their son.

'They'll be trying me out to see how I shape somewhere else.'

'Are you pleased?'

'In a way. But then it shows they're not sure, otherwise they would have appointed me straight into the managership. Still, they haven't written me off.'

'What sort of place is it?'

'Don't know. We'll find that out when they write.'

'You'll accept?'

'Yes. I can't do otherwise.'

'You'll ring now? Straight away?'

'When I get to work. It will save me the cost, and in any case they'll not be in their offices at quarter to eight in the morning.'

'Congratulations, Dad.'

'Thanks, son. I'll try to be a credit to you.'

At The Firs party an air of formality reigned.

The men wore lounge suits, while the women had agreed on ankle-length dresses. The meal was leisurely and Alice helped Elsie to serve. Surfaces gleamed under powerful lights; linen was starched; a silver épergne dominated the table. Flowers massed in hall, in dining and drawing rooms.

Stephen expressed satisfaction at the brilliance, saying he hated restaurants where he could not see what he was eating.

'That's all of them,' said Gerald.

They laughed; Alice wondered where he had gathered his information.

Adrian knew nothing of Top Fare's offer to Gerald, as they expected. Stephen seemed, to their surprise, interested in the commercial world and questioned Fowler with vigour while the ladies were out. The host sipped his claret, distant. Gerald, as he put it later to his wife, was 'in his eyeholes' and explained his problems and solutions with real penetration. 'Clever old chap,' Gerald admitted. 'He knew the right questions.'

They retired to the large drawing room, sat in easy chairs in lavish warmth. Elsie inquired about Peter's progress at school. Adrian asked if the boy would put himself to bed, and it was Gerald who explained that his wife had laid down a timetable for the evening.

'Ah, but will he keep to it?' Adrian, mischievously.

'Within a few minutes, I believe,' Gerald answered.

'There's real faith in that "I believe."'

Stephen described the progress of his new volume, claiming that the appearance of one book spurred him to fresh work. Elsie had decided that they would stay through the Spring and Summer, at least, in the bungalow. Adrian said, charmingly, that he ought to leave The Firs but was too idle to set the process in motion.

They talked of holidays. Adrian was going to America, the Youlgraves to Iceland.

Elsie encouraged Alice to talk about Spain. She and her husband obliged, amusingly. Stephen, hearing that Gerald spoke Spanish, said that it was a language he did not know but wished he had learnt.

'I've enough French and Italian and Latin to find some sort of enjoyment of the originals as long as there's an English translation attached.'

Gerald inquired what Stephen read, and confessed he had never troubled himself with poetry, English or Spanish. 'I just want to order a drink, to tell somebody to clear off, or change my sparking plugs.'

'Yes,' said Youlgrave. 'Yes. "Tonight I can write the saddest lines."'

'Who's that?' Adrian.

'Neruda.' The professor lifted his head and then recited very distinctly, lifting the words from the deep bottom of a pool:

Escribir, por ejemplo: 'La noche está estrellada,
y tiritan, azules, los astros, a lo lejos.'

'You must forgive my amateurish pronunciation,' he added.

They were impressed, sat silent. Perhaps it was the wine, the unaccustomed food, the heated rooms against the winter

214

outside, the fellowship, but they felt the jewelled sadness of the verse in a strange tongue.

'I don't know whether it's my sort of poetry, even,' said Stephen. 'I don't know, really, if I want to find out.'

'Knowledge, knowledge,' his wife said, 'is what I lack.'

They did not know as they sat there in the brilliance that within twelve months Gerald would have moved his family with success to London, that Adrian would have decided to stay in California, that Stephen would be dead of a heart attack, and Elsie left in the next, mild winter to find herself again, to write up the diary of her conversations with her husband for publication in the States.

'Say it once more,' Gerald demanded. 'It's out of this world.'

This time Stephen began with the line he had first translated. "'Puedo escribir los versos más tristes esta noche",' and continued in the same solemn voice. Again they were silent, though they broke soon and easily into happy trivialities, important people.

At midnight they stood at the front door.

'No blue stars here,' Gerald said.

'No stars at all that I can see.' Elsie.

The Fowlers slipped into their car. Wind touched the cold branches of trees. Again last words of thanks and pleasure were exchanged.

'Right away, driver,' Adrian called, best railway fashion. He waved Gerald's car on.

The three stood in the chill on the steps looking down at an empty drive.

'All change,' said Adrian, taking Stephen's arm, patting Elsie's hand, ushering them in.

'Small change,' she answered, heading the party.